HIGH SPIRITS

Books by Carol J. Perry

Haunted Haven Mysteries

High Spirits

Be My Ghost

Witch City Mysteries

Caught Dead Handed

Tails, You Lose

Look Both Ways

Murder Go Round

Grave Errors

It Takes a Coven

Bells, Spells, and Murders

Final Exam

Late Checkout

Murder, Take Two

See Something

'Til Death

HIGH SPIRITS

CAROL J. PERRY

Kensington Publishing Corp.
www.kensingtonbooks.com

KENSINGTON BOOKS are published by

Kensington Publishing Corp.
119 West 40th Street
New York, NY 10018

All Kensington titles, imprints, and distributed lines are available at special quantity discounts for bulk purchases for sales promotion, premiums, fund-raising, educational, or institutional use.

This book is a work of fiction. Names, characters, businesses, organizations, places, events, and incidents either are the product of the author's imagination or are used fictitiously. Any resemblance to actual persons, living or dead, events, or locales is entirely coincidental.

To the extent that the image or images on the cover of this book depict a person or persons, such person or persons are merely models, and are not intended to portray any character or characters featured in the book.

Special book excerpts or customized printings can also be created to fit specific needs. For details, write or phone the office of the Kensington Sales Manager: Kensington Publishing Corp., 119 West 40th Street, New York, NY 10018. Attn. Sales Department. Phone: 1-800-221-2647.

The K and Teapot logo is a trademark of Kensington Publishing Corp.

ISBN: 978-1-4967-3138-8 (ebook)

ISBN: 978-1-4967-3137-1

First Kensington Trade Paperback Printing: November 2022

10 9 8 7 6 5 4 3 2 1

Printed in the United States of America

For Dan, my husband and best friend

Amazing the things you find when you bother to
search for them.
—Sacagawea

HIGH SPIRITS

Chapter 1

Maureen Doherty knelt on soft gray carpet and carefully lifted the corner of a large plastic storage box marked "Christmas Ornaments." It was the first of several similar containers lined up on the living room floor of Maureen's top-floor suite at the Haven House Inn in Haven, Florida. Her golden retriever, Finn, nudged her hand, giving an impatient "woof."

"Take it easy, boy," she told him. "These decorations are old. They might be breakable. We have to be gentle." She lifted a rounded, paper-wrapped article from the box, stripping away blue tissue.

"See? Look. It's a snow globe. Isn't it pretty? There's a polar bear inside." She shook the globe, watching tiny white flakes drift in the miniature winter world, placed it on the coffee table, and reached into the box for another parcel. She unwrapped a square metal box, with colorfully rendered Santa pictures on four sides, along with a red-knobbed handle. When she turned the crank the music box began to play "Here Comes Santa Claus."

"Cute," she said. "I love it. This will make a great centerpiece for one of the tables in the dining room."

"Woof," Finn agreed.

Presenting the Haven House Inn at its festive best for the oncoming holidays was important to Maureen. This would be her first Christmas as owner-manager of the century-old hotel on the gulf coast of Florida. It was, in fact, Maureen's own first Christmas away from her native New England, and the sight of colored lights strung among palm tree fronds and Santa hats perched on the heads of pink plastic front-lawn flamingoes provided a source of some culture shock. She returned to the task of selecting appropriate decorations from the containers that had been so painstakingly packed by her predecessor and recent benefactor, Penelope Josephine Gray.

A red-nosed Rudolph and a plump Frosty the Snowman joined the other figures on the coffee table and Maureen dug more deeply into the plastic box. "Ms. Gray's habit of saving everything helps us out on the decoration budget," she told Finn, as she unwrapped a delicate clear-glass angel with a golden halo. An oblong package, tissue-wrapped as were the rest of the articles but tied with a narrow blue ribbon, seemed too small and too flat to contain anything centerpiece-worthy. She put it on the coffee table with the intention of opening it later, when the plastic boxes had been emptied.

The late Penelope Josephine Gray had been more than a saver of everything. She'd been a downright, out-and-out, absolute hoarder—and Maureen had inherited not just a vintage inn, but a king-sized storage locker full of things the old woman had deemed "too good to throw away." Some of those things, like the collection of Christmas décor, provided a delightful surprise.

Actually, the ownership of Haven House Inn had been a total surprise too. Maureen, recently unemployed with the closing of Bartlett's of Boston department store where she'd enjoyed a ten-year career as a sportwear buyer, had never before heard of Ms. Gray when the lawyer's letter arrived, informing her that she'd inherited the place, lock, stock, hoard—and ghosts.

It took a while for Maureen to grasp the fact that she was suddenly a property owner.

It had taken a little longer to accept the part about the ghosts. After all, tales of hauntings of old hotels are not uncommon in Florida. Or in Boston. Or just about anywhere. But until a couple of months ago, Maureen had not been a believer in spirits or specters or apparitions or ghosts by any other name.

Things change. People adapt to their surroundings—even when those surroundings include some undeniably otherworldly beings.

Maureen reached into the box, this time finding a dainty silver bell. She turned it over in her hands. "Sterling silver," she announced to the dog, then gave the bell a gentle shake, enjoying the tinkling tones. "Very nice." She placed it on the table with the other finds, frowning when a jingling *ding-dong* sounded in the room even though the silver bell now lay absolutely still. Finn gave a soft "woof."

"It's just Lorna." Maureen glanced across the room toward her desk where the push button on an old-fashioned brass counter bell moved rapidly up and down. At Maureen's request, Lorna Dubois, a long-deceased movie starlet, now preceded her startling sudden appearances in the suite with a courtesy warning jingle.

The room seemed to shimmer for a moment as the blond Jean Harlow look-alike began to take shape. As usual, Lorna appeared in black and white, just as she had in long-ago films.

She surveyed the articles lined up on the coffee table. "Christmas shopping?" she asked. "I like the Rudolph."

"Shopping in Ms. Gray's collection," Maureen said. "I'm looking for things to use as centerpieces on the tables in the restaurant—to give it a festive look for the holidays."

"Huh," the ghost scoffed. "The best thing you can do for that old room is demolish it—like they do on those house-and-garden shows you watch."

I know it's pretty much outdated," Maureen admitted, "but hey, some of the tourists think it's charming the way it is."

"They're just being polite," Lorna insisted. "It needs a whole re-do. Maybe you could get Gordon Ramsey to stop by and fix it up for you. New paint and carpet and everything. Maybe a beach theme."

Maureen closed her eyes, picturing the big room in soft blues and grays. That would take care of the windows, walls, and floor. She'd definitely keep the round tables and the real linen white tablecloths. The rewired player piano would stay too. The bar could use some work, though. She'd ask Ted about updating that part of the room. He'd been a bartender before she'd promoted him to "executive chef." The man knew food, for sure, and between his menu ideas and her promotional abilities, in the short time she'd been in Haven, they'd nearly doubled the lunch business.

"I don't think Gordon Ramsey is going to stop by anytime soon," she said. "But I like the beach theme idea. It makes sense with us being right down the street from the Gulf of Mexico. Maybe a Tiki bar would be fun too. I'll bet there's probably enough stuff in Penelope's hoard to decorate the place. I know I've seen a couple of old round life preservers and some bleached-out wooden oars in the storage locker. I'll think about it. Maybe after the holidays we'll do something."

"Too bad they ran through all of Penelope's money before you got here. You could have just written a check for it all." Lorna sighed a long, dramatic, movie-actress sigh. "I've always liked money."

Lorna was right about Penelope's money being gone. The lawyer handling the estate, Larry Jackson, had explained that the old woman had inherited the inn a long time ago, much the same way Maureen had acquired it—from an unknown benefactor. The major difference was the fact that when Penelope got it, it had come with a great deal of money. The inn was still standing, such as it was, but sadly, all of the money had disappeared—the result of decades of wasteful management.

"No sense crying over spilt milk—or long-gone money," Maureen said. "I'm not going to give up and sell the place, no matter what anyone else thinks. Naming the suites after the famous people who've slept in them is beginning to get some attention. How about the nice photo feature about the Babe Ruth Suite in the *Orlando Sentinel*?"

"I liked it a lot," Lorna said. "So did the Babe."

Maureen nodded, not surprised by the ghost's reference to the late baseball great. According to Lorna, Babe Ruth was in the habit of visiting the L&M Lounge on Haven's Beach Boulevard whenever the Rays and the Yankees played in St. Petersburg. "Glad he approved. The Humphrey Bogart Suite is nearly ready. According to an old guest register he spent a weekend here when they were shooting *Key Largo* back in 1948. We've got some great publicity photos of him with Lauren Bacall for the suite décor."

"Well, every little bit helps," Lorna acknowledged. "Mind if I wear your halter-topped white silk dress tonight?" Maureen wasn't surprised by the request. Lorna often "borrowed" clothes—or rather what she called "the essence" of the clothes. The actual garments remained in Maureen's closet, while Lorna appeared in the same outfit, perfectly fitted to her slim starlet body.

"Help yourself," Maureen said. "Something special going on?"

"Waltz night over in St. Augustine at the Casa Monica Hotel," Lorna said.

Maureen wasn't surprised. The beautiful 1887 Mediterranean Revival hotel was famous among ghost hunters for the late-night waltz music that seemed to play out of nowhere while a roomful of ghosts waltzed gracefully in the lobby. "Got a date?" she asked.

"Kind of. I ran into an old flame recently. Can I wear your white shoes with the rhinestone heels?"

"Sure. Have fun." Maureen had learned shortly after her arrival in Haven that, although many of the Sunshine State's older attractions, like the Casa Monica, didn't object to the publicity that accompanied hauntings, most of the residents of Haven were adamantly opposed to the "ghost hunters," fearing that attention from television shows and magazine articles would spoil the peaceful, pleasant life they enjoyed in their quiet gulf-side small town. The amusement parks and major highways had long ago bypassed Haven and folks there preferred to keep their city—and their ghosts—to themselves.

Chapter 2

It took a couple of hours for Maureen to sort through the boxes, but when she'd finished, the coffee table, the top of the matching blond wood sideboard, and the seat of one beige armchair were covered with the festive results of her search. She'd rewrapped the remaining objects and carefully repacked them for future use. It must have taken Penelope Josephine years to accumulate the excellent assortment—and Maureen was confident that it would take years to properly display all of them in the inn.

Carrying the decorations she'd chosen for the first-floor restaurant dining room would take more than one trip in the Haven House's elegant, brass, glass and polished wood elevator. She packed her selection into three canvas bags—also part of her predecessor's hoard of things "too good to throw away." The unopened oblong package remained on the coffee table. She picked it up, balanced it on one hand. "It's light," she told the golden. "Looks like it might be letters. Do you suppose old Penelope had a lover? And that these might be her love letters?"

The idea of the old woman having a lover was too tantalizing to resist. Maureen, with just the tiniest bit of discomfort, untied the ribbon and pulled apart the tissue on one end of the small bundle. Finn woofed and looked away. "What?

She left everything to me. I have a right to look at her letters." Finn lay on the carpet, covering his eyes with his front paws.

"Stop that," she told the dog, and removed the first envelope, yellowed with age. She opened it carefully, inspected it, then laughed out loud. "Christmas cards," she said, returning the package to the tabletop. "It figures. She saved Christmas cards along with everything else. I'll check them out later. Old cards might be valuable to a collector. We need all the money we can get."

Maureen picked up one of the canvas bags. "I'll take the first two down, Finn," she told the golden. "You stand guard over the other one, then I'll take you for a walk. Okay?"

Finn woofed agreement. "If the cats come home, try to keep them out of the decoration bag," she said. Along with the inn and all its financial troubles, Maureen had also inherited Ms. Gray's two cats, Bogie and Bacall. She unlocked the white paneled door with the round cat door at its base and stepped out into the long corridor. Hers was the only apartment on the inn's top floor. Elizabeth Mack, the former manager of the place, had called it, with a dismissive sniff, "the penthouse." It had been Elizabeth who'd run the place darned near out of money, and was now in jail, facing several charges—including the murder of a previous ghost-hunter guest. Elizabeth would get what she deserved and Maureen was left with the biggest challenge of her life: to bring the neglected old hotel property back to the vibrant place it had once been—a place where movie stars and sports heroes had come to vacation.

She pressed the DOWN button and the shiny brass accordion-style doors slid open. She watched with pleasure through etched-glass windows as the cage descended two stories within the brick-walled enclosure. *I love my elevator*, she thought, lifting the canvas bags, one with each hand, and stepped out into the reception area with its white wicker furniture and bright yellow walls. *How much prettier will this room be with beachy blues and greens, grays, and tans?* It would take time and a lot of work but her confidence grew almost daily. *We can do this,* she told herself, and pushed open the louvred doors leading to the restaurant.

Leo, the backup bartender, waved from across the room. Several of the large round tables were already full with the early lunch crowd. Maureen had considered getting smaller tables but had decided to encourage diners to eat together with others instead of sitting by themselves. The idea had worked out nicely. Now people from the various Beach Boulevard businesses lunched together regularly. Some had started referring to the Haven House restaurant as the "Lunch-time Chamber of Commerce." When Maureen had first arrived in Haven to collect her inheritance, the dining room restaurant had been called Elizabeth's. Even though Penelope Josephine Gray had named it after the queen of England, deleting the name from the menus and removing the sign from the door had been done soon after Elizabeth Mack, the disgraced former manager, had been arrested.

Smiling, nodding to customers, replying to cheerful greetings, she crossed the room. "Is Ted in the kitchen?" she asked Leo as she approached another louvred door.

"Sure is. Need help with those bags?" he offered.

"Nope. I've got it. It's some of Ms. Gray's Christmas decorations for the dining room. There's a nice Rudolph in here too, for the bar," she called over her shoulder, and pushed open the door to the kitchen.

The Haven House kitchen was a model of efficiency—and had been ever since bartender Ted Carr had taken over as executive chef. As soon as Maureen arrived she'd found that several of the inn's employees were also "guests." That is, Penelope Josephine Gray had permitted certain employees to exchange their labor for rent. Ted was one of these. Elizabeth had been one too. Perhaps the most surprising of the work-for-board staff were Molly, Gert, George, and Sam. Although the four senior citizen residents spent much of their time in rocking chairs on the inn's big wraparound porch, they served as an always-willing household staff. Softhearted Ms. Gray had never raised the rent on any of them and, so far, neither had Maureen.

"Got a minute, Ted?" Maureen asked. The brown-eyed, brown-haired chef looked up from a bowl of fresh salad greens he was tossing and smiled.

"Of course. What's up?" He glanced at the bags she carried. A stuffed Frosty the Snowman peeked over the top of one. "Are you playing Santa Claus a little bit early?"

"Not exactly. I found all of these wonderful old Christmas decorations in Ms. Gray's stash. I've picked out a dozen for centerpieces for the round tables in the dining room. I think we'll need to work them into flower arrangements." She placed the bags on a long butcher-block table. "Can you recommend a florist?"

Walking toward her, Ted wiped his hands on his apron. "Sure can. Petals and Kettles. It's a combination florist and tea shop. It's not far from here. One street over from the boulevard."

"That sounds like fun. I've seen their ads in the paper but haven't met the owner yet."

"Owners," he corrected. "Leslie and Warren Brown. Nice young couple with some original ideas about promotion."

"That's something we could use around here," she said. "I'll call them. Can I put these things in one of your cabinets until we figure out how to display them? There's one more bagful upstairs."

He flashed his fresh-faced, honest smile. *No wonder he'd made big tips when he was tending bar.* "Sure. Use whatever space you need," he offered. "I was just about to take a break. I'll help you bring them down."

"Okay," she agreed. She'd almost refused the offer. After

all, she was perfectly capable of carrying a canvas bag full of light decorations down a short elevator ride. She valued Ted's opinion, though, and her conversation with Lorna had started thoughts about improving the inn's décor spinning through her head. Ted would surely have some ideas on updating the look of the place. He might even have some suggestions on how to pay for it.

Ted washed his hands and turned the salad-making chore over to Molly, who often helped out in the kitchen. He followed Maureen through the dining room and out into the reception area. "Sooner or later, these yellow walls have got to go," he said, making a face.

"Exactly what I was thinking," she said. "I've been daydreaming lately about some new concepts for the overall look of the place. What do you think about a beach theme? Lots of blues and greens and grays—with maybe some sunbleached flotsam and jetsam to hang on the walls in the public areas. Do you like it?" The pair stepped into the elevator and Maureen pushed the button for the top floor.

"I do," he said as the cage moved upward. "I'd like to see it start in the restaurant dining room. The pale green draperies you bought to replace those old dark ones was a good start." He was right. She'd used up a good chunk of her severance pay from Bartlett's of Boston on the much more attractive pastels and the improvement was obvious.

"The new drapes let in more light, but it shows how much the walls need paint," she said. It could be expensive, repairing dings in the walls and woodwork and buying paint. "We're just barely keeping up with expenses as it is. Any bright ideas on how to round up some more money?" They'd reached the third floor and heard Finn's welcoming "woof" from behind the door.

Maureen unlocked the door. "Oh look, Ted. Your favorite cats are in here too." Ms. Gray's rescue cats, Bogie and Bacall, looked down from their perches on the cat tower in front of the big picture window. Bogie was a big tiger-striped gentleman cat who looked as though he'd experienced some tough times. Bacall, on the other hand, was a princess. Pure-bred French Chartreux, all gray with copper-colored eyes. Both cats were fond of Ted, who'd fed them outside the back kitchen door when they'd refused to come inside during the long time between Ms. Gray's death until several weeks after Maureen had come to live at the inn.

"Do you have time to come into the kitchen and have a cup of coffee with me? We could maybe crunch some numbers and figure out how to paint those walls and still pay the bills and buy groceries."

With a glance at the third canvas bag on the floor beside the door, Ted headed to the kitchen and eased his slim frame into one of the blond-wood chairs at either end of the red-and-white enamel-topped table while Maureen slipped a coffee pod into the Keurig machine. In minutes, with two mugs of coffee between them, she sat facing Ted. Maureen was good at figures. She'd had to be for her job at Bartlett's.

"Maybe we can figure out some kind of tie-in with those Christmas movies they'll be running at the Paramount Theater. Did you know that Penelope Josephine Gray was a member of the Paramount's original board of directors? Dinner and a Movie. We'll buy a block of tickets and give one with each dinner," she said. "I think Penelope Josephine would like the idea and the new owner won't mind. He's planning to sell the old place."

"How much do the movie tickets cost?"

"Around ten bucks, I think, for the evening showings, less for the matinees," he said. "Maybe we could pair that with one or two of our regular twenty-dollar dinners and offer a twenty-nine ninety-five special. The first movie starts in a couple of days." There was enthusiasm in his voice.

"Sounds good. We can promote it with flyers all over

town," she said. "Maybe we can get the movie critic at the *Tampa Bay Times* to do a feature on the old movies and mention us in it."

"It would be good if we can set up an interview with the old guy who's the projectionist. Used to be in the movies himself."

At her questioning look, he added "Decklin Monroe. He checked in last night. Met him in the bar. Drinks vodka martinis. Not too many people these days know how to operate the old two-reel projectors. But he does."

"I saw his name on the guest register this morning, and looked around to welcome him, but Gert told me he'd already left for the theater. I had no idea he'd been in movies himself."

"Long time ago, but hey, the inn is starting to attract some really interesting guests. We've got no place to go but up." Again, that endearing smile. Maureen was happy to have him on her side.

"I'm glad you agree about the beach theme for the inn. I think that, along with rooms named after the famous guests who've slept there, we'll attract some new interest." Her tone was hopeful, if not completely convincing.

"We've got this!" *His* tone was thoroughly optimistic, and made her smile too.

"I know you're busy and I have errands to do, so we'd both better get moving." She stood and walked with him to the door, Finn walking between the two. She picked up her purse from the couch. "Bye-bye Finn," she said. "Be a good boy."

The golden crouched in front of the door and began to whine. "I think he wants to go with you." Ted stooped and patted the dog. "It's a nice day for a dog to ride with his head out the window, isn't it, boy?"

"Oh, okay. You're right. He loves riding. I'll get his leash.

See you later, Ted." She picked up the leash from behind the kitchen door and clipped it to Finn's collar. The whining stopped and the tail wagging began in earnest. "I have an errand to do, Finn," she told him. "This isn't just a joyride." The dog practically pranced in anticipation as the two walked down the two flights of stairs and out the back way to where the Subaru was parked.

Chapter 3

Deciding to stop some other time at Sherwin Williams for paint samples and Jo-Ann's for fabric swatches, Maureen headed directly for the tearoom/florist's shop Ted had suggested. Finn—head out the window, ears flapping—was clearly having a good time. The Christmas-themed centerpieces would need to be created well before any significant changes would be made in the inn's restaurant. *Petals and Kettles is such a cute name,* she thought. *I'm sure I'll like the Browns.* She hadn't phoned ahead, and hoped that Leslie or Warren Brown would be on the premises.

The bright blue–painted cottage was on a pretty street parallel to the boulevard. Maureen pulled into a vacant spot in front of the building. "This won't take too long, Finn." She rolled the windows partway down and locked the doors. "I'll be right back." She admired the sign over the front door depicting an old-fashioned tea kettle filled with wild flowers. A good-sized display window showed an assortment of fresh floral arrangements along with an array of porcelain teacups and packages of more varieties of tea than Maureen had ever dreamed existed.

She pushed the blue door open and smiled when the door chime played "I'm a Little Teapot." The place smelled wonderful, whether from whatever exotic tea was brewing in the cozy dining room on her right, or from the colorful display of flowers and plants in the room on her left, she couldn't tell.

"Welcome to Petals and Kettles," called a petite woman from behind a cash register in the flower shop. "Tea or posies for you today?"

"Probably both. If we can sit where I can see my car. My dog came along for the ride." Maureen introduced herself and learned that the dark-eyed beauty was Leslie Brown. She'd taken photos of most of the Christmas decorations and she and Leslie sat together over tea (a fragrant hibiscus variety) in vintage wire ice cream parlor chairs at one of the dainty marble-topped tables. The room was lighted with delicate crystal-prismed chandeliers above each table. Maureen had a clear view of the Subaru from where she sat as the two discussed the best ways to display Penelope's old-time treasures along with appropriate holiday foliage and blooms.

After half an hour they'd decided on a dozen designs for the tables and one for the bar. They'd agreed on a simple, traditional look that took into account Maureen's slim budget as well as the fact that the arrangements needed to be low enough so that guests could see across a table over them. Holly, red berries, and pinecones along with red and white carnations combined with plaid ribbons and a few woven baskets would provide most of the basic supplies. Maureen had at first envisioned red roses, but Leslie Brown had gently suggested that carnations would cost less, last longer, and the general effect would be just as nice. They agreed that either Leslie or Warren would prepare the arrangements at the shop and that they'd be ready in plenty of time for the legendary Twelve Days of Christmas, and that the shop would supply fresh carnations when the original ones wilted. Maureen wrote a check for the deposit, the two shook hands, each of them seemingly happy with the agreement. Leslie insisted on walking to the car with Maureen, especially to meet Finn.

"We'll plan for the Twelve Days of Christmas to coincide

with one or two of the old movies at the Paramount," Maureen said, as Finn enjoyed some ear scratching and head-patting from the woman. "We're planning some special Dinner-and-a-Movie events at the inn."

"Perfect," Leslie agreed, accepting a lick on the nose from Finn. "Warren and I have talked about doing a tea-themed movie night here some time. The only one we've come up with for sure so far is *Tea for Two* with Doris Day."

"I'm sure there are lots more of them," Maureen said. "Maybe you could ask Decklin Monroe. He's the projectionist the Paramount hired for the twelve days. He knows how to show the old two-reel movies so he's probably seen millions of films. He's staying at the inn. I'll be glad to introduce you."

Leslie flashed a dimpled smile. "Oh, thank you. We've already met Mr. Monroe. He's a dear, isn't he? He was a friend of my parents' many years ago. He stopped by for tea yesterday. My mom was here and they had a nice chat—reminiscing about old times. He's quite the tea connoisseur. He's agreed to look up tea movies for us. He says he thinks there's a nice Japanese tea ceremony in one of the Karate Kid movies."

Hesitant to admit that she hadn't herself yet actually met the projectionist, Maureen thanked her hostess, said that she looked forward to working with the Browns, confirmed an appointment for the following day for delivering the chosen thirteen items from Ms. Gray's Christmas hoard, and left the attractive blue shop. From where she stood beside the car, she could see past the blue building and what appeared to be a matching small cottage behind it into the parking lot behind the Paramount Theater. Maybe the projectionist would still be there. She climbed into the Subaru, mentally checking "find a florist" off her to-do list.

For as long as Maureen had been in Haven, the movie house had only been open on weekend evenings and special occasions, showing a variety of favorites like *Psycho* and *Rear Window,* and currently, according to the sign on the marquee, *Dumb and Dumber.* She felt as though she might identify with the latter, since so far, resident housekeeper and long-ago Las Vegas showgirl Gert, chef Ted, and the local tea house proprietors knew more about her new semi-famous tenant than she did.

There were few cars in the designated parking lot behind the theater. Maureen surmised that at one time there must have been many more spaces for moviegoers, and wondered what the current owners of the Paramount intended to do with the overflow. She saw one with California plates. Decklin Monroe had been in movies once—maybe the nicely restored vintage Plymouth coupe was his. There was an exit door from the theater facing onto the parking lot. Maureen gave the door handle a gentle tug. The door swung open, emitting a rush of air-conditioned air. "Hello," she called, "is anybody here? Mr. Monroe?"

She was answered by the booming sound of an organ chord, then another, until the series of unrelated, discordant harmonies ceased and a quieter series of tones issued from the darkened theater, then stopped abruptly.

"Hello?" A masculine voice sounded from the blackness. "Sorry if that startled you. Scared me too. I just remembered there's a Wurlitzer organ in here. I'm Monroe. Who's there?"

Maureen remained standing in the pool of light just inside the door. Shielding her eyes and peering inside, she tried to determine what direction the voice had come from. "I'm Maureen Doherty," she announced. "From the Haven House Inn."

There was the sound of footsteps, a few muffled clicks, and several lights went on—one of them a spotlight illuminating the stooped figure of a man standing in the corner of a curtained stage. "Hi, Maureen. Pleased to meet you. Come aboard." The figure beckoned. A few more clicks and all of the houselights in the long room blazed.

Maureen had attended several movies in the old theater, but had never seen it fully lighted before. "Wow. This place is bigger than I remembered." She took a hesitant step toward the man. "How many seats?" she called. "Do you know?"

"Two hundred and fifty," came the answer, "although most of them are pretty beat up."

She nodded agreement, noting the worn red fabric seats. He turned off the spotlight, leaving only the aisle lights glowing. "They don't look so bad with the lights dimmed." He joined her beside the open door. His lined face was deeply tanned, hair snowy white, a Ron Jon Surf Shop T-shirt revealing a slim, frail body. She wondered how old he was. Seventy? Eighty? Ninety?

"People don't seem to mind," she said. "It's kind of shabby-chic, you know?"

"I guess you could look at it that way," he said, "but I'm thinking of buying the place, so I have to think about costs of bringing it up to snuff. New seats, new carpet, fix some leaks in the roof. The building inspector says the public can't use the balcony at all until the stairway is repaired. That's fifty unusable seats." He waved long, bony arms, taking in the entire room. "Quite a project."

She smiled at the use of the old expression. She was having her own experience in trying to bring an aged structure "up to snuff," whatever that meant. "I'd heard something about it being for sale," she told him. "It's certainly an interesting piece of property. It'd be nice to fix it up so a new generation can enjoy it. The newspaper said there's an out-of-town corporate owner. It's sort of on some kind of lease to the college."

"That's right," he said. "The youngsters in the Haven City Junior College movie club have been running it as a fund-raiser. They mostly show artsy-fartsy film festival things they can get free. Once in a while they get hold of a real movie. The owner is footing the bill for the twelve Christmas movies. They hired me to work with the kids so nothing gets screwed up. I think it's kind of a test to see if they can attract a good audience by showing some classics. If it works, it makes the place more valuable."

"So the price goes up," she observed.

"It would," he agreed, "but I think I know where I can get some backing. I have some meetings set up. I'll just have to make a good impression, do a good job of convincing the money people that I can make a go of it. If I did it, I wouldn't have to depend on showing only old-time films and freebies. I'd be able to get the new releases." A gentle sigh. "Quite a project," he said again.

"I know what you mean," she sympathized. "The Haven House Inn is *my* project. Progress is slow." She echoed his sigh. "And expensive."

"Oh, you're the owner? I like the place. Needs work, but it has good bones."

"I inherited the inn," she said. "As a matter of fact, the woman who left it to me was on the board of directors of this theater. I inherited her membership along with the inn, but I guess that doesn't mean much now that the Paramount has a new owner too." She appreciated the thought about the inn's good bones. "I'm glad you like the inn. Thanks. I'm thinking about doing a Dinner and a Movie event. We'd buy a block of tickets for a Christmas movie and pair it with a dinner."

The old man nodded. "I'll check out the list of movies and try to pick out one of the best ones for you."

"Thanks so much. Do you have the list? The first one is scheduled for day after tomorrow." Was she being pushy? "I'm only asking because I'm working on ideas for some floral centerpiece ideas using a collection of old-time Christmas decorations," she explained. "Maybe we can match up some of the decorations with one of the movies." She paused briefly, then added, "I'm working with your friends at Petals and Kettles."

"Sweet couple," he said. "I get it. You could use a reindeer decoration with *Prancer.* Or a snowman with *Frosty.* So you collect old ornaments?"

"Not exactly. I inherited a collection as well," she said. "They seem to suit the place so I may as well make use of them."

"I know what you mean. Seems that the Paramount has a stash of the old two-reel films that have been here for years. Somebody saved them even though I'm sure they were supposed to be returned to the studios. One of them turned out to be *Remember the Night*, an old 1940 Barbara Stanwyck Christmas comedy. I plan to start with that one for the first night."

"Wow. I'll bet none of the TV stations even have that one for their Holiday movie lineup."

"I'm pretty sure they don't. It's one of those two-reel old-timers. Not too many guys these days know how to switch the reels without interrupting the movie. I'm good at it. That's why they hired me." He stood a little straighter. "Everything now is digital so they don't need the complicated projectors. But this place has the old projector, and a bunch of films."

"Any other famous movies?" she wondered.

"I don't know yet. I haven't had a chance to take a good look beyond the Stanwyck one. I believe all the others are single reels or digital. To tell the truth, I'm a little creeped out by the place. You know about the Paramount ghost?" He tipped his head to one side, frowning. "Or aren't you a believer in such things?"

Loaded question. How to answer? "I try to keep an open

mind about it," she said. "I've heard some talk about haunted buildings in Haven. Is this supposed to be one of them?"

"Yes. A man. He was shot here back in the seventies. Sitting in an aisle seat, minding his own business, watching *Animal House*." He shook his head. "Then, boom. Gone."

"Who was he?"

He shrugged. "Nobody. Some kind of small-time hoodlum."

Her voice still hushed, Maureen asked, "Did they catch the killer?"

"Don't know. They say the man's ghost has been seen in the same seat, watching a movie. Row four. Aisle one. First seat."

"How does anyone know it's him?" Maureen wondered, feeling doubtful.

"When the houselights come up, he disappears. And, oh yeah, he only watches comedies."

"Have you seen him yourself?" she asked.

A short burst of laughter. "Of course not. Like my mother told me, there's no such thing as ghosts!"

My mother told me the same thing, Maureen recalled. *But Haven has taught me something different.* She didn't disagree with Decklin Monroe. Her mother had taught her respect for one's elders too. Besides, how does anyone explain Lorna and Billy Bedoggoned Bailey and Babe Ruth and the other . . . er . . . manifestations without sounding like a total nut job? Her thoughts about Haven's ghost population were interrupted.

"What do you say? Want to come up to the projection booth and see how everything works? Where the magic happens?" Decklin offered. "Maybe watch a short subject?"

"Sorry. Not today." She pointed to the Subaru where Finn watched from the open passenger seat window. "I have my dog with me." Anyway, was it even safe to walk into an empty building with a strange man—even if the man was old and bent and obviously somewhat fragile?

"Oh, bring him on in," Monroe said. "A little dog hair can't harm anything in this old place. Housebroken, isn't he?"

"Of course." She made a quick decision that she'd be safe—especially with Finn at her side—retrieved Finn from the car, and whispered, "He's an old guy, Finn. Between us, we could take him if we had to."

"Woof woof," Finn agreed. She locked the car door and entered the theater, leaving the parking lot door wide open, and fell into step behind the man, casting a backward glance at aisle one, row four. Cautiously, with the building inspector's warning in mind, the three climbed a flight of stairs to the balcony, then passed through a nearly hidden door at the rear of the upper tier of seats. Another flight of stairs. Narrower. Darker. Decklin Monroe flicked on a flashlight, making the climb easier and less creepy. Monroe went first, Finn behind him, Maureen holding tight to Finn's leash.

"I found a box full of usher's flashlights," he said. "They've come in handy." He pushed open a paneled door. "Here we are." He pressed a switch and the small room was illuminated. Maureen was surprised. The projectionist's booth was surprisingly cozy, carpeted, with a comfortable-looking upholstered chair beside a long table bearing what she recognized easily as projectors. One was a larger version of the one her grandfather had used to show what he called "home movies"—jittery, mostly black-and-white footage of people and places *his* grandfather had photographed. She felt a moment of sadness, wishing now she'd paid more attention. Perhaps her folks had saved the movies. She'd be sure to ask next time she talked to them. A pair of taller projectors she recognized as the reel-to-reel ones she'd heard about, but had never seen close up. She pointed to one. "This must be the ones that take two reels at a time. Your specialty."

"You're right." He tapped the smaller projector. "Want to see a couple of quick short subjects? I have this one all loaded up. Take the soft chair. You can see the screen through that little window." He pointed. Finn had already made himself comfortable on the carpet beside the designated soft chair.

"I'd love to see it. Wow. Everything but the popcorn."

"Actually, even the vintage popcorn machine is in the lobby. Still in working order," he said. "Maybe next time . . ."

"Next time," she agreed. "Meanwhile, what are we watching now?"

"Three Stooges."

A comedy, she thought. "A Three Stooges movie!" she exclaimed. "Awesome."

The theme music for the film began: "Three Blind Mice." She focused her attention on the distant, glowing screen, forcing herself not to look at aisle one, row four, aisle seat.

Chapter 4

Maureen had really enjoyed the film and Finn seemed to have liked it too. Decklin ran another one. Maureen giggled and Finn wagged his tail. The slapstick comedy was still funny, the corny jokes still bringing a laugh or a groan. When THE END flashed on the screen and the music stopped, she turned to face the old man. "That was fun. Thank you, Mr. Monroe. Maybe popcorn, next time?"

"Absolutely. I make it with coconut oil and real butter. Ordered the coconut oil special. For the real old-time movie popcorn taste. Please call me Decklin—and do we know each other well enough for me to call you Maureen?"

"We do," she said. "I'd better get going back to Haven House. I expect I'll see you there later?"

"Yes indeed." He handed her a flashlight. "Here, Maureen. Take one of these. I have a whole box full. You can find your way out, can't you? I'd escort you but these old legs can use a rest and I have some tidying up to do here. I might give the Stanwyck film a quick run-through just to be sure it's intact."

With only the slightest hesitation, she took the flashlight. "Sure I can. I mean, no problem. Down the stairs, across the balcony, down the unstable stairs, and out the door. Got it."

She gave him a quick salute with the light. "See you back at the ranch, Decklin."

He was already hunched over the tall projector, removing the large top wheel of the thing. "Uh-huh," he said, clearly absorbed in what he was doing, forgetting her. She pulled open the door, made sure the light was burning brightly, and with Finn going ahead, started down to the balcony, across to the stairs, down that flight, and onto the main floor of the theater where the aisle lights glowed in neat, parallel rows. She hurried toward the shining red word EXIT and the still-open door.

Glad of the sunlight, she pulled the door closed behind her, wondering why she was so relieved to get out of Haven's Paramount Theater. She hadn't seen anything in the least disturbing while she was inside. Decklin Monroe had been charming. Finn had seemed to like him and the movie both. There had been no shimmering shadows, no sudden drops in temperature, certainly no manifestations. *No ghoulies or ghosties or long-leggedy beasties or things that go bump in the night!* She comforted herself with the old Robert Burns quote, and headed for her car.

The sensation of relief was short lived when she recognized the man leaning against the Subaru door, watching as she approached. Officer Frank Hubbard. What did he want? There surely couldn't be any parking restrictions in this almost empty lot. She slipped the flashlight into her purse and faced him. "Good afternoon, Officer Hubbard. Anything wrong?" Finn woofed softly and moved forward, placing himself between Maureen and the policeman.

"Now what would make you think anything is wrong, Ms. Doherty? Nothing at all. At least nothing I know of unless you want to tell me why you're in a closed-up, smelly old theater on a nice day like this?"

"Not that it's any of your business, Officer," she spoke as politely as she could manage, "but I was here to welcome a guest at the inn. Mr. Monroe is the new projectionist here. He's busy inside right now but I'm sure he'd be glad to show you around." Maureen knew that her "none of your business" remark was a bit flip, and regretted saying it as soon as the words had crossed her lips. She tried to make amends with a softened tone. "Mr. Monroe is thinking about renovating the old place. He has some good ideas. It would be good for Haven, having a full-time movie theater. 'First-run films,' he says."

"You were in there quite a long time, Ms. Doherty," Hubbard announced. "Seems like we're both checking up on your new guest."

"I wasn't . . . what do you mean, 'checking up'? This was what we in the hotel business consider a 'courtesy call.' I always try to greet my guests in person. I wasn't there when he checked in." She spoke quickly, not trying to disguise her annoyance. The man could be insufferable sometimes.

"Don't get huffy, Ms. Doherty. Maybe checking up isn't the right thing to call it? What would you call a nice-looking young woman being holed up in a run-down old movie house with a guy old enough to be her grandfather for . . ." He looked at his watch. "For one hour and seven minutes."

Shoot. The movies alone had taken about half an hour. Wait a minute. He was timing her? What was going on here?

"Why on earth do you want to know? If it's any of your business, most of the time I was watching some old movies. Ever hear of the Three Stooges?"

"Sure. He showed you movies? Why?"

"Because that's what he does, Officer. He shows movies." She moved toward the driver's side of the Subaru, tugging Finn's leash. "If you'll excuse me? I need to get back home and walk my dog."

He didn't move. "What do you know about this guy? Besides that he shows movies?"

"Ted says he used to be an actor. That's it. That's all I know."
She unlocked the car door.

"Ted, huh? Did he mention that Monroe has a record?"
He stepped away from the car. He didn't look as though he
expected an answer, and didn't get one. Maureen climbed
into the driver's seat, opened the passenger-side window for
Finn, checked her surroundings, and drove slowly, carefully,
out of the lot and onto Beach Boulevard. She glanced at the
rearview mirror more than a few times on the ride back to
the inn. No patrol car in sight.

She parked the Subaru in the back lot behind the inn, in
the space marked MANAGER. Elizabeth's name had been spray-
painted out. Maybe sometime when money wasn't an issue,
she'd have a proper new sign painted. The kitchen door was
the closest one to the lot, and making her way through the
front porch guests sometimes took more time than she had to
spare just then. Finn was getting anxious for his afternoon
walk to the beach. She knocked first, even though she owned
the place, then pushed the door open.

Something smelled wonderful—not unusual from executive chef Ted's department. Gert was busily stirring the contents of a huge black iron pot.

Shakespeare's old song of the witches flashed through her
consciousness. *Double, double toil and trouble / Fire burn
and cauldron bubble.* She shook the silly thought away, trying
not to connect the recent encounter with Officer Hubbard
and "double toil and trouble." Senior citizen ex-showgirl
Gert was no witch and Maureen didn't want to hear any more
information about Decklin's past troubles anyway.

"Hi, Maureen. Did you get the flower arrangements figured out?" She was glad to see Ted. His crisp white chef's
jacket was just as fresh and clean as it had been hours ago,
his hair as neatly combed. He bent and put his arms around
Finn's neck. "Did you have a good time, boy?"

Finn said, "woof."

"Arrangements are all figured out," Maureen said, "and Ted, the Browns are so pleasant and cooperative. I'll take the ornaments over to Petals and Kettles in the morning. I'm sure they'll all fit into the Subaru. Then I'll need to ask George or Sam to bring the truck over to pick up the finished products."

"No problem. That'll be on the first day of the Twelve Days of Christmas promotion, right?

"Right. Lunch smells amazing. I'd stop and taste but I'm sure Finn is getting anxious."

"It's corn and chicken chowder. We had chicken left over from yesterday's grilled chicken breasts. Throw in a few cans of corn, some fresh veggies and cream—and along with rolls and salad it's a whole new lunch entrée."

"I like the way you think, Ted," she told him. "Food recycling like that helps a lot to save the money we need."

"Learned it from my mother," he told her. "Wise woman. Good cook."

Maureen knew that Ted's mom had once run a seafood restaurant near the sport fishing docks. She wondered for a brief moment if Ted's wise mother, like Decklin's mother—and her own—had told him there was no such thing as ghosts. She didn't ask, and—at Gert's insistence—accepted a spoonful of chowder.

"Fabulous," she said. "Save me a bowl. I'll be back shortly. Gotta change my shoes and take Finn to the beach." She hurried toward the elevator. The dog walking wouldn't take long and she'd have plenty of time for lunch. After all, nobody was timing her. "One hour and seven minutes," she muttered aloud. "The nerve of the man!" She often talked to Finn and sometimes read to him too. He seemed to enjoy both. As soon as the elevator doors parted she dropped the leash and followed as he trotted toward home. She changed quickly into sneakers and shorts and the two took the stairs down to the lobby. She'd pushed the green door to the porch partly open when Gert greeted her with a stage-whispered warning.

"Just in case you're interested, that cop, Hubbard, is parked right out front, sitting in his cruiser, as if he's keeping an eye on the place. You might want to duck out the side door—that is if you want to."

"Thanks, Gert. I will."

Gert wasn't through. "What does he want? If you don't mind my asking."

"I don't know," Maureen said honestly. "But it has something to do with our new guest. Mr. Monroe."

"Oh, that." Gert had a wise look on her wrinkled face. "Might have known he'd dig *that* up again."

"What?" Maureen whispered back. Too late. Gert had already closed the door, leaving her employer inside the lobby, wondering. As Gert had suggested, she cut through a short corridor, past the guest laundry and the ice machine, and out to the side door—which had a round cat door at its base, giving Bogie and Bacall easy access to the inn when they didn't choose to come in the "penthouse" window. She peeked around a tall pink hibiscus. Gert was right. There he was, parked directly in front of the inn, paper coffee cup on the dashboard, just like a TV detective on a stakeout.

Chapter 5

Finn tugged at his leash. It was the urgent kind of tug that meant he truly had to go. If she cut through a few backyards, maybe she could get to the beach without Hubbard spotting her, or maybe she'd just brazen it out and march right past the cruiser. He'd parked facing in the wrong direction, so it would take a minute for him to catch up with her—if that's what he meant to do. She wished there was time to go back inside the inn and get Gert to tell her exactly what was being "dug up" again. Finn woofed. There was no time to spare.

So head up, shoulders back, leash in one hand and plastic doggie-doo bag in the other, she moved past the hibiscus, onto the sidewalk, in full view of Officer Frank Hubbard—if he happened to be looking her way.

He wasn't. His attention was clearly fixed on the front porch, where George and Sam sat in their usual rockers, staring right back at him. Maureen took a tentative step forward. Maybe she was going to sneak right past him. Would have too, if Finn the Friendly hadn't greeted the two porch-sitters with a short burst of happy woofs. Hubbard snapped his head around so fast he almost spilled his coffee.

By the time he'd executed a totally illegal U-turn, Finn and Maureen were all the way down the boulevard to the Haven Bookshop, where owner Aster Patterson waved from her patio. As often was the case, Aster's choice of wardrobe was distinctive. Today she wore quilted ski pants with what looked to Maureen like a pink satin bed jacket. Stopping for a visit was out of the question and she upped her pace toward the beach. The cruiser got there at the same time she did. Hubbard leaned from his window. "In a hurry, Ms. Doherty?"

She pointed to the golden, who'd just assumed the position for doing what came naturally. "No, sir," she said politely. "But my dog was."

He frowned, got out of the car, and approached her—cautiously. She turned, cleaned up after Finn, and walked toward the receptacle provided for it. He followed. "Couple of questions," he said.

"Do I need my lawyer?"

"No. Want to get rid of that?" He pointed to the plastic bag.

"It'll keep," she said. "What do you want?"

"I've heard that you had a visit with the Browns before you went to see Monroe, the old pal of Leslie Henshaw's—now Mrs. Brown's—daddy. Care to explain that?"

"I ordered some flowers." *Mrs. Brown's daddy? What does he have to do with anything?* She held the offending plastic bag a tiny bit closer to the officer. "Is that all?"

He took a step back. "You knew the two men were acquainted?"

"No. I don't know much of anything about either one of them. I just met Mr. Monroe today and never even heard of Mrs. Brown's father before." She dropped the bag into the container. "I've promised the dog a run on the beach. Unless you'd care to join us . . . ?" She looked down at his polished, laced-up black shoes and was sure he'd turn down the invitation.

"I'll try to keep up," he said. He bent down, took off the shoes, tucked his socks inside, put the shoes under his arm, and fell into step beside her. "Let's just get this over with, so I don't have to waste the taxpayers' money chasing you all over Haven."

They'd reached the sand. Astonished, she faced him. "This must be important," she said, "but I've already answered your questions. I've told you everything I know." Finn tugged, ready for his run and she broke into a jog. Hubbard kept up with her.

"Cold case," he said. "I read them when I have spare time. Kind of a hobby. Anyway, there was a murder that happened here in Haven forty-odd years ago. Murder in Haven is pretty darned unusual."

"I'm sure it is." She picked up the pace. "I wasn't here that long ago. I wasn't even born."

"I know that. But for the first time in darn near half a century, two persons of interest are now back in Haven. Monroe and Henshaw were both in Haven when that murder happened. Why do you think that is, Ms. Doherty?" He puffed a little from the exertion, and half smiled. "We both know you like to investigate murder, Ms. Doherty, and you've managed to make contact with both of these people in half a day. What do you know that you're not telling me?"

She slowed down, despite Finn's urging. "I have no idea what you're talking about. And who got murdered anyway?"

"A nobody. An out-of-town bum name of Putnam. Buddy Putnam. Never found any relatives. The city buried him. Died watching a movie." He motioned back toward the boulevard with his free arm. "In that movie theater back there. Where you were today for an hour and seven minutes."

The ghost on aisle one!

She didn't—couldn't—answer. The remark about her liking to investigate murder wasn't true. She'd helped with an investigation earlier in the year, but she'd had to. It had happened at the Haven House Inn and she'd needed to clear her own name along with other innocent residents and guests. It wasn't anything she'd liked doing.

"Ms. Doherty?" Hubbard persisted. "What about it? Did Monroe tell you about the murder?"

"He said a man was shot in the first seat on row four in aisle one back in the seventies, and that his spirit is supposed to be haunting the theater." She paused, thinking. "Oh, yeah. The man was watching *Animal House*."

"Ghosts!" It came from his lips like a disgusted snarl. "Ghosts again, huh?"

Unfortunately, the death at Haven House had involved a professional ghost hunter. "That's what Mr. Monroe told me. That's all I know about it. And Mr. Monroe doesn't believe in ghosts."

"Have you met Leslie Brown's father? Harry Henshaw?"

"No."

"Her mother?"

"No."

"Do you have plans to . . . uh . . . visit with the Browns again?"

"Tomorrow," she said. "About the flower arrangements they're doing for me." Finn tugged harder. "Is there anything else?" she asked. "We need to run now."

"Nothing more for now." He shifted the shoes from one arm to the other. "I'll be in touch," he said, turned around, and started walking—as though the hot sand burned his feet—back toward the boulevard.

Maureen and Finn took time to stop at the bookstore on the way back to the inn. Aster Patterson, as always, was glad to see both. "Can you stop for a spot of tea and some nice shortbread cookies?" Aster baked those cookies every day. They'd been her late husband Peter's favorite treat and word around Haven was that she baked them in hopes that his spirit would visit her. Unlike so many other sites in Haven, the bookstore, so far as anyone knew, remained ghost-free. Thanks to Maureen and Ted, though, the cookies were often on the inn's lunch menu.

"Just stopping to say 'hello,' " Maureen told her. "Lots to do back at the inn."

"So, what's going on with you and Officer Hubbard?" Aster passed the plate of cookies, despite Maureen's protest.

She ate one anyway. "He's interested in a guest at the inn," she said. "I couldn't help him."

"Oh, that," Aster chewed her own cookie thoughtfully. "Decklin Monroe, huh? Everybody down at the Quic-Shop was talking about it. Somebody said he has a police record here from a long time ago. Drunk and disorderly, they say. How come you spent an hour and seven minutes with the old coot?"

Maureen had ceased being amazed at the rumor mill the local grocery had become, but she *was* surprised at the speed with which this particular rumor had traveled. "He showed me a couple of funny little Three Stooges movies," she admitted.

"Oh, yeah." Aster nodded, smiling. "The Three Stooges. I always loved them."

Maureen returned the smile, reserving comment. At least they weren't talking about Leslie Brown's parents, she thought. Aster pushed the cookie plate forward again, and Maureen declined, remembering the bowl of chicken corn chowder awaiting her. "Thanks, Aster," she said. "Gotta get going. Lots to do."

"Business pretty good?"

"Getting better." This time it was Maureen who tugged on the leash, urging Finn away from the shop window where he was visiting with the shop's black cat, Erle Stanley Gardner. "See you later, Aster," she called, fearing that the next revelation might be from the inn's profit and loss sheet.

*   *   *

Once, again, she used the side entrance and by the time she'd passed the ice machine, the clink of china and the hum of conversation from the dining room told her that the lunchtime promotions were working. She peeked through the louvred door. The room was nearly full. She and the golden rode the elevator up to the third floor. She fed Finn hastily, changed from shorts, T-shirt, and Nikes to a more business-like white shirt, navy denim skirt, and flats, and returned via the back entrance to the kitchen.

"I saved you some chowder," Molly called. "Good thing I did. We almost ran out. We're doing coffee ice cream with chocolate sauce and shortbread cookies for dessert. Want some?"

Maureen patted her tummy. "Already had cookies," she said, accepting the steaming bowl of chowder. "I'll just eat this right here."

"Ted's in his office. Why don't you take it in there?"

"Okay. I will." A small desk bearing a laptop with a bulletin board on the wall above next to the walk-in refrigerator had been dubbed "Ted's office." She made a pretend "knock knock" motion. "Hello, Ted? Can I come in?"

"Come in." Ted stood to greet her. "Is everything okay? Gert said Hubbard was lurking outside, waiting for you. What's going on?"

It was a relief to be able to talk to someone she trusted about the day's strange happenings—from her own perspective, unfiltered through the rumor mill at the Quic-Shop Market. As carefully and accurately as she could, between rich spoonfuls of chowder, she told him about her courtesy call at the theater, her meeting with the Browns, and her two encounters with Frank Hubbard. "What do *you* think is going on?"

"He ran on the beach with you?" Ted half smiled.

"I know. Weird, isn't it? He seemed to think it was that important—whatever 'it' is."

"So there's a connection between Mr. Monroe and Leslie's father and Hubbard thinks you might be the connection?"

"I guess so. It's just silly," she said. "Both men have something to do with a cold-case murder that happened at the theater a long time ago. Before I was born. So how can I be connected to it?"

"You aren't, of course." His calm voice and concerned expression made her feel better. "Relax. We'll figure this out."

She liked his use of "we."

"I stopped to visit with Aster." She finished her chowder and pushed the bowl away. "That was delicious. Anyway, the Haven rumor mill is all cranked up on this already. Aster even knew the part about my spending an hour and seven minutes in the Paramount Theater with Monroe."

"The Quic-Shop?" He grinned.

" 'Fraid so." She spread her hands in a helpless gesture. "I don't even shop there."

"Most everybody does," he said. "Beer, cigarettes, lottery tickets, basic groceries."

"I don't use the first three and the groceries are too expensive," she reasoned. "Anyway, I depend on the restaurant to feed me and I order Finn's dog food online."

"I don't shop there either," Ted admitted, "but my name turns up occasionally at the Quic-Shop too. I mean, how come everyone in town knows that you and I meet in front of the Casino every morning and run on the beach together? By now they probably know that you ran today with Hubbard." Short laugh.

"I guess some of it comes from right here inside the inn," she reasoned. "Our resident porch-sitters don't miss much."

"They're all on our side," Ted assured her. "Gert and Molly, Sam and George—they love this place. They love you. We're in good hands."

She liked his use of "we" again. "Thank you for the lovely lunch. I'm off to get some paint samples for future consideration. See you at dinner."

The trips to the paint and fabric stores proved time consuming, but successful. The paint store had not only the expected color chips, but also provided sample jars of each color she chose. It turned out that the clerk at the fabric store was an old friend of Ms. Gray's and could hardly contain her joy at the idea of refurbishing the dining room. She clipped samples happily from the selected lengths of yard goods, and even suggested a few materials Maureen hadn't thought about.

It was close to sunset when Maureen returned to the inn. She used the front door this time, greeting guests and residents as she walked between the rocking chairs. She peeked into the dining room, where dinner guests already crowded around several of the tables. Perhaps she'd come downstairs later for the evening meal—and perhaps a cocktail to celebrate the end of a busy day.

She entered the elevator, tapped the UP button, and began the slow upward ride. Maureen was thoughtful, visualizing Christmas centerpieces, when she felt a jolt. The elevator had stopped. She peered through etched-glass sides, seeing gray brick wall. It had stopped between floors.

"Oh, I say. I'm sorry. Did I do that?"

The man's voice came from behind her.

Chapter 6

Maureen whirled around, turning in the direction the voice had come from, facing the man. He was tall, quite handsome in a slicked-back hair, narrow-mustached, tweed-jacket sort of way. Also he was shimmering, his edges not quite distinct. There was the faintest scent of pipe tobacco in the air. Ordinarily, she would have screamed—or at least felt some sort of fright—but his appearance was so similar to Lorna's that she knew immediately that her elevator mate was other-worldly in nature, even though he appeared in full color, not black and white. She was more annoyed than frightened. "You probably did, somehow. Who are you and why are you in my elevator?"

"I beg your pardon. This is your lift—or as you Americans call it, your elevator? This *is* the Haven House Inn, is it not?"

"It is," she agreed, "and we seem to be between floors."

"I'm sorry," he said again. "I have an affinity for lifts and this is a wonderful one. I'm Reginald Yardley and I have an appointment in the penthouse." He reached past her and pressed the button marked 3. "Here we go." The elevator whirred to life and began to rise.

"I happen to be going to the penthouse too," Maureen said. "I'm Maureen Doherty and I live there."

"Ah!" His smile was a thing of orthodontic beauty. "Yes.

Lorna mentioned you. Her roommate, I believe. Charmed to meet you." He didn't extend his hand, nor did Maureen extend hers. Shaking hands with a ghost was unsatisfactory to say the least—your hand went right through theirs and the place where his hand should be was freezing cold. The elevator cruised to a stop and the doors parted. "I'm here to pick up my date."

Maureen remembered the borrowed dress and shoes. "Waltz night in St. Augustine?"

"Exactly. They have a delightful elevator there too, though not so fine as this one." He made a sweeping, courtly gesture. "After you, Ms. Doherty."

She moved into the long hall, pausing until he caught up with her. The idea of a ghost behind her back was somehow disturbing. She listened for Finn's expected welcoming woofs. The hall was quiet. She walked a little faster toward her suite. *Never mind the following ghost.* She called for the golden even before she'd turned the key in the lock. "Finn! It's me!"

"Take it easy, Maureen." It was Lorna's voice. "We're right here. I was reading Finn a nice dog story. *Greyfriars Bobby.*" A soft "woof" from Finn verified his presence. She pushed the door open and accepted Finn's apologetic wet doggy kisses. The book in Lorna's hand disappeared like smoke as she recognized Maureen's companion. "Reggie! You're early. I guess you've met my roomie?"

"We met in the elevator," Maureen said. "It's getting cool out. Maybe you should borrow my faux mink jacket. Let's go in the bedroom and you can try it on. Excuse us, Mr. Yardley." *Lorna has some explaining to do about that roommate story.* For the second time that evening, Maureen had a ghost following behind her as Lorna, with a wave and a blown kiss in Reggie's direction, followed her through the kitchen and into the bedroom.

"Okay. Since when is this your home address?" Maureen felt silly just asking the question of a ghost.

"Since you ask, it's the only homeplace I've had since that night back in 1975 when I was doing Summer Stock down at the Haven Playhouse, tripped over an electrical cord, and took a header downstage center and broke my neck." Maureen knew the story of Lorna's untimely and quite ungraceful demise at the age of sixty-five. "I told you. I was staying at Haven House at the time. All my clothes and stuff were here, so I decided to stay."

Maureen nodded understanding. "I knew that. I'm getting used to you popping in and out, and I rather liked the fact that I can tap on the pushbell and get you right away if I need to talk to you. I guess I just hadn't thought of you as a 'roommate.' The subject never came up before."

"Is it okay, then? I can stay?"

"Where else could you go?" Maureen wondered.

"I'm not sure what would become of me," Lorna admitted, "and I would rather not find out just yet."

"Okay, then. You can stay. But absolutely no having boyfriends sleep over."

"I promise. Anyway, he haunts a room over at the Casa Monica. Thanks, Maureen. Now can I try on that mink?"

"Faux mink."

"I'll never tell," she said and, in the wink of an eye, the illusion of the soft brown jacket was draped over her shoulders. "All right, Reggie," she called as she left the room, hips swaying, "here I come. Ready or not."

Once her ghost-guests had shimmered away, and she'd promised Finn that she'd see if Aster had a copy of *Greyfriars Bobby* at the bookstore, Maureen kicked off her shoes and sat on the sofa. The package of Christmas cards was still on the coffee table. She picked it up and untied the narrow blue ribbon. "If these are old enough, they may be worth a few bucks," she told Finn. It might be enough to make the difference between plain cotton and real barkcloth for dining room seat covers.

The first envelope, of good quality ecru paper, was addressed—by typewriter—to Penelope Josephine Gray at the Haven House Inn. It bore a Miami postmark, and a 1968 date. She rifled through the others, all addressed to Ms. Gray, all in the same typeface. There were a few 1970s, some 1980s, and a couple of 1990s. The postmarks showed several Florida cities. "Not really old enough to be antiques," she muttered, then brightened. "Hey, Finn, maybe they're signed by somebody famous." She opened the envelope carefully, removing a colorful greeting card. A snowy Christmas scene on the front, a brief printed greeting on the inside. No signature. She looked at the envelope once again. No return address.

One at a time, she opened the envelopes, and one at a time found similar cards. Each one had a traditional design—some Santas, more snow scenes, some cute animals. Each card bore a friendly, warm holiday greeting. None was signed. None bore a return address.

She reached the last envelope. This one was a plain, blank white oblong. No address, no postmark at all. "Maybe this was one Penelope meant to mail to somebody," she told the dog. He moved a little closer to the couch, watching with interest as she attempted to lift the flap. Surprised, she realized that this card was sealed. "Shall I open it?" she asked aloud, more to herself than to Finn.

Finn answered anyway. "Woof."

"Of course. You're right. It's mine. Everything here is mine." Carrying the blank envelope and leaving the others on the coffee table, she went to the desk, picked up the letter opener from the desk set she'd used in her office at Bartlett's, and carefully opened the envelope.

This card was different. No sleighs in the snow, no Santas, no bunnies or kitties. No red and green holly or candy canes there either. A drawing of a quarter moon and a star were at the top of the blue card. The verse was printed in dark red. She'd seen a similar card quite recently. It hadn't come in a sealed envelope, though. It had come from an animated machine in an amusement park.

She'd entered the arcade at South of the Border, immediately drawn to the flashing lights of a true-to-the-original Zoltar fortune-telling machine. It had looked exactly like the one she remembered from the old movie *Big*. After a satisfying moment of blinking, pinging, and chiming, the card had inched out from an oblong golden portal. The rhyme on that card had begun:

> *With a message from the dead*
> *On a journey you've been led.*

She'd saved that card. It, along with a coin she'd found on the floor on her last day at Bartlett's, were by themselves in the smallest drawer in her big, beautiful, blond Heywood-Wakefield bureau. The card she'd just found in a stack of old unsigned Christmas cards that had been saved by Penelope Josephine Gray began with exactly the same words. It had the same drawing of a quarter moon and a star. She lay the card on the coffee table—facedown. She didn't want to read the rest of the message.

"Maybe later," she told Finn. "Maybe now I'll go downstairs and enjoy a nice dinner—and maybe a glass of wine. Then, if I feel like it, I'll read the damned thing."

Finn gave a soft "woof" and put his head on her knee. She scratched behind his ears, gave him a pat and a little kiss on top of his head, and slipped the shoes back on.

Chapter 7

Maureen couldn't help looking around in the elevator on the way down to the dining room. She was alone, no company—earthly or otherwise—and no tobacco smell either. If she had occasion to meet Reginald again, she'd remind him that Haven House was a no-smoking establishment. When she reached the lobby she was pleased to see that there were still a few folks waiting to be seated. *No sense taking up a dining room seat that a paying customer might want*, she thought. *I can just as well grab a bite at the bar.* After greeting each of the waiting guests, she made her way around the edge of the long room to the bar, pleased to see that Ted had changed from chef's jacket to his bartender red vest and was busy topping off a Bloody Mary with a fresh celery stick. She knew he'd already been working most of the day in the kitchen. *I'd give him another raise if I could afford it*, she thought, selecting a stool, noting that the piping around the leather cushion looked worn.

"Hi, Maureen." He caught her eye and moved to where she sat. "What's your pleasure?"

"That Bloody Mary looked awfully good, and I haven't eaten since lunch. What's on the pub grub menu tonight?"

"How about a roast beef sandwich au jus on Hawaiian bread?"

"Perfect," she said, realizing it was exactly what she wanted even if she hadn't known it.

She'd sipped the drink and had just taken her first bite of her sandwich, savoring the just-right meat, the rich, hot juice, the soft white Hawaiian bun, when someone sat on the stool beside her.

"Good evening, Maureen."

I hate it when someone speaks to me when I have a mouthful of food, she thought, dabbing at her lips, glad that Haven House still used cloth napkins. She faced Decklin Monroe, nodding as pleasantly as she could while chewing.

She managed a polite "Hello, Decklin. Nice to see you again," took another sip of her Bloody Mary, and wished he'd go away. She didn't want to think about the old theater—with or without the ghost. She didn't want to dwell on Frank Hubbard's questions or the projectionist's connection to a long-ago murder. She wanted to relax, enjoy her dinner, watch Ted mixing a fancy drink, flipping a shaker around and balancing a bottle on his arm. But, of course, Monroe didn't go away. He signaled Ted that he wanted to order. Ted acknowledged the raised hand with a nod and a smile, poured something green and frothy into a rocks glass, placing it before the obviously impressed customer, and approached the two. He put a Bud Lite coaster in front of the man. *Mental note: Order Haven House coasters—as soon as budget allows.* "Hi, Mr. Monroe. The usual?"

"Right, Ted. Vodka martini." He turned, facing Maureen. "Great bartender you have here. It's a simple drink—three ingredients. Supposedly anyone can make it—but this man"—he pointed to Ted—"makes a perfect one."

Ted once again manned the shaker, pulled a martini glass from the freezer, prepared the concoction—using, she noted, the top-shelf brands—poured it, topped it with a slice of lemon, and placed the finished drink on the coaster. "Here you go, Mr. Monroe."

Maureen once again concentrated on her dinner, hoping Decklin Monroe would enjoy his perfect martini in silence. No such luck. "I enjoyed our short time together at the Paramount," he said. Her mouth full once again, she nodded.

"I understand the local constabulary found our meeting interesting too." He sipped his drink. She sipped hers, searching her mind for something noncommittal to say. Nothing came. He continued. "He actually timed us. An hour and seven minutes, I've heard in several places." He didn't look pleased.

She wasn't pleased about it either. "Quic-Shop store, I suppose?" she said. "That's where most of Haven's rumors find a home."

"Molly and Gert each asked about it." A half smile. "They tried to be subtle."

"That's hard to picture," she said, returning the smile. Subtlety wasn't the strength of either woman.

"Everybody at the market seemed to know about it. Not a speck of subtlety there." He finished his drink and signaled Ted for another. "What is he looking for?"

Maureen saw no point in keeping what Hubbard had told her a secret. "He's opening up a cold case. He's interested in the murder you told me about. The man on aisle four in the theater. He mentioned you and another man. Harry Henshaw."

"He's really digging around, huh? Do you know Harry?"

"No," she said. "I believe he's my florist's father."

"Right." He lifted his glass, as though in a toast. "The old crook set them up in business."

Maureen had no ready answer.

"I like Gert," he said, indicating an abrupt change of subject.

"I like her too," she said, trying hard to make any connection between the housekeeper and Frank Hubbard's cold-case questions.

"We knew some of the same people," he announced. "Important people."

"Harry Henshaw?" Maureen asked, still searching for some continuity in this conversation.

He made a face. "Harry? Harry was small time. No, Gert spent a lot of time in Vegas back in the sixties. So did I. Frankie, Dean, Sammy. We knew 'em all."

Pretty sure that if Gert had ever known Frank Sinatra, she'd have told everybody about it by now and unable to think of an appropriate response, she concentrated on her sandwich. "Umm. This roast beef is delicious. You hungry, Decklin?"

"Looks good," he agreed. "Can I put it on my room tab?"

"Absolutely," she agreed, deciding while he placed his order to pursue the show business direction the conversation had taken. "Were you acting when you were in Las Vegas or had you started your projectionist career by then?"

"I was still working in films in the sixties. Went to Vegas to gamble in those good old days. When my looks started to go, I went back there and worked a Keno game in one of the smaller clubs," he said. "Ran some stag flicks and did some part-time stage work. No more movie parts. Not even as an extra. They wanted the young guys. Not like now when they can still be working in their nineties." He sipped absently on his drink. "Times change."

"You could still do stage work if you wanted to, I'll bet," she told him. "You're quite distinguished looking." She didn't add "for your age."

"You think so?"

"Sure," she said. "You ought to check with some of the dinner theater places over in St. Petersburg or Tampa."

"Maybe I will," he said. His sandwich arrived just as she finished the last bite of hers.

"Good. I'll see you later. I need to take my dog for his

evening walk." She stood, waved a good night to Ted, who was busy serving both the bar and the dining room orders.

She shared the elevator with a couple headed for the second floor. They were staying in one of the updated suites and were enthusiastic about it. "We're in the Babe Ruth Suite," the woman said. "We had no idea that the Babe was so in love with this area—that he had hit the longest ball ever hit in a Major League game not far from here."

"Yep. March 25, 1934." Maureen recited the fact from memory. She'd researched the Babe's time in Florida carefully, with particular attention to local lore. She didn't, however, mention that Babe Ruth might be seen late at night, after hours, just down the street at the L&M Lounge. Maureen was delighted to hear that they were pleased with their suite, and told them so. "If you want to take a little ride over to St. Petersburg, you can see the mansion Babe Ruth had for his Winter Estate back in 1928," she suggested. "It's not open for tours or anything, but I'll bet you could snap a picture. It's in a beautiful neighborhood on one of St. Petersburg's old redbrick streets." She scribbled an address on the back of her business card, wondering if the Babe might show up in a photo.

When the elevator door slid open on the third floor, Maureen was relieved to hear Finn's joyous welcoming "woof." She took that to mean there'd be no shimmering starlet reading *Greyfriars Bobby* to her dog. That, though, triggered two more. One, she'd promised to get a copy of the book because Finn loved hearing her read aloud to him, and two, there was a blue card facedown on her coffee table that she didn't want to read—aloud or otherwise.

"I'll combine the two," she told herself as she hurried down the long corridor to her suite. "I'll read it to Finn, That'll make it easier." She accepted the golden's enthusiastic welcome home with some ear-scratching, and a loving kiss on the top of his head. "We'll go for our walk in a few minutes," she told him. "Maybe if the bookstore is still open we'll get that book about Bobby you liked." She sat on the couch, the dog at her feet, and reached for the blue card, touching it lightly, still not picking it up. "But I'll read something to you now. Would you like that?" Finn gave an agreeable "woof," brown eyes focused on her face. She lifted the card, stared at it for a long moment, and began to read aloud.

With a message from the dead
On a journey you've been led
Now there's more for you to learn
Questions, rumors, deep concern.
Not your normal cup of tea,
Be prepared for land and sea
A frightening, foreboding feeling
Darkness, silence, images reeling
Strange and difficult indeed you may find it;
But the message that you need is behind it.

ZOLTAR KNOWS ALL

Chapter 8

Maureen sat quietly on the couch for a long moment, the blue card in her hand. Finn lay at her feet, eyes alert. She stood. "Well, Finn. I'll put this away and get your leash. Maybe the bookshop is open." Once in the bedroom, she opened the small drawer containing the first card and the coin, added the new card, then closed it. Changing back into Nikes and shorts, she pulled Finn's leash from its hook behind the kitchen door and returned to the living room. "That's that. Out of sight, out of mind, right, Finn?" She clipped the leash onto his collar and hoped what she'd just said was true. "We'll worry about that silly thing later. Let's go see if we can get your book." They used the stairs this time rather than risk sharing the elevator with guests, and opted for the side door route too. She warned Finn to be quiet with a finger to her lips and tiptoed past the soda machines and the guest laundry and out into the dark, cool yard. "Good boy." She patted his head. "I guess I'm not feeling very sociable tonight."

Before moving onto the sidewalk, she peeked out from behind the now-familiar hibiscus, looking for the also-familiar police cruiser. She looked up and down the street. "The coast is clear," she whispered, and she and Finn headed toward the beach.

The lights were out at the bookstore. "Tomorrow, Finn," she told him, "we'll get your book." They hurried toward the Second Glance thrift store. Lights were out there too. She peered in the window, wondering if the store cat, Petunia, was inside. Mr. Crenshaw, the store owner, had told Maureen that he stayed away from the store after dark. He claimed it was haunted at night by an opera singer who wasn't very good at her craft.

Curious, Maureen listened. Nary an aria. Maybe some other time she'd hear the singing ghost for herself.

They reached the Haven Casino and, after looking up and down the sand, Maureen unclipped the leash from Finn's collar. "I think it's okay for you to take a little run, Finn. I'll be right behind you." Running felt good. The cooling breeze from the gulf felt good. This should clear her head of unwanted thoughts.

But, of course, it didn't. That blue card. Another Zoltar card without a Zoltar machine anywhere in sight. It didn't make sense—at least most of it didn't. She paused in her run and closed her eyes for a few seconds, trying to remember the words on the blue card.

With a message from the dead; on a journey you've been led . . . Yes, that's the same as the words on the first card in my bureau. What about the next lines? She furrowed her brow. "I think I've got it," she whispered.

Now there's more for you to learn; questions, rumors, deep concern.

Finn was by then trotting along beside her at an easy pace. "I get the rumors part, Finn," she told him. "The rest of it is plain old gobbledygook. Everybody has questions. Everybody has concerns. Like, where is the money going to come from to fix up the inn?"

They ran together in silence for a bit—a little faster, Finn slightly ahead, but looking back at her every few seconds. They changed direction and headed back toward the Casino, arriving together, she slightly out of breath, the golden panting happily. "You're a good smart dog, Finn," she told him. "I don't care what those guide dog people said." The golden responded with a satisfied "woof."

There were a few folks strolling along Beach Boulevard. Some shops were still open and some of the strollers carried bags, indicating to retail-savvy Maureen that there was business to be had in Haven after dark. The marquee at the Paramount was brightly lighted, promising TWELVE DAYS OF GREAT CHRISTMAS MOVIES. She quickened her pace, anxious by then to get back to her office—to put some more time into plans to make the inn pay for itself. She didn't realize until she heard Finn's low growl that the police cruiser was behind them, moving slowly. No red and white lights. No siren. Just creeping along like a stalker.

Angry now, she stepped deliberately in front of the car, forcing him to stop short. She moved to the driver's side, waited for him to roll down the window. By this time a few of the shoppers and strollers had noticed the confrontation. She didn't try to lower her voice. "What do you want, Officer Hubbard? Why are you following me around?"

"You're the main contact we have to the Putnam case. I figure sooner or later you might lead us to the killer." He tapped his temple. "Innocently, of course. I know you had nothing to do with it."

She gave an exasperated sigh. "I know absolutely nothing about the Putnam person. And if you want to talk to Mr. Monroe or Mr. Henshaw, go follow them around."

"They aren't talking. See, I figure that you might not know what you know, so you might figure it out. you being pretty good at snooping yourself. Buddy Putnam's the dead guy in aisle four. You know?"

"No I don't know."

"Yeah, well, he was nobody important, though. Small-time hood."

Oops. She'd heard a similar description of someone else recently. Harry Henshaw. From Decklin Monroe. She stood erect. Looked Hubbard straight in the eyes.

"Listen. If you don't stop harassing me, I'll have to report you to somebody higher up."

"Well, we're just a little kind of substation here. I'm it just now. I had an assistant once but he quit. I do my best with what I've got. And right now, you're all I've got. Hey, I'll stop bothering you if you'll share what you find out from Monroe and the other guy. All I've got on Monroe is an old 'disturbing the peace' arrest. Nothing on Henshaw. Did anyone tell you that both Monroe and Henshaw were in Haven the day that Buddy got offed? No? Neither one of them will give me the time of day. They know I have no grounds to pull them in for questioning when all I have is a hunch." Small smile. "Can you do that? Share with me?"

"Share what? I talk to Mr. Monroe about movies. I've never even met the tea shop man." She backed away from the window. "If you want to talk to me, you can call, make an appointment, and come to my office."

"Okay. I'll do that. But you know what I mean. You figured out who killed that ghost hunter before I had the first clue." He began to accelerate the cruiser. "You've got some kind of a gift or something, Ms. Doherty. I've seen it in detectives before. It's like a 'feeling' you get, right? There's a killer still loose somewhere—maybe right here in Haven. I need your help." She watched him pull away.

What was it the Zoltar card had said? *A frightening, foreboding feeling*? She tried to shake the thought away. The inn looked pretty from the sidewalk. Christmas lights on the palm trees, little candles in the windows, even a decorated Christmas tree on the far end of the wraparound porch. That was where the ghost hunter had been found dead in a rocking chair and nobody wanted to sit there anymore.

Maureen counted more than a dozen guests in rockers on

the porch as she approached the inn—Molly and George and Sam in their usual spots at the top of the stairs. It was a pleasant-looking group, and she pulled out her phone, indicating that she meant to take a photo. Everyone in the group nodded, smiling agreement. (She always asked permission before taking photos, including guests; not everybody wanted evidence of where they were—or who they were with.) She'd been snapping pictures both inside and outside the inn with the thought of someday—when she had more time—making a scrapbook. *I'll get another shot later when Gert is here. She must still be working in the kitchen,* she thought. *I'll have to talk to her about Decklin Monroe. I wonder if she knows anything about Buddy Putnam—and maybe I'll check out that crazy Sinatra story. Hubbard had said there might actually be a killer loose here in Haven. Maybe, if I can, I should help him after all.*

She made her way up the steps, greeted Molly, George, and Sam, then spoke a few words to each of the inn guests congregated there. Finn stopped and greeted each one too, receiving plenty of head scratches, pats, and "good boys." Decklin Monroe wasn't among the porch-sitters. She wondered if he was still at the bar. She took the stairs to the third floor, avoiding the elevator again, not sure how Finn might react to a ghost rider in the etched glass confines. The two entered the suite, happy to see that both Bogie and Bacall were perched on the cat tower. "See, you'll have company while I go back downstairs for a little while," she told him. She put the leash back on its hook, checked hair and makeup in the bathroom mirror, and left the suite.

The dining room was nearly empty except for a group at one table lingering over coffee. Decklin was in the same seat at the bar where she'd last seen him. His companion, on the stool Maureen had occupied earlier, was Gert. The two appeared to be in deep conversation, heads close together, his white and hers dyed coal black. She hesitated, not wanting to intrude, selecting a seat a discreet distance away from the two, but still within earshot. Ted hurried toward her.

"Hi, Maureen. Leo's just about to take over for the late shift. Can I join you on that side of the bar?"

"Sure can," she said, patting the stool beside hers, just as red-vested Leo pushed open the door from the kitchen.

"What can I get you, Ms. Doherty?" he asked.

"I think I'll just have a cup of coffee, Leo."

"Same for me." Ted slid onto the stool beside hers. It appeared to Maureen that the pair at the end of the bar hadn't noticed her at all.

"What's going on over there?" She tilted her head in the direction of Gert and Decklin.

"Dunno. Soon as Gert came out of the kitchen she headed right for him. Like they had a date. He's been buying her drinks ever since. Odd couple."

"Maybe." Maureen poured cream into her coffee. "Maybe not so odd. Decklin says they knew each other in Vegas a long time ago."

"Knew each other in the Biblical sense?" Ted grinned. "You think?"

"I don't know. Could be. The showgirl and the actor? Why not?" She lowered her voice. "I think we're far enough away from them that they won't overhear us. Can I talk to you about something?"

His expression was completely earnest. "Sure. You know that. What's wrong?"

"Nothing wrong, really, that I can put my finger on—just some strange things. Hubbard followed me again tonight when I took Finn for his walk."

Ted put his coffee cup down hard enough to spill coffee into the saucer. "He has no right to follow you—to stalk you. What does he want? Is he trying to make a pass or what?"

"No. Nothing like that. He's investigating what he calls a 'cold case.' It's about a murder in the Paramount Theater a long time ago. He thinks Decklin Monroe and Leslie's dad are involved somehow."

"What does that have to do with you?"

"Apparently, both men were here when a man was shot while he was watching a movie at the Paramount. Back in the seventies. Now they're both here again and Hubbard thinks that I can help him . . ."

"Why you?

Maureen's laugh was nervous. "It's silly, really. He thinks that, because I helped to figure out who killed the ghost hunter last Halloween, I have some kind of special 'gift.' That I get 'feelings' about murder—and, Ted, he thinks there may be a killer loose right here in Haven."

Ted's fist was clenched. "And what does he want you to do about it?"

"He wants me to tell him what I find out about the two men. What I 'feel' about the case." She leaned closer to him. "What do you think I should do?"

"What do you know about them so far?"

"Not much of anything." She smothered a laugh. "I think Decklin is a nice old man with an interesting job and a bit of a drinking habit. I've never met Leslie's daddy. And the dead guy at the theater is supposed to be a ghost who only watches comedies."

"Feelings?"

"Just annoyance at Hubbard. Nothing about Decklin or Harry Henshaw."

"Mr. Henshaw set up Petals and Kettles for Leslie and her husband," Ted said. Everybody seems to think he's a pretty nice dad."

"Seems so. I guess if I run into anything that sounds important, I'll let him know. Can't do any harm, I guess."

"Just be careful, Maureen. Don't get yourself too involved." He muffled a yawn. "Sorry. It's my bedtime. See you on the beach in the morning?"

"See you there. Good night."

Maureen left a tip for Leo and moved toward the lobby, trying to avoid eye contact with the two at the end of the bar. Neither one even looked up. Both had full glasses in front of them. *I hope Decklin will be in good enough shape to run the first-day-of-Christmas movie tomorrow night*, she thought, *and that Gert will be on hand to help with tomorrow's lunch.*

Once again she shared the elevator with guests—a nice couple from Nashville who'd spent their honeymoon at the inn twenty years ago Christmas Eve. She thought, not for the first time, of how many people she'd already met in the short time she'd been in Haven who had fond memories of the Haven House Inn, including the two from Nashville, and others—like Lorna and Billy Bedoggoned Bailey, who liked it so much they kept coming back long after they were dead.

Chapter 9

As she'd expected, Ted was already waiting in front of the Haven Casino, immaculate in white shorts and T-shirt, hair shower-wet and curling a bit over his tanned forehead. She'd worn pink, top to bottom—shorts, shirt, and sneakers. The passing thought that they made a cute couple crossed her mind—but of course, they weren't actually a "couple."

"Good morning, boss lady," he said. "Where's Finn?"

"He's still sleeping. I guess he got tired out from the extra run last night." *Or maybe Lorna got home late from her date and read him more of the dog story.*

The two moved onto the hard-packed sand at the water's edge and began to jog toward the distant fishing pier. It looks as though we'll have a full house for our Dinner and a Movie night," she said. "I'm excited about it."

"Customers are loving the idea too. Dinner with us at six, then a walk down the boulevard to the Paramount for an old Christmas movie. I understand that most all of the inn guests signed up, and quite a few of the local people too." Enthusiasm showed in his voice. "George will be ready with the truck this morning at nine to take you to pick up the table arrangements."

"I'll be ready," she promised. "The dining room is going to look amazing."

"We're all set for a buffet lunch on the porch. Casual but fun," he said. "The girls—I mean Gert and Molly, of course—have made some little flower arrangements for each table with wildflowers from around the grounds along with some candy canes. Take your time putting the centerpieces in place. You're doing a great job making improvements around the inn, Maureen. I'm glad you're not going to sell the old place."

"Not if I can possibly avoid it." She moved out ahead of him. "Race you to the Long Pier Fishing Charter sign!" She was sure he'd win the race but the exertion was fun anyway. As she'd expected, Ted was leaning against the weather-beaten sign advertising Haven's fleet of fishing charter boats when she reached it, pretending he'd been there for hours. The sign itself had a special significance for Maureen. Her parents had taken a picture of her when she was twelve, standing in front of that sign, proudly holding the fish she'd caught. They'd had that fish for dinner, prepared at a small local restaurant. The strange thing was, Penelope Josephine Gray also had a print of that picture. It had been in a small silver frame in her office. And Ted had told her that his mother had owned a small restaurant across from the fish pier. *But this entire journey has been a series of strange things, hasn't it?* They turned and headed back toward the Casino at a slower pace, in companionable silence.

Finn was wide-awake when she returned and, as expected, was ready for his morning outing. "Okay," she said. "I need to change and get going with my day. I'll see if Gert or Molly or one of the guys can take you." She called Sam's cell first, since he was usually the first one to arrive at the four-rocker location in the morning. He agreed immediately and was happy to come upstairs right away to pick up the golden.

"There. That was easy. Sam will take you for a nice walk," she told Finn, who gave a short "woof" that she took to mean "Okay." Sam would be able to return Finn home after his walk, since he had master keys to all the room in the building because of his houseman duties. She grabbed the leash from its hook and put it on the coffee table, moving aside a small stack of pictures she'd printed out for use in that "someday" scrapbook. A *rat-a-tat-tat* knock on the door announced Sam's arrival.

"Come on in, Sam," she said, pulling the door open. "I appreciate this. I may be out for a while, so please just stick him back here when you're finished." She handed him the leash. He attached it to Finn's collar, then glanced back at the pile of photos on the coffee table.

"You looking through the old woman's picture collection?"

"Picture collection? These are a few of some I've been taking around the place. I'm thinking of making a scrapbook someday. Did Penelope collect pictures?" She laughed. "Lord knows she collected everything else."

"Yeah. She worried that people might have lost things or left things behind by mistake, you know? She always thought they might come back for them and be happy that she'd saved them." Sam laughed too. "Like the warehouse full of stuff you're still trying to get rid of. Well, you know that picture machine at the Quic-Shop? Where you make copies of pictures? Sometimes people leave their pictures in the machine by mistake. She found out the store just throws them away after a while, so she started bringing them all back here. She even used to put the pictures she liked the best in little silver frames and put them around the place, in case someone might recognize something in the photo. Her stash must be somewhere around the place. Guess we just haven't dug it up yet."

Questions, rumors, deep concerns.

Sam had given her a possible answer to a major question. *If the Quic-Shop had a machine back when I was twelve*, she thought, *that could be where Penelope got the picture of me with that fish.*

As soon as Sam had left with Finn, she opened her laptop, anxious to see what Wikipedia had to say about those big yellow picture makers. Her fish picture would have been taken around 1999. Sure enough, Wiki said that the machines were introduced in the "late nineties." Maureen realized she'd been holding her breath. She relaxed against the couch cushions with a long sigh. *A question answered.*

The clock showed eight-thirty. With no more time to spend on personal questions and answers, she hurried through the morning shower-shampoo ritual. She skipped the hair dryer. Her short blond hair didn't look bad damp and always seemed to air-dry quickly in Florida's warmth. A short-sleeved mini dress in black-and-white print with side pockets and black sandals would be cool and comfortable until evening when she planned a semi-glamourous, toned-down Lorna Dubois look for Haven House Inn's first Dinner and a Movie event.

She rode down in the elevator alone, popped into the kitchen to tell Ted she was on her way to meet George, and—as promised—stepped into the Haven House Inn truck at exactly nine o'clock. She was pleased to see that George had remembered to put the tonneau cover on the back of the truck to protect the arrangements on the return trip, thankful for the inn's quite unorthodox but fiercely loyal household staff.

"Ever been to the Petals and Kettles shop before, George?"

"Sure. Elizabeth used to buy flowers from them. Ms. Gray liked fresh flowers around the place," he said. "Leslie and Warren are good kids. The mom is nice too. The old man is kind of a grouch."

Maureen helped remove the tonneau top, hoping the thirteen arrangements would fit into the wide truck bed. She and George entered the Petals and Kettles shop, both smiling as the chimes played "I'm a Little Teapot."

"Wow! Would you look at that?" George exclaimed.

Wow, indeed! The entire expanse of counter space in the

shop, along with the tops of two desks and the checkout area, was covered by thirteen colorful, beautiful, Christmas floral arrangements—each one with its own unique vintage ornament at its center. They were alone in the fragrant shop. "Hello?" Maureen called. "It's Maureen from Haven House."

"Coming," a woman answered. Maureen didn't recognize the voice. Slim, petite, with silvery white hair perfectly coiffed, the woman hurried on tiny high-heeled feet. "Hello. I'm Katherine Henshaw—Leslie's mom. Her father and I are visiting from New York. We rarely get to Florida so I've been enjoying this lovely weather all week. My husband just got here recently. I hope you like what Leslie and Warren have done with your wonderful Christmas theme."

"Like it?" Maureen almost wanted to hug the woman. "These are beyond wonderful!" She stepped back for a better perspective. Each of the precious vintage decorations was surrounded by tiny twinkling lights and centered on a low bed of spruce branches, holly, pinecones, artificial red berries, and fresh red and white carnations. "Are Leslie and Warren here? I'd like to thank them personally."

"They're both in the tea shop. I'll get them. Busy this morning. Lots of people are in town for that special movie show, I guess, and Christmas poinsettia houseplants are flying out the door too. Dad and I can take over in there and send them over here." Katherine Henshaw turned in a swishy swirl of floral asymmetrical silk. Maureen's department store buyer brain kicked in, recognizing Veriko's pricey handiwork. Whatever Mr. Harry Henshaw did for a living to keep his wife in top designer fashions, she was sure it wasn't what Decklin Monroe had described as "small time."

Katherine Henshaw had mentioned her husband, the generous parent who'd given the young people Petals and Kettles. Maybe she'd get a peek at the man, so at least she'd know what the person Hubbard was so interested in looked like. Maureen took a tentative step toward the tea shop.

Through a latticework archway she saw that several of the marble tables with their cute ice cream parlor chairs were occupied. Leslie, wearing a pink pinafore, moved gracefully between the tables, bearing a tray laden with an assortment of flower-sprigged china teacups. Warren stood nearby, manning a variety of copper teapots and kettles while a tall, balding man carefully wheeled a two-tiered pastry cart between the tables.

Katherine Henshaw approached the man, spoke softly to him, and after a brief conversation among the four, Leslie untied her pinafore, handing it to her mother while Warren took over the pastry cart. Leslie and the man Maureen assumed was Harry Henshaw made their way through the arch and into the flower shop.

"Hi, Maureen," Leslie greeted her. "Please meet my dad, Harry Henshaw. You've already met Mom, I see. Hi, George. You know my dad, right?"

Maureen extended her hand and Harry Henshaw grabbed it in a hearty handshake while giving a brief nod in George's direction. Maureen tried to figure out how old the man was. If he was one of Decklin Monroe's contemporaries, he had to be at least in his eighties. She chalked up the smooth complexion and firm jaw line to excellent plastic surgery. There was no doubt that he could afford it.

"Well, Ms. Doherty, what do you think of our kids' handiwork? Pretty darned good, right?"

"It's all wonderful," she said, handing her credit card to Leslie. "Better than I'd even imagined it could be." She gestured toward the tea shop area. "I see you're awfully busy. George and I will just load these into the truck and get out of your way. These centerpieces will add just the touch we needed for our Twelve Days of Christmas promotion."

"Maureen's Haven House is tying in special dinners and the vintage decorations with some old-time Christmas movies at the Paramount Theater, Dad," Leslie explained.

"That old dump still open?" he asked, smiling.

"Just for old movies and mostly just on weekends," Maureen told him. "The movie club young people from USF man the projectors and the popcorn machine. It's kind of a fund-raiser to buy equipment for their visual arts department. They don't get any of the first-run films, of course. This Twelve Days of Christmas event is something special."

"Sounds like a good promotion for your inn," Henshaw offered.

"We're excited about it," Maureen said. "They were able to get some really good old movies like *It's a Wonderful Life* and *A Christmas Story,* and the University recommended a professional projectionist who'd given an excellent Zoom presentation for their department."

"We met him," Leslie said. "Decklin Monroe. He stopped in for tea one day and he and Mom had a nice chat about old times in Haven. Do you remember him?"

The change in Harry Henshaw's face was remarkable. In an instant his smile faded, jaw tightened, eyes narrowed. Without speaking another word, the man stormed through the latticed arch, seized his wife's arm with what must have been a painful grip, and pulled her through a doorway and out of sight.

"Mom! Dad!" Leslie gasped and followed the pair.

Maureen and George looked at each other, then carefully, quietly, pretending not to have noticed what was happening in the next room, began the process of carrying the arrangements, two at a time, out to the waiting truck.

Chapter 10

Once the truck began to move away from the curb, George was first to speak. "Holy Moly, Ms. Doherty," he said. "What the heck was that all about?"

"None of our business." Maureen spoke firmly. "I'd really appreciate it, George, if you didn't talk with anybody else about this. I wouldn't want it to be the latest news at the Quic-Shop, if you follow me."

"Gotcha," he said, "but I hope Mrs. Henshaw is okay. That old man always had a mean temper. He grabbed hold of her pretty hard. I bet it'll leave a bruise."

"I'm sure Leslie and Warren will settle him down. I'm going to call Leslie, though, and make sure everything is all right. I hate seeing a man treat a woman like that."

"Me too," he said. "She's such a nice person. Always was. And she still looks great."

"What? You know Mrs. Henshaw?"

"I wouldn't say that. I just remember her because she was so pretty. She wouldn't remember me. Hell, I was just a wharf rat. Kate was a local girl. Didn't you know that?"

"Kate . . . Katherine . . . Mrs. Henshaw is from Haven?"

"Long time back. Heck, she was even Miss Haven in a beauty contest once. I think she went to high school with Gert. Then she ran off with Henshaw. She couldn't have been more than seventeen. He was darned near forty." He shook his head.

"I wonder what made Mr. Henshaw so angry with her."

"Beats me," he said. "It might have something to do with our famous new guest. Monroe."

Maureen was sure George was right, but thought better about saying so. No need to supply more rumor material for the local grapevine. George's information about Katherine Henshaw was interesting. She'd ask Gert about it. She wasn't about to mention it to Frank Hubbard, though. Right now she didn't want to concentrate on anything but table arrangements. "Let's take these in through the side door," she said. "They're going to serve lunch on the porch today. No sense giving guests a preview of coming attractions, as they say in the movies."

As quietly as they could, Maureen and George carried the pieces into the empty dining room, placing each one on a table. When George left the dining room to get the thirteenth one, unbidden, the player piano whirred to life and began plinking a ragtime version of "It's Beginning to Look a Lot Like Christmas."

Billy Bedoggoned Bailey is pleased, she thought. George returned and, moving a few bottles aside, placed the last arrangement over the bar. "Everything looks really good, Ms. Doherty," he said. "The girls—Gert and Molly, I mean—are working on an extra decoration for the lobby. It's supposed to be a surprise for you."

"I promise to be surprised," Maureen told him, "and I love the way you all are helping make the inn better." Then, as she'd promised, she called Leslie Brown's phone number. The young woman answered on the first ring.

"Oh, Maureen, I was going to call you. I'm sorry I didn't get to say goodbye when you left—and sorry you had to see that little unpleasantness between my parents."

In my world, that was more than "a little unpleasantness."
"Is everything okay over there now?" Maureen asked. "Is your mother all right?"

"Oh, of course. Daddy is still so possessive about her. They've kissed and made up." There was a brief laugh. "You'd think at their age he'd not get all jealous about her just talking to another man. They're still so crazy about each other."

"Is that what it was? About your mother and Mr. Monroe chatting about old times in Haven?"

"That's all it was." Long sigh. "I'm so sorry you had to see it."

"All's well that ends well, I guess," Maureen said. "I just wanted to tell you how very much I appreciate your work on the centerpieces. They're absolutely perfect. I hope you'll come over to see them."

"We'll be there tonight for Dinner and a Movie," Leslie said. "Warren and I, and Mom and Dad too. We haven't told Dad yet. It's a surprise."

"Wonderful. I'll see you all, then." Satisfied that the dining room décor was as perfect as it could be—at least for *this* Christmas—Maureen stepped inside the elevator. Did she detect the lingering odor of pipe tobacco? She looked behind her. No one—worldly or otherwise—shared her space. "Imagining things," she muttered and entered the hall leading to her suite. A happy "woof" told her that Finn had arrived ahead of her.

She greeted the golden with the requisite scratchings, pattings, and loving words. The cats Bogie and Bacall looked up at her from the couch, with accusatory looks implying that she'd interrupted their naps. She gave each one a pat on the head, then reached for the push bell on her desk. She had a few questions that might require input from "the other side." She tapped the bell that summoned Lorna Dubois.

Within a few seconds the blond apparition shimmered into place. "What's up?" Lorna asked, sitting beside the cats. Bacall immediately stood, stretched, and walked through Lorna to the other end of the couch.

"Doesn't that bother you? When Bacall does that?"

Lorna shrugged a satin-clad shoulder. "I humor her. She thinks it's funny. Cats are weird. At least she knows I'm here. Bogie pretends he can't see me. That's annoying." She stuck her tongue out at the big striped tiger cat, who—as usual—pretended he didn't see her. "Anyway, you rang?"

"I did," Maureen said. "I'd like to hear your take on a few things that are going on in Haven."

"Shoot," said the ghost. "I'm all ears."

"You said you died in Haven in 1975, right?"

"Sure did."

"There were a few things happening here at around that time that you might have some firsthand knowledge about."

"Try me. I have a good memory."

"Okay. How about this?" Maureen sat beside Lorna. "A shooting at the Paramount Theater."

"Easy one. Buddy Putnam got offed. Small-caliber bullet. Probably used a silencer. It was in all the papers." She smiled. "Used to be more than one paper back then. *The Saint Petersburg Times*, *The Tampa Tribune*, the *Clearwater Sun*. Plenty of news." She cocked her finger as though pulling a trigger. "Poof. No one heard it. Right into the back of his skull."

If it was in all those papers Hubbard surely knows all that.

"Did you ever hear that maybe Harry Henshaw and Decklin Monroe might have had something to do with it?" Maureen asked.

"I'm pretty sure the cops questioned both of them. Bad blood between the three of 'em." Lorna stabbed the air with one finger. "They traveled in a rough crowd. Nobody was too surprised that Buddy got shot. Poor jerk was minding his own business. Watching a movie."

"*Animal House,*" Maureen said. "He loved comedies. They say his spirit haunts the Paramount. Did you know that?"

"I've never run into him there," she said, "but it wouldn't be unusual if he did."

"It wouldn't?"

"Not at all. A couple of ghosts haunt the Florida Theatre over in Jacksonville. Look it up." Lorna leaned back and Bacall strolled through her again, winding up in Maureen's lap. "Anything else you want to know about?"

"Harry Henshaw," Maureen said. "Did he and Decklin Monroe get along?"

"I never actually met either one of them," she said. "They were a little younger than me. Besides, by then I was stage. They were movies. Big difference. Decklin was an almost-over-the-hill actor. Henshaw was a producer, among other things. Big bucks. I knew Buddy, though."

"What was he like?"

"Run-of-the-mill big city hoodlum. Chicago, I think," she said. "As far as I know, Decklin and Henshaw were from there too. Buddy was sort of a sweet guy. I even went to a movie at the Paramount with him once. We sneaked in through the side door. He got a kick out of being crooked even when he didn't need to. No family. The city had to bury him. Nobody really cared, so there wasn't much of an investigation into who shot him."

There is now.

"I've heard that Gert went to school with Harry Henshaw's wife," Maureen said. "Her name is Katherine. I met her today. She seems very pleasant, but I saw him treat her rudely. Did you know her?"

"I heard he had a young wife. Saw her once. Never met her. Did you ask Gert?"

"Not yet. Everybody around here is busy getting ready for Christmas. Tonight's the start of the Twelve Days of Christmas promotion." Maureen smiled. "You and Reggie ought to stop by."

"Thanks for inviting us. Maybe we will. Formal? I need to know what to wear."

"Kind of first-nighter style. I'm wearing a long dress," Maureen said. "And tell Reggie this is a no-smoking hotel. I'm serious. You two have to stay invisible. I don't want my guests scared."

Lorna crossed her heart. "We'll be good. I promise. Was there anything else you wanted to talk to me about? When you rang I was in Memphis—Charlie Rich's birthday bash."

"Charlie Rich? Country and Western singer, right?" Maureen searched her memory for song titles.

With a condescending look and an eye roll, Lorna helped her out. "Ask Alexa. She'll play some for you. Try 'The Most Beautiful Girl,' or 'Behind Closed Doors.' Ring any bells?" She pointed to the push bell on the desk. "Besides that one?"

"Yes. I remember now. My mom was a big fan. Have fun at the party. Thanks for coming." She waved to the fading silhouette. "See you tonight." Lorna had already disappeared when she corrected herself. "I mean, I'd better not actually *see* you tonight."

She took Lorna's advice on two subjects. She hummed along as Alexa played "The Most Beautiful Girl," and read aloud to Finn about the Florida Theatre's ghost. It turned out, according to an article in *The Florida Times-Union*, that the theater, which dated back to 1927, had long been rumored to be haunted. Two seats in the upper balcony—E1 and E2—had attracted the attention of today's ghost hunters. A $10 million restoration project included replacing 1,950 seats. But the two haunted seats were retained and refurbished. " 'We did not want our ghost to be homeless,' " said the theater's president.

"If Decklin or anyone else buys the old Paramount, I hope they'll keep the end seat on aisle one, row four," Maureen told Finn, "so Buddy won't be homeless."

"Woof," Finn agreed.

Chapter 11

Maureen had splurged on a Victoria Beckham jersey midi dress in bright red. It had spaghetti straps, a thin silver belt, and side slit pockets. She posed, turning back and forth in front of the full-length mirror. "I think it's just right for the occasion," she told the golden. "Festive but not frou-frou at all. I like it—and I'm sure Lorna will want to borrow it." With strappy silver sandals and a single silver bangle bracelet, it was the look she wanted. Simple and elegant.

"Okay, Finn," she said. "I'm ready to go downstairs. I wish you could come with me but I'm afraid this is a no-dogs-allowed thing." He whined softly. "Maybe I should have bought you a doggy tuxedo and you could have been my escort. Would you like that?" Finn lay flat, covering both eyes with his paws. "I didn't think so. I know you don't like dressing up. Wish me luck. I'll bring you a doggie bag after dinner, before we all walk down to the theater."

She chose the stairs instead of the elevator, taking her time, thinking as she walked about the progress she'd made with the inn so far, and how much more she'd need to do before the place might actually be in a good position financially. "Baby steps," she told herself. "Just keep moving forward."

There was a small lighted Christmas tree on the white wicker table in the front lobby. Shells and sand dollars and bits of coral, some sparkling with silver glitter, dangled from green branches, a gold-painted starfish at its top. Gert and Molly stood nearby, identically clad in black skirts, white blouses, and red aprons, obviously watching for her reaction. Maureen didn't have to pretend surprise. The little tree was the perfect touch for the lobby area. There were tears in her eyes as she embraced the two women. "I absolutely love it," she said. "It's beautiful. Thank you so much for all you do for me—for Haven House."

"Glad you like it," Gert spoke brusquely, while wiping her own eyes. "We gotta get to work. Ted's got me handing out menus and Molly's doing bar back duty."

"We love you," Molly whispered, then, following Gert, darted through the louvered door into the dining room. Maureen, in her position as hostess for Haven House Inn's first Twelve Days of Christmas celebration, remained in the lobby, beside the tree, greeting guests as they arrived both from outside and from within the hotel. Inside the dining room Ted, handsome in dark suit and Christmas red-and-green–striped tie, directed guests to their reserved seats.

Maureen was happy to see Leslie and Warren come through the green door from the porch with Katherine between them. Maureen looked behind them. "Isn't Mr. Henshaw with you?"

Leslie shook her head. "Poor Daddy. Right after lunch he began to feel bad. He's home in bed with some stomach medicine. We phoned and cancelled his reservation right away. I know you probably have a waiting list."

"We do, and I appreciate your calling. I'm so sorry he won't be with us, but I can hardly wait for you all to see how great the centerpieces look. Ted will show you to your table." As the group passed by, Maureen observed Katherine, fashion-trained eyes appreciating the black long-sleeved column gown on a darned-near-as-perfect-as-Lorna's body—it might even be a vintage Dior—complemented by a black Saint Laurent's handbag that had sold for more than a thousand dollars in Barnett's couture department and a floaty black silk scarf. The shoes were soft black Capezios like the ones Lady Gaga and Katy Perry had been wearing lately. The woman was absolutely stunning. No wonder her husband was crazy about her.

It didn't take long for the room to fill up, with every seat at the dozen round tables filled. The porch, which had been set up with smaller tables for lunch, took the overflow. Leo was behind the bar with Molly at barback position. Some of the regular extra waitstaff from the community was on hand. The player piano tinkled Christmas tunes. Everything was moving along smoothly. She stood beside Ted just inside the louvred door to the lobby and felt herself beginning to relax

"The dinner part of our Dinner and a Movie seems to be going perfectly, Ted," she told him. "Your menu is just right and everyone looks happy. I hope the movie part is just as smooth. I haven't seen Decklin this evening."

"He grabbed a sandwich a while ago and left early for the theater," Ted said. "Don't worry. He was sober, all spiffed up, and excited about the old movie he's showing tonight."

Ted had planned the dinner service so that there'd be plenty of time for "first-nighters" to arrive at the Paramount in time for the showing. Decklin had prepared to start the show with a Bugs Bunny cartoon, followed by a newsreel showing President Truman lighting the White House Christmas tree in 1952, back when crowds were permitted on the grounds to watch the ceremony. As a special feature the college movie club had prepared a "preview of coming attractions" with clips of the eleven holiday movies to come. Then the main feature, *Remember the Night*, would be shown. Maureen had rented a few brightly colored open golf cart–type vehicles for those who preferred riding the short distance down Beach Boulevard to the theater, while Ted and Maureen followed, heading up the mini-parade of those who chose to walk. It was a festive and excited group that arrived under the brightly lighted marquee of Haven's vintage Paramount Motion Picture Theater, where framed black and white photos of stars Barbara Stanwyck, Fred MacMurray, and Beulah Bondi decorated the covered entrance and twin spotlights moved in a back-and-forth rhythm across the night sky.

A pretty usherette unhooked a red velvet rope divider, admitting the crowd to the lobby. Two local teenagers in rented uniforms served as ushers and Sam, in suit and tie, took tickets. Considering the age of the place, it looked pretty good, Maureen thought. The carpet was clean. The candy counter was stocked with old-time favorites—Sky Bars, Necco Wafers, and Black Crows—and the popcorn machine was lighted and ready to fill red-and-white–striped boxes with complimentary, buttery white puffed kernels. Seats hadn't been assigned because the hundred or so in the ticketed audience wouldn't begin to fill the cavernous theater, so they were free to select their own seats on the main floor. The stairway to the balcony had been roped off with velvet dividers and prominent NO ADMITTANCE signs. Maureen and Ted had chosen seats in the last row of the center aisle so that they had a good view of everything.

Decklin had thoughtfully arranged for a local organist to play some carols on the old Wurlitzer organ while the moviegoers filed in. The organ could have used a tuning, Maureen thought, but the general effect was quite lovely. She checked with Sam, who reported that he'd collected ninety-six tickets. Every one who'd bought a ticket from Haven House Inn had shown up. Great. She noticed that the aisle seat in row four was still vacant when the house lights dimmed, signaling the beginning of the first night of Christmas in Haven.

The audience laughed along with the antics of Bugs Bunny, Daffy Duck, and Elmer Fudd. They fell silent while President Truman lighted that long-ago tree, surrounded by a holiday crowd, while war still raged in Korea. The coming attractions were greeted with applause for each one. It was time for the main feature. Maureen settled back in her seat, watching as the opening credits ran. *So far, so good.*

The theater was quiet, the story holding the audience's attention as the heroine played by Stanwyck gets arrested for stealing a bracelet from a New York City jewelry store. Christmas is a few days away and the assistant DA, played by MacMurray, has the trial postponed so that she won't get a sympathetic jury. But he feels sorry for her having to spend the holiday in jail, so at the last minute posts bail. The story had reached a point where MacMurray starts a fire in his wastebasket as a distraction, when Ted tapped Maureen's arm, then pointed at his watch and whispered, "The movie runs ninety-four minutes. We're coming up on the halfway point—forty-seven minutes. Decklin told me that this is where the big reel switch happens. He's really proud of the way he does it. 'Seamless,' he told me. 'You won't even notice a skip in the action.' Let's see if we can tell when he switches reels."

They each leaned forward in their seats, focused on the big screen ahead. Ted whispered the count as the last couple of minutes ticked by. "Forty-five, forty-six, Forty-seven. Now."

The screen became bright white. A rhythmic *flap-flap-flap* sound echoed throughout the darkened theater. Maureen stood immediately. So did Ted. "Something's wrong," she said, moving into the aisle.

"I'll go up and see what's going on with Decklin," Ted said. "See if you can grab a mic and tell everybody we have a technical error. Maybe see if you can get that organist to play something."

"Do you know how to get to the projection booth?" Maureen asked.

"No. Where is it?"

"It'll take longer to tell you than to go myself," she called over her shoulder, already running toward the balcony stairway. "I know the way." Glad she hadn't worn heels, but sorry she hadn't brought the flashlight Decklin had given her, she ducked under the velvet rope, and with only the slightest pause walked quickly and carefully up the stairs, then made her way to the almost hidden door in the back wall. She pulled it open, admitting what scant light there was. Heart pounding, she raced up the narrow stairway. "Decklin! Decklin! Are you all right?"

She saw right away what was wrong with the projector. The first reel had ended. The final strip of celluloid flapped back and forth in the light. Decklin sat, unmoving, in the comfortable chair beside the tall machine.

Images reeling. Zoltar knows all.

From far below she heard Ted's amplified voice. "A little technical glitch, folks," he said. "This is a genuine 1940s movie and we'll patch her up as fast as we can. Meanwhile, let's enjoy a little Christmas music from the magnificent Paramount Wurlitzer."

"Joy to the World" rang out while Maureen looked into Decklin's face. A trickle of blood oozed from a small wound in his forehead. Eyes wide, he wore a look of surprise. There was no need for her to touch him. He was, without doubt, quite dead. She backed away and retraced her steps down to the balcony, trying to think calmly. She'd left her phone in her purse on the aisle seat. She needed to call 911 right away.

She hurried down the stairs, walking even more carefully this time. A collapsed staircase was all she needed just now. The audience had begun singing along with the organ music: ". . . and heaven and nature sing, and heaven and nature sing . . ." the words rang out. She quickly arrived at her seat and reached for the phone. Ted was doing a good job keeping the audience occupied. If police stormed into the building right now, how would this crowd react? A run for the exit? There were two main exits—one with double doors to the lobby and an outer door to the street as well as the exit leading to the parking lot. What if people headed for different exits and ran into each other? Panic? There'd been far too many headlines about people being trampled to death in crowded theaters and concert halls, and she'd already no-ticed quite a few children in this audience.

She slid the phone back into her purse and began to walk, slowly, deliberately toward the front of the theater, glad she'd told the golf cart drivers to stand by, and for the inn staff to remain on duty for returning moviegoers. *We'll empty the theater first. Then call for help. Decklin isn't going to get any deader if we wait a few minutes.* Ted raised a quizzical eye-brow when she stood beside him, fake-smiling at the audi-ence.

"May I have the mic?" she whispered. Silently he handed it to her, at the same time signaling the organist to stop playing.

"Hi, everybody. I'm Maureen Doherty from the Haven House Inn. I guess you've noticed that we have a bit of a technical glitch with our old movie." A ripple of laughter ran throughout the theater. "Sorry to announce that twentieth-century movies don't respond really well to twenty-first-century fixes. In short, we can't get the darned thing started." Another ripple. "Those of you who purchased Din-ner and a Movie tickets from Haven House Inn, I'm inviting you all back to the inn. I'll buy the first round of drinks." Applause greeted that announcement. "Those who bought tickets from the box office are entitled to a full refund." She continued. "The golf carts are parked outside and it's a lovely evening in Haven for a moonlight walk. So let's get this party moving!" She reached for Ted's hand and started down the center aisle toward the exit.

He leaned close to her. "What's going on?" he whispered. "Where's Decklin?"

"He's upstairs, and he's dead with a hole in his forehead.

We've got to clear this place out in a hurry," she said, walking faster. "Then we've got to call 911."

He frowned, not questioning further. He pushed the door to the lobby open, then continued toward the outer doors, pushing them open, beckoning the following crowd to exit the theater. Actually, it didn't take long at all before the last couple climbed into a golf cart and started along Beach Boulevard. Sam and the ushers led the walkers and Ted directed traffic while Maureen retrieved her phone, dialed the inn, and alerted the staff that the crowd was headed their way. Only then did she call 911 to report that Decklin Monroe was dead.

Chapter 12

Maureen held the phone to her ear, telling the 911 dispatcher, as calmly as she could, who she was, where she was, and that she'd found the projectionist at the Paramount Theater dead in his chair in the projection room. She answered questions as succinctly as she was able to. Yes, she was sure he was dead. She described the round hole in his forehead, the trickle of blood. No, she hadn't touched anything and no one else had gone into the projection room. Yes, she'd wait for the police to come. She replaced the phone in her purse, glad to see Ted approaching. Without even thinking about it, she reached for his hand.

"You okay?" he asked.

"Not really," she said.

"It's good that you got the people out before the cops arrive," he said.

"I don't know what Frank Hubbard will think about it, but I didn't see any point in yelling 'Murder!' in a crowded theater."

"Murder," he repeated. It wasn't a question. "It must have happened after the newsreel and the short subjects," he reasoned. "During the first reel of the feature."

"Had to have been. He never got to flip from one reel to the second one."

"Forty-seven minutes," Ted said. "Somebody was up there with Decklin during the first forty-seven minutes of *Remember the Night*. I don't suppose this old place has security cameras?"

"Nope. And from where I sat, people were running up and down the aisles constantly tonight—for candy or popcorn or for the restrooms or whatever."

"It could have been practically anybody, then, unless somebody saw somebody else going up the stairs to the balcony and could identify them," he said. "Hubbard's going to want to question every person in tonight's audience."

"He would have kept us all here all night," Maureen reasoned. "He can just as well do the questioning later."

A siren sounded in the distance. "Speak of the devil," Ted said. "Here comes Hubbard now." Ted was right. The uniformed policeman climbing out of the cruiser was Frank Hubbard, and he did not look happy as, followed by two more uniformed men, he approached the pair.

"Why am I not surprised to see you, Ms. Doherty? Found another body, did you?"

"Yes, sir," she agreed. "It's Decklin Monroe. He's in the projectionist's booth. And he's dead."

"Well, the EMTs and the medical examiner should be right behind me. You're sure he's dead?" Not waiting for an answer he moved past Ted and Maureen and pulled open the double theater doors. "Where's all the people?" he whirled to face them. "I thought there was a movie show going on here tonight."

"There was," Maureen explained. "I sent them outside in an orderly way before calling you." She repeated what she'd told Ted. "It didn't seem like a good idea to yell 'murder' in a crowded theater."

He shook his head. "Bad choice," he said. "How do you know he was murdered? In fact, how did you know he was dead? Maybe you could have saved him by calling 911 a little faster." A black van pulled up in front of the Paramount, followed by an ambulance. "Here's the ME and the medics. Let's go take a look." He led the way into the dimly lighted, now empty theater, the blank screen still glaring white, the film still flap-flapping in the silence. "Where did you say the deceased is?"

"I'll show you," Maureen said and headed for the staircase to the balcony. She explained that the staircase might be unsafe, then didn't speak as she led the strange parade single file up the stairs—two EMTs with a stretcher, the medical examiner with a black bag, Frank Hubbard, two deputies, and Ted.

"There's another stairway up to the projection booth," she said. "Do any of you have a flashlight?"

Somebody did. The group crowded into the small room. Decklin Monroe still sat in his chair, just as Maureen had described. One of the EMTs touched the man's wrist, shook his head.

The medical examiner moved forward, focused a light on Decklin's forehead, lingering on the still shiny blood. "Small-caliber bullet." He moved Decklin's head gently forward. Maureen looked away. "No exit wound. The shooter probably used a twenty-two—not enough power there to exit the skull. He hasn't been dead very long—about an hour or so, I'd guess. Let's take him downtown. I'll get a better idea then."

"He was killed within forty-seven minutes from the time the movie started," Ted offered as the EMTs lifted Decklin from his chair onto the stretcher

"How would you know that?" Hubbard demanded. "Unless you witnessed it." Ted explained about the length of the movie and the time the reels needed to be changed. The officer was silent for a long moment, then turned to face Maureen. "So you, on your own, Ms. Doherty, without notifying authorities, decided to empty a crime scene of what, a hundred, hundred and fifty witnesses? Send them out the door to God only knows where when one of them might be a killer? Am I correct, Ms. Doherty?"

Maureen had done exactly that and knew she had some serious explaining to do. "I did what I thought made sense at the time," she said. "I was worried about a panicked race for the exits. There are two double doorways in the front of the building and another on the side. Anyway, this was a paid admission event. I have names and addresses, e-mails, and credit cards of everyone who was here from the inn. Chances are they're all still at the inn, enjoying drinks on the house. I'm sure the theater box office has accurate records too. The whole thing was on a reservation basis."

"Wonderful. So, well after the fact, I have to go to your inn and interview a bunch of drunks. Then find everybody else who bought a ticket." He pulled out a phone and barked orders for an officer to go to the inn and make sure nobody left the premises. "Secure the room Monroe was staying in. Post a guard." He aimed a stern look in Maureen's direction. "And use the sirens. Let's get going." He ordered the deputies to secure the projection booth and to designate the entire building a crime scene, turned and headed for the still-propped-open theater entrance. "Ms. Doherty, you will ride with me. Mr. Carr, please assist the deputies, do what you have to do to help them lock up around here, then join us at the inn."

Hubbard took the wheel of the cruiser, Maureen in the passenger seat. "How many people were in the audience, Ms. Doherty?" he asked. "Do you know?"

"We sold ninety-six tickets and everyone showed up. It looked like there was maybe another hundred people there." She looked out of the cruiser window, noticing several people she recognized from the dinner, strolling along the sidewalk at a leisurely pace, some even stopping to look into shop windows. "Besides that," she continued, "there was a ticket taker, three ushers, the organist, two helpers in the lobby for the popcorn and the candy, and Ted and me."

"You're sure about that?"

"Yes."

"Nobody left the theater during the movie?"

"I . . . I don't think so."

"And nobody wandered in off the street during the movie?" Hubbard had raised his voice slightly. "You're sure nobody wandered in off the street, climbed up the balcony stairs, and killed the projectionist?"

She wasn't sure at all. But, she reasoned, even if that had happened, keeping the audience in the theater wouldn't have changed anything one way or the other. She told him so.

"It would have made my job a lot easier," Hubbard insisted, "to have had everyone in one place. But you, Ms. Doherty, have never been interested in making my job easier." He pulled the cruiser to a stop in the no-parking area in front of the inn, tucked a brown notebook under one arm, climbed out and walked around, and opened her door. There were already two other police cruisers parked in the lot beside the building. The temporary tables and chairs had been removed from the porch, and the rocking chairs had been replaced. All were empty. Maureen and Frank Hubbard climbed the stairs. A uniformed officer opened the green door. Another officer stood outside the doors to the dining room. A NO EXIT yellow tape blocked the elevator and stairwell.

"Everybody in the restaurant?" Hubbard asked.

"There are still some empty seats in there," the officer reported, moving aside so that Hubbard could look into the dining room. Maureen was surprised by how quiet the place was. There was a hum of conversation coming from inside the room. She'd halfway expected to hear guests and movie-

goers complaining loudly about being detained. The door behind them opened and several stragglers came inside. Then a
few more showed up. Finally all of the seats at the round tables were filled.

"It's about time," Hubbard snapped. "Okay, Doherty, settle them down, get me a table and chair, grab your ticket sale
records, and we'll start taking statements."

Chapter 13

It looked to Maureen as though most of the folks who'd had dinner there earlier had returned to their original seats at the round tables. The overflow people were at the bar or seated in folding chairs around the edge of the room. George brought one of the tables used earlier on the porch and two straight-backed chairs. Hubbard stood in front of the table. "Ladies and gentlemen, I am Frank Hubbard, Haven Police Department. As you probably know by now there has been a suspicious death at the movie theater. Since all of you here are possible witnesses to a crime, I'll need to take preliminary statements from each of you." He sat, placing a small recorder on the table, opening his notebook, and producing a pen from an inside pocket. "One tableful at a time, Doherty," he said. "Let's get started." He'd dropped the courteous "Ms." and she didn't blame him.

Maureen summoned the first eight tablemates. Still chatting with one another, they stood in a loose line in front of Hubbard, some still holding bar glasses. The process took less time than Maureen had thought it might. Hubbard inspected IDs from each one, cross-checking with the information Maureen had collected earlier. He asked where each had been seated in the theater, whether they had seen anyone leave or enter during the films. He asked if they had known Decklin Monroe personally. He asked for phone numbers and e-mail addresses in case he had further questions. Some of the guests got permission to return to their rooms, but most, apparently curious and interested in what was going on, went back to their seats at the round tables. Molly, still in waitress uniform, continued to serve drinks and coffee.

The second table was called up for questioning. Leslie, Warren, and Katherine moved forward. "So sorry about all this," Maureen whispered as she led them toward Hubbard. "This whole thing has turned out to be a disaster from start to finish."

"I'm sorry too," Leslie said. "I hope this won't take long. Mother is anxious to get home to make sure Daddy is all right. He finally answered his phone the last time she called and says he's fine, but she's worried."

"Of course she is," Maureen said, observing the older woman, who appeared calm. "But since you're all right here in town I'm sure Officer Hubbard won't keep you any longer than he has to. And of course you all knew Decklin Monroe, which makes it all the more troubling for you. I'm so sorry," she said again, and moved on to the next ones in line. She was pleased when the officer guarding the dining room door opened it.

Ted stood in the doorway, then approached the table where Hubbard sat. "The theater is secure," he said. "Here are my keys. The owners have another program scheduled there for tomorrow night. Do you think you can finish your site examination by then?"

"I already have a team there. They'll work through the night. If I can count on cooperation from Ms. Doherty and all these people"—he waved one hand—"maybe I can speed things up. Tomorrow night should be all right."

Hubbard recognized Katherine Henshaw's last name. "Related to Harry Henshaw?" he asked.

"My husband," she told him. "He was supposed to come with us tonight, but he was sick."

Hubbard's pen remained poised in midair. "Sick?" he asked, peering closely into her face. "Sick how?"

She smiled. "Tummy ache. He threw up his lunch. He's fine now. Thank you for asking." Another sweet smile.

"You're welcome," Hubbard growled, clearly recognizing her subtle dig at his manners. He turned his attention to Leslie and Warren. "I understand that the deceased was a customer at your tea shop. Right?"

All three nodded.

"Did any of you notice any activity near or on the staircase leading to the balcony?"

"No. We were on the aisle on the opposite side of the theater," Leslie offered.

"Did any of you leave your seats during the show?" He leaned forward then, his eyes fixed on Leslie. "For any reason?"

"I didn't," Warren said, "but the girls went to the restroom during the newsreel."

Katherine waved a small hand. "I did," she said. "I got up twice to call Harry. And once to stock up on Harry's favorite candy. Most places don't carry it. He hates it when he runs out. I was so worried about him—being sick and all."

"Did he answer your phone calls?" Hubbard's gaze was then fixed on Katherine.

"No, he didn't at first." Her eyes were downcast. "I was so worried."

"And the second time you called? Did he answer then, and do you remember what part of the show you were watching?"

She smiled. "Yes. He answered. He was feeling much better. I don't remember about the movie, though. I'd sort of lost interest in it, you know? Of course I've seen it several times before and anyway, I like the color movies better."

"Me too," he said. "I'll talk to your husband when he feels better. Like later tonight." He looked at Warren again. "Mr. Brown, I'd appreciate it if none of you leave town without telling me, hear?"

Warren agreed. "Yes, sir. We have a couple of businesses to run. And it's Christmastime. We can't even leave the store."

The conversations with other guests were in a similar vein. He checked IDs, cross-checked with Maureen's records, and asked if they were acquainted in any way with Decklin Monroe. He asked if they'd seen any activity near or on the balcony staircase and if they'd left their seats during the show. Only a few knew Decklin—mostly from talking to him at the bar—and almost everyone recalled leaving their seats at least once. Two people thought they'd seen someone on the staircase leading to the balcony.

"Man or woman? Tall or short? Fat or thin?" Hubbard wanted to know. Neither person could give a description.

"It was just a shape," one of them said. "Like a shadow."

Maureen couldn't help thinking of the man from the first seat, aisle four. Maybe he got bored and changed seats after the Bugs Bunny cartoon. The couple from the Babe Ruth Suite reported that each of them had left their seats. She'd visited the ladies' room and he'd visited the candy counter twice. "They have candy out there I haven't seen since I was a kid. I bought a whole bag full." Maureen's merchandising background was immediately alerted. *Find out where the theater gets that candy and start selling it at the inn.*

By the time Hubbard had reached the end of the line that night, he'd only found a handful of people who'd had any connection at all with Decklin other than casual conversation at the bar or on the porch. Ted had met him shortly after he'd arrived at the inn and had served him at the bar. Maureen had spent that notorious hour and seven minutes with him at the theater. Katherine Henshaw had a longer acquaintance to report, although except for a brief chat in the tearoom, she didn't recall seeing or hearing from him in many years. The Browns only knew him as a knowledgeable tea drinker. Gert told Hubbard—and anyone else who'd listen—about the old days when she was a showgirl in Vegas, and how she was pretty sure she remembered him from back then. Hubbard asked some pointed questions about the time Decklin and Gert had spent together drinking, which elicited some improbable tales about raucous good times with the Rat Pack.

After a while the guests and neighborhood people began to drift away and Hubbard announced that he'd follow the Browns back to their home, as he intended to question Harry Henshaw in person—tummy ache or not.

"But Officer Hubbard, Daddy hasn't seen that man for years," Leslie protested. "I've never even heard his name mentioned in our house."

"Just doing my job, young lady," Hubbard said. "I'll be as brief with your father as I can be—since he was too sick tonight to attend the movie show with the rest of you. What's your address, please?"

"Leslie and I live upstairs, over the shops," Warren said, reciting the address. "Mother and Dad are staying in a little guest house we built out back."

Hubbard scribbled in his notebook. "Nice," he mumbled. "Convenient so that the in-laws can come and go as they please, without interrupting the business." He stuck the pencil and notebook into his inside pocket and headed for the front door, then turned, facing Maureen. "We'll try to finish up at the Paramount in time for tomorrow's movie, Doherty.

I'll arrange for a thorough search of Monroe's rooms here at the inn tomorrow morning. It shouldn't take long. Good night."

Maureen spoke a hurried "Goodbye" to the departing family, thanking them once again for the beautiful Christmas arrangements and thinking how much she'd like to listen in on that interview with Harry Henshaw. *Tomorrow's movie! I owe all ninety-six of my movie-going guests either a refund or another movie,* she thought. *Maybe we can buy another block of seats for tomorrow night.* She dialed the theater, reached an automated voice recording, and, fingers crossed, bought one hundred seats for *Home Alone.* Next she called the young man from the USF movie club, hoping he'd be available for the rest of the week, and that he didn't mind working from the site of a recent crime scene.

"Thanks, Ms. Doherty," he said. "We heard about the old guy getting killed. The school has already contacted the theater owner and, well, like they say, 'the show must go on.' I thought you might call. I'm not afraid to do it and the movie club needs the money, but my mom had a fit so here's the deal." He paused, and Maureen heard a deep intake of breath. "I can only do it if my dad can come with me. He used to be a Marine, you know. And he has a license to carry concealed in Florida, so if all that is okay with you, I can do it as long as I don't have to do any fancy reel-changing like the old guy did."

Maureen, immediately and gratefully, agreed. "I understand that all the rest of the films are just like the ones you do on weekends—single reels and maybe some that are digital—and thanks so much for agreeing on such short notice." *Having an armed ex-Marine on the premises isn't a bad idea either.* A few guests still lingered in the dining room, mostly at the bar where Leo continued working, the player piano tinkling Christmas songs in the background.

Ted, having supervised a quick and efficient cleanup of the tables, approached Maureen. "How are you doing, boss lady?"

"I don't like being called 'boss lady.' "

He looked crushed. She hadn't meant to be so blunt. "Oh Ted, I'm sorry. That sounded snarky—but, well, it's true." She sat on the stool at the very end of the bar.

He smiled then, sat on the stool next to hers, and raised his right hand. "I'll never say it again. But seriously, how are you doing? It's been a tough night. Anything I can do to help?"

"What a mess. Tonight was an absolute train wreck. I've bought tickets for tomorrow's movie for all ninety-six of those people, and I suppose I'll have to refund the money to those who can't stay around for the substitute show." She put her elbows on the bar and put one fist under her chin. "So with a refund we'll lose money on all those dinners, and if they take the tickets for *Home Alone*, I'm still out the money for tonight's dinners too."

"I don't think you have to do a full refund—just the price of the movie," he said. "There are unsold seats on all the rest of the twelve nights, and I can put a few more tables on the porch starting as soon as the cops are through with whatever they're doing."

"That'll help." She didn't sound convinced. "Hey! Maybe we should do some matinees. A Lunch and a Movie promotion. Can do?"

"Can do," he said, grinning. "That'll work. Lots of people don't like driving at night anyway, and the Lunch and a Movie will cost less to prepare. See? We can do this. We're a great team." He offered a fist bump.

She liked the sound of that "we." She gave his fist a tap. She liked the idea of the two of them being a team too. The player piano made an abrupt switch from "Good King Wenceslas" to "Side by Side." Was Billy Bedoggoned Bailey listening to the conversation? The lyric about not having a barrel of money certainly matched the situation. And the part about not knowing what's coming tomorrow worked too. Beside all that, the old song didn't fit into the Christmas song rotation at all. With a nod and a smile, she faced the empty piano bench, hoping that Billy could see her, even if she couldn't see him.

Chapter 14

Maureen and Ted had talked about being a team, and about how it would take teamwork to get everything regarding the Twelve Days of Christmas promotion back on track—and showing a profit. Within hours of the happenings Maureen had designated "a train wreck," a team had formed solidly around the two. Molly and Gert had, without being asked, joined Ted in the kitchen for a darned-near-all-nighter of preparation for the next night's dinner, along with tentative plans for at least one lunchtime matinee special. Sam arranged more chairs and tables on the porch. The college was delighted about the proposed matinee ticket sales. Maureen had called all of the resident and local people who'd been at the Paramount and left a message that the inn would offer the next night's movie as a replacement.

Maureen took a break between designing and printing flyers about the matinees in her office to ride up to the third floor to check on Finn. He woofed a happy hello when she turned her key in the lock, and Maureen wasn't surprised to see Lorna on the couch, Finn at her feet, and a book on her lap. *It must just be the "essence" of a book,* Maureen realized. *Otherwise, it would sink right through her.*

"Oh, hi," the ghost said. "We're just finishing up with

Greyfriars Bobby. Next we're going to start *Call of the Wild.* That St. Petersburg Library has plenty of the books I loved when I was a kid."

"Finn loves being read to," Maureen told her. "Sorry to say, I've never read either of those."

"Yeah, well, I was a kid a long time ago. Times change. You were probably reading *Clifford the Big Red Dog* or *The Hundred and One Dalmatians*," Lorna said. "You've been gone quite a while. How did the shindig at the Paramount work out? We decided to skip it—wait for a night when they had a better movie."

"Not well. Not well at all." Maureen sat in one of the beige armchairs, kicked off one shoe, and rubbed her foot. "Just for starters, Decklin Monroe got killed while he was running the feature film."

"The Barbara Stanwyck one? Why? It wasn't *that* bad."

Maureen half smiled. "I don't think they're looking for a film critic. Seems that somebody got up into the projection room and shot poor Decklin in the forehead. Then I got in trouble with Frank Hubbard because I cleared out the theater before I called the cops."

Lorna tilted her head to one side. "So they wouldn't panic and step on each other trying to get out?"

"Right. That's the way I saw it too. Hubbard thinks I do things just to make his job harder. Anyway, now we have to give refunds to the inn guests who got cheated out of the movie, and give them rain checks for another Christmas show. Probably for tonight," Maureen told her. "We're going to a matinee lunch or maybe more for what's left of the twelve days. To try to make up for the loss. What do you think?"

"About the Stanwyck movie? Or about old Decklin getting himself shot? Or about lunches?"

"About Decklin, mostly—although I guess my question

was about the lunches. You said you remember Decklin from when he was here back in the seventies—before you . . . um . . . departed."

"I remember him being here in Haven," she said, "but it wasn't like I palled around with him or anything like that. He and that Henshaw guy were kind of high-powered for little old Haven. They were into gambling and maybe even drugs. Made trips back and forth to Las Vegas and New York. My looks were pretty much gone by then, so even if I was in the same room with them they didn't pay any attention to me."

"What about Buddy Putnam?"

She gave a shimmery little smile. "Poor Buddy. Yeah. I hung around with him some. We used to meet at the L&M Lounge sometimes at night after my play was over. He worked for those guys sometimes, but they didn't exactly socialize, you know what I mean?"

"I think so," Maureen said. "Do you know what kind of work he did for them?"

"Not really. He didn't talk about himself that much. I know he did what he called 'running errands' for Mr. Henshaw sometimes. It had to do with moving money around, I think like finding legit businesses and parking the money there."

"Money laundering?" Maureen had heard the term and had a fair idea of what it involved. Money acquired from illegal dealings could sometimes be manipulated so that it appeared to have come from reputable sources.

"Money laundering. Is that what they call it now?" She giggled. "Yeah. I guess it was something like washing dirty money."

"There must have been a lot of talk about Buddy getting shot in the movie theater," Maureen reasoned. "Were there a lot of suspects—because of his line of work?"

"Funny thing about that," Lorna said. "I hadn't thought

about it in years, but it seems to me that both Decklin and Harry Henshaw were questioned about it, but they both had solid alibis. Seems to me I remember that Decklin got drunk and started a fight with Harry. I'm pretty sure Decklin got arrested."

That would be the drunk and disorderly charge, Maureen thought. "Did Decklin go to jail?

"Nah. The cops just dropped the case. I mean, Buddy was nobody to them."

"Did you ever meet Mrs. Henshaw? Katherine?"

"Nope. Never did. Buddy pointed her out to me once. She was really pretty. Young. 'Beautiful Kate,' Buddy called her. I think he had a crush on her."

Lorna picked up the Jack London book. "Weird, isn't it? Now somebody else gets shot in the same movie house and both Decklin and Harry are in Haven again. Only this time Decklin's dead. Weird."

"Woof," Finn agreed, wagging his tail, impatient to hear about a big, kindhearted dog named Buck.

"I guess I'll go back downstairs, Lorna. You seem to have everything under control here." Maureen closed the door softly behind her and walked quickly down the corridor to the elevator. When she returned to the dining room she found her team—Ted, Molly, Gert, George, and Sam—all gathered at the bar, looking quite relaxed, with Leo serving as bartender.

"Come on. Sit with us," Sam called. "We've been talking about what a good job you've been doing with the old place."

Gert moved one stool over, patting the stool next to her, leaving a space for Maureen to sit beside Ted. "Here you go, dear. You sure are a big improvement over Elizabeth. She didn't mind letting the inn—our home—go to ruin. She was all for selling it. Putting us out on the street."

Maureen sat on the offered stool. "I have a feeling you guys would have been okay no matter what happened here, but I'm glad to have you with me. I haven't had time to properly thank you all for your help with this Twelve Days of Christmas mess—and Gert, the tree you and Molly decorated is gorgeous." She signaled to Leo. "Since none of us have to drive anywhere, I'm buying the next round, including an Irish coffee for me." That brought smiles and raised glasses.

"So, Maureen, has that cop been bothering you any more after we left?" Gert didn't bother to lower her voice. "Such a pain in the butt."

"Not much. He's not happy with me because I emptied the theater before I called him, but at least he said he'd try to finish up in the Paramount in time for tomorrow night's movie. The cop outside Decklin's room will be here all night I suppose, and they'll search it in the morning."

"It'll be good if they get the Paramount finished," Ted offered. "Then we can plan Lunch and a Matinees for the weekend. That'll give you time to get the word out and give me time to figure out food for lunch."

"Let's all keep our fingers crossed. Hubbard followed the Browns home. He's planning to interview Harry Henshaw tonight—stomachache or not." Maureen savored her first sip of Irish coffee.

"The man is a bulldog," Molly said. "He never gives up once he thinks he's on to something. Poor Harry is in for it."

"His wife was quite worried about him," Maureen said. "She was anxious to get home."

"Sweet Kate," Gert said. "She's a year older than me but you'd never know it, she's still so pretty."

"That's one high-maintenance woman," George grumbled. "Henshaw has enough money to keep her looking good. Clothes, facelifts, and all that."

Maureen silently agreed, thinking of the woman's fashionable wardrobe and unlined face. "George said you went to high school with her, is that right, Gert?"

"Yep. She was a year ahead of me. Smart as a whip and pretty too." Gert pushed her glass in Leo's direction for a refill. "We all figured she'd be going to college, but darned if she didn't up and marry that Henshaw guy right after her graduation. She was only seventeen and he must have been thirty-odd. Gave her an engagement ring with a rock as big as a robin's egg."

"Her daughter says they're still madly in love," Maureen said.

"I believe it." Molly signaled Leo and tapped the rim of her glass. "Some women just marry the right guy and live happily ever after."

Maureen thought of her own parents, happy together in their California condo, married for more than forty years. "I agree," she said. "Some women are just lucky that way." *Maybe someday I'll be that lucky too.* She finished the last tasty sip of her Irish coffee, told Leo to put whatever the others wanted onto her tab, muffled a yawn, wished the others a good night, and headed for the elevator. She pressed the button for the third floor, thinking, as the glass-and-brass cage rose, about the many famous people who'd ridden up and down in it through the years. *I wonder*, she thought, *if some of them still drop by Haven as ghosts sometimes, like Babe Ruth or Vice President Charlie Curtis or Reggie Yardley, or poor Buddy Putnam in his lonely seat at the Paramount.*

Finn gave a sleepy "woof" as she approached her door. Lorna had apparently left and the golden was curled up on the floor in front of the couch where she'd been reading to him. He looked up as she entered, stretched, and trotted toward the bedroom.

"I'm right behind you Finn," she said. "It's been a long, long day. There's nothing in the world that could keep me awake much longer tonight."

Except wondering how Harry Henshaw will react to being questioned by Hubbard.

Chapter 15

Maureen felt the beginning of a return to normalcy with the morning routine of running on the beach. When she and Finn returned to the inn, she welcomed the sight of George and Sam in their usual rocking chairs, in their accustomed positions at the head of the stairs. The extra table setups had replaced quite a few of the rocking chairs, but the quartet had managed to maintain their front row spaces. Molly's and Gert's chairs were empty but a couple of towels tossed over the seats warned others away.

"Hey, Ms. Doherty," Sam called. "They're making eggnog French toast for breakfast this morning—special for Christmas."

"That sounds wonderful," she said. "I can hardly wait." Ted had met her as usual in front of the Casino, but had cut his run short, explaining that with all the rooms filled, he'd be extra busy with the breakfast service. Molly and Gert were undoubtedly helping in the kitchen. She waited by the green door to the lobby while Finn greeted the two men and a few others who'd found rockers. She dashed through the lobby, where the smell of coffee and bacon wafted temptingly from the dining room, and hurried up the two flights of stairs to her suite.

She'd just showered, dressed, and fed Finn when her house phone rang. The landline phone had been one of Elizabeth's better ideas. If there was no one available to man the reservation desk in the lobby, the calls could be switched to the office or to the penthouse suite.

"Hi, Maureen. It's Leslie Brown. I noticed last night that some of the flowers in the centerpieces had wilted. I'm on my way over with some fresh carnations. Is that all right?"

"Of course, Leslie," Maureen said. "I'll meet you in the lobby. Do you have time to have breakfast with me? Chef's special. Eggnog French Toast."

"That sounds good." The young woman's voice sounded strained. "Yes. I'll make time."

Maureen waited beside the lobby Christmas tree, admiring once again the beach-themed decorations. *We could probably sell decorations like these year-round. We really need a gift shop.* Her retail background brain kicked in once again. *Old-time candy. Shell craft. Maybe some beachwear.*

Her visualization was interrupted when Leslie appeared, arms laden with green tissue–wrapped blooms. The young woman wore a pink smock with *Petals and Kettles* embroidered on the breast pocket. "I realized on the drive over that your dining room might be full if that breakfast is as delicious as it sounds. I may have to stay for a while to spruce up the arrangements as the tables clear."

"Can I help you carry those?" Maureen reached toward the flowers, inhaling the sweet scents of carnations. "It's early. I'm sure some of the tables are still unoccupied."

Leslie handed her nearly half of the tissue-wrapped blossoms. "Here you go. Maybe we can put them in water while we wait."

"Sure. Follow me to the kitchen. I'm sure we have something that'll work."

Arms full, Maureen pushed the door to the kitchen open

with one elbow. The spotless room was a study in efficiency. Two waitresses, Shelly and Jolene, stood ready to pick up orders beneath the long warming lamp, while Ted and Molly worked at the grill and Gert plated the orders.

"Need a vase for those?" Ted looked up from the grill with a smile. "Second cabinet from your left. Top shelf. Take your pick. Penelope Josephine Gray had a taste for very large flower arrangements."

Maureen shifted the flowers to one arm and pulled open the designated cabinet door. Ted was right. There were at least ten giant containers. Maureen handed her flowers back to Leslie and used both hands to lift the tall glass vase. Filled with water it easily accommodated the blooms.

"This'll work fine. Thanks, Ted," she said, following Leslie back to the dining room where only three of the round tables were occupied. They sat at the first empty one. Leslie pulled the centerpiece toward herself and went to work replacing wilted blooms with fresh ones while Maureen gathered the discarded petals and tissue paper, putting them into a trash bag.

They worked in silence for several minutes. Then Leslie began to speak, slowly, levelly. "It was terrible," she said. "Poor Daddy."

"He's still quite ill?" Maureen questioned.

"He's feeling better, but the way that man—Hubbard—talked to him. So rudely."

Maureen could sympathize. Hubbard's "bulldog" reputation was well known, and Maureen could personally vouch for that. "I understand," she told Leslie. "Once Officer Hubbard gets an idea in his head, it's darned near impossible to get him to let go of it. Is he somehow blaming your dad for what happened at the Paramount last night?"

"Daddy tried to explain. He'd been so sick all day. We'd all kept checking on him, bringing him herbal tea, trying to make him comfortable. Mother didn't even want to leave him to go to the dinner and the movie, but he convinced her to go ahead. He said he'd just play computer games or watch TV or something and that he'd be all right if we left him home alone." She laughed a wry little laugh. " 'Home alone.' That's tonight's movie, isn't it? It's one of Warren's favorites.

"Officer Hubbard wanted to know if we were *sure* Daddy was sick and not lying about it," she continued. "How do we *know* he really was throwing up? How do we *know* he had diarrhea? For goodness' sake, Maureen, does he think we followed him into the bathroom?" Leslie wiped her eyes with a piece of tissue paper. "It was horrible."

Maureen handed her a white cloth napkin. "What is Frank Hubbard suggesting? That your father wasn't really sick, that he went to the Paramount and somehow got into the projection booth and shot Decklin while the movie was running without being seen?" Maureen tried to picture the man she'd seen at the flower shop carrying a gun and tiptoeing up the stairs to the balcony. It seemed unlikely, even in a dark theater, but could it be possible?

"I guess that's what Hubbard thinks." Leslie poked bright carnations into the greenery with a little more force than necessary. "He had poor Mother in tears, and I could barely keep from telling him what I thought of him. Good thing Warren was there. He answered the rude questions as politely as he could and at the same time tried to keep Daddy from getting himself in even more trouble by calling the policeman an incompetent moron and worse."

The two moved to the next table. "Did Hubbard actually accuse your father of anything?" Maureen handed Leslie a few flowers, and brushed some fallen petals into the bag. "I mean, he didn't actually say 'murder,' did he?"

"No. Nothing like that, really. It's just the way he asks questions. And the way he looks at you—like he doesn't believe a word you're saying. You know?"

Oh yes! I know. "Yeah. He's tough to talk to, but don't take it personally. He talks to everybody that way." Maureen paused. "I'm sure your father has some good attorneys."

"Yes." Leslie's expression brightened. "They're local. Jackson, Nathan and Peters. You know them?"

"Sure do. Nora Nathan represented me not too long ago when Frank Hubbard thought *I* might have had something to do with killing somebody."

"You? That's not possible." Leslie pulled a small pair of shears from a smock pocket and began trimming the stems of the blooms. "You wouldn't hurt a flea."

"Finn will tell you, I'm very hard on fleas." Maureen smiled. "But Hubbard is thorough. He thought I'd had the opportunity to kill a man right on the porch of this inn."

"The ghost hunter," Leslie recalled. "It was all over the news. And Hubbard suspected *you*? That's hard to believe."

"It was for me too. That's why I'm telling you not to take his questions too personally. Wait 'til he gets around to questioning some of the people who were in the audience last night. He'll scare each one of them to pieces, then move on to the next person on his list."

Leslie seemed to relax some as they moved from table to table, refreshing each centerpiece. By the time they reached the last one, the conversation turned to more pleasant topics like weather and tourists and clothes, and the newly freshened tables had begun to fill up. Jolene appeared and asked if they'd like to order.

"What do you say, Leslie?" Maureen asked. "Does Eggnog French Toast sound good? Let's finish up here, put this vase back in the kitchen, have some breakfast, and get acquainted. I've been in Haven such a short while I've barely met anybody outside of the inn."

Leslie glanced at her watch, an understated stainless Gucci. "Sure. I still have a little time. I'll call Mom and tell her I'll be a little late getting back. Can we sit at one of those little tables outside?"

"Good idea. Why don't you go out and grab a table while I put the vase away?"

Ted greeted Maureen as soon as she entered the kitchen, reached for the vase, emptied and wiped it, and returned it to its top shelf position. "What happened at the Henshaw house last night?" he whispered. "Did Leslie tell you anything?"

Maureen glanced around to see if the kitchen staff was listening. Of course they were. She kept her voice low. "Just about what you'd expect. I guess there was pretty intense grilling of her dad from Hubbard. Leslie is outraged, her mom in tears, Warren holding everybody together. No accusations, but Mr. Henshaw has lawyered up. Leslie is staying for breakfast. We're on the porch. Join us if you have time."

Wry smile. "Fat chance of that."

The young florist was enjoying a mug of coffee when Maureen returned. "Good coffee," she said. "And that breakfast sounds good too."

"Coffee, huh? Not your normal cup of tea?" As soon as she'd spoken, she uttered a slight gasp and sat down quickly. *Not your normal cup of tea.* Words from the Zoltar card. What did they mean?

"You okay?" Leslie leaned forward. "Is anything wrong?"

"No. Nothing at all. I need some of that good coffee too." She signaled to Jolene, ordered Eggnog French Toast for two and more coffees.

"Decklin Monroe was staying here at the inn, wasn't he?" Leslie cut her French toast into neat little squares and took a dainty bite. "Did you get to know him at all?"

"Not really. He was nice, though. He showed me around the theater and even played a few short films for me to demonstrate how the projectors work."

"That would creep me out," Leslie announced. "I mean,

up in that dusty old place with a complete stranger. Were you scared?"

"Of Decklin? No. Well, maybe a little at first. He was easy to talk to. Gert—one of my . . . um . . . my household staff— talked to him for hours."

One raised, arched, surprised eyebrow. "Really? What did they find to talk about?"

"According to her, they talked about Las Vegas. They both used to work there." Maureen remembered the two, heads together at the end of the bar.

Were the old days in Vegas all they talked about? Does Gert know something about Decklin Monroe that we don't know?

"This is yummy," Leslie said, swirling a piece of her toast around in butter. "I guess your Gert had better be ready for a lot of questions from Officer Hubbard about murder, then, won't she?"

"I'm guessing you're right about that," Maureen agreed. "He talked to her for a while last night and he'd better be ready for some more tall stories about the Rat Pack."

Chapter 16

It was nearly noon and Maureen was behind the reception desk in the lobby of the inn when Frank Hubbard telephoned to announce that he'd finished his work at the Paramount and that she could go ahead with plans for the movie. "We'll have to tape off the stairs to the balcony and the projection room. No admittance to anyone except the college kid and his dad. There'll be an officer at the foot of the stairs to make sure no one else gets up there."

"Thanks. I appreciate you finishing it up in time for tonight's show," she said. "The officers you sent to examine Decklin's room finished about an hour ago," she told him. "So our housekeeping staff will have it ready for guests later today."

"I know you probably need the income," he said, "trying to keep that old ruin of a place in business."

"You've got that right," she admitted. "Did you learn anything about who might have killed Decklin?"

"Think I'd tell you if I did? You'd be surprised at how much we've already learned and we don't have the medical examiner's report yet. Yes, ma'am. A professional team can learn a lot with some bright lights and a good vacuum cleaner." He gave a little snort of laughter. "To tell the truth there wasn't much to vacuum up. The guy was a snacker. A couple of soda cans, an empty popcorn box, gum wrappers, candy. Cleanest that projection room and stairway have been since they built that place back in the forties."

"Well, thanks again," she said.

"I may want to talk to you and that cook of yours again. Stay around so I can find you."

"We'll be here." She put the phone down. Hubbard had sounded really pleased with himself, and he'd finished his investigation of the theater much faster than she'd dared to hope he would. She'd be willing to bet that he'd found something important—and she hoped he'd figure out who'd killed Decklin soon. Being in a small town where everyone knew a murderer was running around loose was definitely bad for business. She wouldn't be surprised if there'd be a pile of cancelations for dinner and the showing of *Home Alone* and she hated the thought of refunding more money.

Quite a few of the reservations had been for inn guests. She began the chore of calling the suites, leaving the message that Dinner and a Movie was on for the evening, that there'd be a police guard at the theater, and that a wonderful meal, and a famous funny movie along with a cartoon and a vintage newsreel for twenty-nine ninety-five was a hard bargain to beat. She sent an e-mail blast to the others who'd made reservations and was pleasantly surprised when by two in the afternoon none of her guests, and only a dozen of the others who'd reserved tickets, had cancelled.

It was time for Finn's afternoon walk when she shared the elevator on the way upstairs with the couple from the Babe Ruth Suite. "Oh, Ms. Doherty," the woman gushed. "This is all so exciting. We've called all of our friends to tell them to watch the papers about the Christmas movie murder. I even snapped a couple of pictures outside the Paramount for my Facebook page. Just think: We must have been right there when it happened. It was so interesting, being questioned by the nice officer. I hope they'll catch the killer before we all have to go home."

Since when is murder a tourist attraction? "Yes. We all hope so," Maureen agreed. "I'll see you tonight." Were the papers actually calling Decklin's death "the Christmas movie murder"? Maybe there were even videos circulating on social media of her telling people to leave the theater. She sincerely hoped not as the couple got off on the second floor.

As soon as the elevator began to chug upward, she smelled the pipe smoke again. Whirling around, she studied the interior of the cubicle. There was, of course, no smoke there. *It must be the essence of smoke,* she decided, but even that was unacceptable in the ancient wooden structure. "Reggie!" She spoke aloud. "I don't want to have to tell you again. This is a no-smoking hotel." The odor immediately disappeared. The doors parted and she stepped out into the hall. "That's better," she said and walked to her suite, listening for welcoming "woofs."

Lorna was just inside the door. Finn, Bogie, and Bacall lined up in a row behind her. "Oh, hi, Maureen. Hi, Reggie," she said. As Maureen watched, Reggie shimmered into view, clad this time in jodhpurs, tall boots, a slim-fitting jacket, white ascot at the throat, and a tweed cap. Lorna raised perfectly shaped eyebrows. "Riding to the hounds?" she asked.

He rolled brown eyes. "The hunt requires a red jacket, silly girl. No. Playing polo today. By the way, Maureen, I just heard about this 'Christmas movie murder' you've got going on here. You personally cleared the murder scene, hey?"

"Where did you hear that?" Maureen hung her purse over the arm of a beige chair, wondering if Reggie had decided to take up residence at Haven House Inn and was wandering about, listening to random conversations.

"I stopped by the local grocery store," he said. "I needed

some hairspray. Everybody was talking about it. Quite the excitement for your little hamlet."

"Naturally the Quic-Shop," Maureen said, while at the same time wondering how the *essence* of hairspray would work. "What did you hear? Any guesses as to who the killer might be?"

"There's some wagering going on," he said. "The smart money seems to be on some sort of out-of-town, big city hit man. It seems that Mr. Monroe had business dealings with some unsavory characters. Did you know that?"

"I knew very little at all about him," Maureen insisted. "Some incidental chats about movies, or how Haven had changed since he was here last."

Reggie adjusted his cap. "Ah, yes. The unpleasantness about being intoxicated and starting a ruckus."

"Drunk and disorderly," Lorna put in. "He got caught beating up on Harry Henshaw. A regular dogfight."

"Woof," Finn said. "Woof woof woof."

"Not that kind of dogfight, Finn," Maureen corrected. "Anyway, if the police dropped the charges it couldn't have been all that bad. He seemed like a fairly even-tempered man to me." *Though I can't say the same for Harry Henshaw.*

"He must have done something to make somebody terribly angry with him, though, wouldn't you agree?" Reggie asked. "Somebody he knew, I'd guess. They say it was done at very close range."

"You're right." Maureen sat on the couch. Bogie and Bacall climbed up and sat on either side of her. "Whoever did it stood right square in front of him." She thought once again of the look of surprise on the dead man's face. "I don't think he was expecting trouble."

"Have you talked to Hubbard about it today?" Lorna asked.

"Yes. He called to say it's okay to show the movie at the Paramount tonight. *Home Alone.*"

Reggie laughed. "*Home Alone*? 'Merry Christmas, you filthy animal!' "

Lorna giggled. "I didn't think you watched American movies."

"I like some of the funny ones," he said.

"Like Buddy Putnam." Maureen spoke softly, almost to herself. "Poor Buddy only watches funny movies."

"Buddy sure didn't see what was coming," Lorna said. "Shot in the back of the head while he was watching *Animal House*."

"*Animal House!*" Reggie laughed again. " 'Toga! Toga! Toga!' I liked that one too. Can Lorna and I go to your movie tonight, Maureen? We don't take up any room."

"Sure you can. I've had hardly any cancellations. But nobody is supposed to go up the stairs to the balcony or the projection room," she warned.

"NoBODY?" Reggie accented the second two syllables. "No BODY?" He winked in Lorna's direction. "We can respect that."

Bacall, apparently bored with the conversation, left the couch, walked through Lorna and climbed onto the cat tower. Bogie ignored Lorna, and the cats, their backs turned to human and once-human, tails hanging down from the top tier, watched whatever was going on in or beyond the Christmas light–trimmed palm trees outside. Lorna, following the cats, shimmered her way to the window, shielded her eyes and peered out.

"Uh-oh, Maureen," she said. "There's a police car parked out there. Looks like your friendly neighborhood cop is back. Do you think maybe he's interested in you romantically?"

"Not a chance," Maureen said, "but I'd better get back down there and see if I can keep him from harassing my guests."

"On the other hand," Lorna suggested, "he may just be

looking for free coffee and doughnuts. Elizabeth had all the cops spoiled and I think maybe Gert and Molly have continued the tradition."

"We can't actually afford to be giving away *anything* free these days, but I guess some leftover coffee and a couple of yesterday's doughnuts won't hurt us." Maureen picked up her purse and pulled open the door. "I'd better get down there and see what he wants."

The elevator was busy so she took the stairs, arriving in the first-floor lobby just as Frank Hubbard came through the green doors from outside. He lifted one hand in a friendly-looking salute. "Oh, hi, Ms. Doherty. Just the person I was looking for. Got a minute?"

"Of course. Shall we go into my office?"

"No need. Couple of things. First, I'll need to keep an officer outside Monroe's room for a while longer. We've got the basic stuff—his phone and wallet and laptop. There's probably nothing of importance in the room but I can't spare the team to properly search it yet. We can most likely free it up for you by tomorrow afternoon. But the main thing is, do you have any reservations left for tonight's movie dinner thing?"

"I do," she said, puzzled. "Are you planning on joining us?"

"Me? No. I don't have time for movies." He looked slightly flustered. "It's for my mother. She and a girlfriend want to come. Can I make reservations for the two of them?"

"Certainly. We'll be glad to have them. Excuse me for a moment. The tickets are in the safe in my office." She unlocked the office door, and closed it behind her. The small safe was located behind an oil painting of a bright red poinciana tree. She lifted the framed picture, tapped in the short combination and selected two of the numbered tickets from the safe, then placed them into a Haven House Inn envelope. She returned to the reservation desk where Hubbard had moved the tall stool reserved for customers from the right-hand end of the counter to the left. She gave him a questioning look. "I like watching that elevator go up and down," he said. That was understandable. She'd done exactly the same thing the previous day, picturing famous guests who'd used it. "Names?" she asked.

"Edith Hubbard and Aster Patterson."

"Aster from the bookshop?" Maureen asked, surprised.

"Sure. You know anybody else named Aster? Anyway she and my mom go way back. Both widows. They find stuff to do together. Pottery classes. Ghost tours. Bridge club. Movies."

Ghost tours?

"That's nice." Maureen placed the numbered tickets on the desk. "Cash or charge?" Hubbard handed her a Visa card, then leaned forward with his elbows on the raised counter, watching her intently as she ran the card. "We start serving dinner at six," she told him, "then we'll all walk together to the Paramount. We have golf carts too, if she'd prefer that."

He returned the card to his wallet and pocketed the tickets. "Thanks. I'll get them both here by six. What time do you think this thing will be over?"

"By eleven, I should say, if all goes as planned."

"If all goes as planned," he repeated. "Good luck, Ms. Doherty."

Chapter 17

That was odd, she thought. *Was that all he wanted? He could have phoned the information about the room guard. Just tickets for his mom and Aster? He could have done that by phone too.* She quick-walked to the green door and stepped out onto the porch, watching as Hubbard approached the cruiser and climbed into the driver's seat. Will he leave, she wondered, or will he hang around, looking for whatever it is he *really* came over here for? She waited, watching for a long moment. Then, the cruiser moved slowly away from the curb, made an illegal U-turn, and headed back down the boulevard, past the Paramount toward the beach. She shrugged, still wondering, and went back inside the inn.

Within less than a minute, George and Sam had followed her to the lobby. "Everything all right, Ms. Doherty?" Sam asked.

George frowned. "Don't like that cop nosin' around here—just lookin' for trouble."

The two looked at her expectantly, an unspoken *What did he want?* hanging between them. She decided to answer it anyway. "He came to say the room guard would be here another day and he bought tickets for tonight's Dinner and a Movie. They're for his mother and her girlfriend," she told them.

"That's all?" The words were spoken in surprised unison. She echoed them. "That's all."

The men, muttering between themselves, returned to the porch. It appeared to Maureen, as they walked away, that both Sam and George had a disappointed slump to their shoulders. She was a little disappointed too. This was the first time since she'd met Frank Hubbard that he'd shown up without subjecting her to a barrage of annoying questions. Something about it just didn't feel right.

Shaking the nagging feeling away, she turned the reservation desk duties over to Shelly, who was putting in some overtime to help pay off her college loan, and pushed open the louvred door to the dining room. It actually did look a lot better in there than it had when she'd first inherited the place. The new light-colored draperies, clean carpet, sparkling windows, and Christmas centerpieces gave a hint of the kind of charm she hoped she could bring to the Haven House Inn.

She glanced over toward the bar in the far corner of the long room. That area could use some updating. The wonderfully old-style wooden bar, heavily carved with fanciful sea creatures and gleaming from regular polishings with lemon oil, needed no improvement, but the red cushions on the bar stools looked shabby and the shelving behind the bar where bottles were displayed had certainly seen better days.

Maureen kept a file in her office marked with a single letter *S*—for "Someday." In it were full-color sketches of half a dozen areas of the inn. These were much-improved images of the front of the building, a guest suite, the inn's lobby, the dining room, the bar, the front porch, and even a small gift shop covering the far end of the porch where the ghost hunter had died. This portfolio had been a gift from a couple of former guests—professional interior decorators Trent and Pierre. They'd already made reservations for the following June—they'd be celebrating Trent's birthday—and she'd promised that she'd try to implement some of the designs in time for their return. *The Christmas movie promotion will make us a little money. I think I'll use some of it for the bar,* she decided. *It's the smallest space but a little upgrade might make a big impression. I'd better take another look at that sketch and get an idea of what we'll need to do—and what it will cost.*

She spread the contents of the portfolio onto her desk, placing the sketch of the bar area at the top of the pile. Trent and Pierre had visualized something more than new seat cushions. The watercolor rendering showed dark wood barstools, in tones matching the rich mahogany of the bar itself, with padded red seats and backs. The utilitarian shelves behind the bar had been replaced by dark wood shelving with carved sea horses, fish, and sand dollars here and there to match the bar décor. The wall behind it was mirrored, reflecting carefully arranged bottles, while in the center of the structure was a large lighted aquarium. It was perfect. But undoubtedly expensive.

If we can only do part of this, I'd like to get Ted's input on what's the best place to start. She pulled her cell phone from the purse and tapped in Ted's number. "Can you spare a few minutes?" she asked. "I'm in my office and I need your opinion on something."

"I'll be right there," he promised. "We're all set for tonight's dinner. No problems. I have something for you to taste anyway."

Within minutes she heard his tap at the door. "Come on in," she called. "It's not locked." He pushed the door open with one hand while in the other he carefully balanced a small tray.

"Whatever that is, it smells beyond wonderful." Maureen approached him, trying to get a better look into the steaming mug on the tray. She could already tell that the mug was surrounded by some of Aster Patterson's shortbread cookies.

"It's wassail!" Ted announced proudly. "You know, from the song." He attempted an off-key rendering of "Here We Come A-wassailing." "I thought maybe we'd serve wassail and cookies after the movie tonight. The weather's getting cooler and it fits the theme. What do you think?"

She took a careful sip. "Marvelous. They'll love it. I can taste orange juice and—what? Apple cider?"

Ted beamed. "Yep. Apple cider from New England and orange juice from Florida. With a whiff of brandy. I thought it was just right for you."

He made it for me?

"They'll love it. I love it." She sipped the hot liquid carefully, nibbled on a shortbread cookie, then put the tray aside, being careful not to spill anything on the artwork. "Here, look. I'm sure you remember these sketches that Trent and Pierre did for us. I've been hoping we could get at least one thing done before they come back next June. I think the bar area—or at least part of it—is doable."

Ted moved closer, their arms touching, and with his forefinger traced the outline of the shelf space behind the bar. "This wall definitely needs improvement. The old shelves got kind of saggy—dangerous, really—and Elizabeth had George bang together some plywood ones, and slap on a coat of dark brown paint. That's the ones that are there now. Let's do as much as we . . . you . . . can afford. The carved woodwork and the mirror and the aquarium would be great. It would make all the difference in the world for the whole dining room."

"Let's work toward that, then. As for the aquarium, I think we'll see Aster tonight. She knows a lot about fish tanks. She has some impressive ones in the bookstore. She could probably even stock it for us with angelfish." Maureen's excitement grew as she visualized the revamped bar. "Trent and Pierre will be so pleased."

"All we have to do is make the money," Ted said. "I'd better get back to my job. I'm glad you like the wassail. I'll pick up the tray later."

By the time Ted had left the office, Maureen had replaced the drawings in the portfolio and had typed "Local carpenters" into the search field on her computer. "No time like the present," she said softly. "I'll need some estimates for tearing that old wall out and building the new one." She reached for the house phone on her desk and dialed the number for the first carpenter's name that showed up.

Within the hour she'd made appointments for three different woodworking companies to come to the inn to make cost estimates for after the first of the new year. Convinced that she'd made a good start on the current to-do list, Maureen returned the S-file to the file cabinet. Next on the list was buying ad space for the matinee lunch in the *Tampa Bay Times* and the weekly *Haven Happenings*. Those arrangements completed, she sat down to e-mail publicity releases to the papers and radio stations. She couldn't afford TV advertising but sent releases to the local stations anyway. She e-mailed the theater owner, requesting the name of the candy wholesaler, telling him about her plans for the matinee Lunch and a Movie feature to help get the film festival on track. He promised to text her the name of the wholesaler. "You seem to have things well in hand, Ms. Doherty," he said. "In the scheme of things, the Paramount Theater isn't of major concern to me as I plan to sell it and have no intention of constantly traveling to Florida. Just use your best judgement on this Christmas thing."

She put her head down on the desk. "There. That's done. I'm tired. My inn is falling apart faster than I can afford to fix it. We made a little money with a dinner-and-a-movie promotion but I might wind up in the hole after all. And poor Decklin is dead and I've ticked off Haven's top cop again."

She fought back tears, then sat up, straightening her shoulders. "I'm doing everything I can," she told herself, "under some darned strange circumstances. Why does everything have to be so difficult?"

Strange and difficult indeed you may find it. The line from the Zoltar card replayed in her mind.

"Okay, Zoltar," she muttered. "You've got that right. Now what am I supposed to do about it?"

Chapter 18

Five o'clock arrived much too soon. Maureen hadn't planned a wardrobe for a second Dinner and a Movie night. What to wear? For a moment she envied Lorna's clothes borrowing technique. A quick trip past Macy's window and she could grab a perfectly fitted, fully accessorized outfit. She scanned the contents of her closet and decided on last year's silk print Tory Burch shirt dress with a fairly new blue cashmere shrug and yesterday's black sandals. Good enough.

Finn had been fed and walked and after a final turn in front of the full-length mirror, she left the suite and hurried down the hall toward the elevator. *Whatever happens tonight,* she thought, *it has to be better than last night's train wreck.* Even before the elevator landed on the first floor she heard the chatter of voices and the *plink-plink* of piano music that signified a good turnout for dinner. She'd done her best at last-minute promotion for the unplanned-for event, but there was little doubt that Ted's menu had a lot to do with the return customers.

The dining room had begun to fill up. Sam, in black pants, white shirt, and red vest held the green doors open for arriving guests. All of the white wicker lobby chairs were occupied and the matching tables held bar glasses and small bowls of cereal, nuts, and pretzel party mix. Everyone looked happy and pleased to be there. The mood was contagious and Maureen felt herself relaxing, smiling, and moving easily among the guests. A peek past the louvred door proved that the Henshaw-Brown family had already been seated, and this time Harry Henshaw was with his family. *Good*, Maureen thought. *He must be over his stomach problems, and from what Frank Hubbard intimated, there was no love lost between Mr. Henshaw and Decklin, so I'm sure he's not mourning the death of an old acquaintance.* Henshaw sat beside his wife, one arm around the back of her chair, his fingers lightly touching her shoulder. She, smiling at something he'd said, touched her hair, her ring catching the light from the centerpiece. Gert was right. That diamond was darn near the size of a robin's egg.

A familiar voice called her name. "Ms. Doherty."

"Yes?" She turned to face Frank Hubbard. He was in uniform, with an elderly woman on each arm.

"This is my mother, Edith Hubbard. I guess you know Mrs. Patterson? Aster?"

"Of course. Hello, Aster." Maureen was pleased to note that Aster's navy blue wool theater ensemble was quite appropriate for the occasion, though the white go-go boots were a jarring note. "How do you do, Mrs. Hubbard? I'm so glad you're both joining us this evening." Maureen extended a hand toward each woman. Aster grasped her hand, holding it tightly. Mrs. Hubbard murmured, "Charmed," and gave a dainty sort of fingertip handshake.

"Hello, sweetheart," Aster said. "I've been dying to go to one of the Christmas movies. I don't get out much, you know, what with the bookshop and the cat and the fish and all. I was thrilled to little pieces when Edith invited me."

"My pleasure, Aster." Mrs. Hubbard smiled at her friend.

"When I get a nice surprise like this, I'm glad I can share it with you."

"Well, then. I guess we're all set." Hubbard backed away from the two women. "I'll be back to pick you up at around eleven. You girls have fun now." He dashed for the exit before anyone answered.

"Take any seat at all, ladies," Maureen said. "Dinner will be served at six. Have a complimentary cocktail if you like." The two, arm in arm, spotted a table close to the player piano where the keys plinked out "Frosty the Snowman." Billy was really getting into the holiday swing of things.

"I'm thinking about putting an aquarium over the bar, Aster," Maureen whispered. "Give it some thought and we'll talk soon."

By six o'clock the dining room tables were filled, and a parade of red-vested servers moved around the room as easily as if they were accustomed to a full house for every meal—which was far from the truth. Pleased with the display of efficiency, Maureen realized that Ted had managed to not only plan and execute delicious, attractive, and cost-effective meals but had somehow managed to train the homegrown Haven staff in five-star-restaurant service as well. *What a guy!*

By the time the after-dinner coffee was served, Maureen had made the obligatory table visits, speaking a few words to each group. She'd chatted briefly with Leslie and Warren and Leslie's parents, being sure to pass on the many compliments she'd had from others in the room about the centerpieces. She'd remembered to ask Harry Henshaw how he was feeling. He said he was fine, that he must have caught some sort of stomach flu. He was happy, he told her, that no one else in the family had caught it.

When she reached the table beside the piano she found Aster and Edith Hubbard chatting easily with their tablemates. This pleased Maureen. Even though her relationship with Edith's son was often rocky, she wanted his mother to enjoy this evening. "We'll leave for our walk to the Paramount soon," she told them. "We have golf carts available if you'd prefer to ride."

"It's such a nice night," the policeman's mother enthused, "I'm looking forward to the walk. When Frank surprised me with the tickets this afternoon I wasn't sure it was something I felt up to doing. And when Aster was free for a last-minute dinner date, well, that was the frosting on the cake. I'm having a wonderful time. The dinner was perfect and I can hardly wait for the movie." Aster added her own enthusiastic comments and the two were giggling like schoolgirls when they walked through the Haven House lobby, heading for the boulevard and a moonlight walk to the movies.

Maureen climbed into the first golf cart, assuring that she'd be at the Paramount to welcome her guests as they arrived at the theater entrance. The spotlights illuminated the night sky over Haven and the white bulbs surrounding the marquee shone Broadway bright. There was already a line at the box office, and George, who'd volunteered for ticket-taker duty, was at his post, looking stern and official. The pretty usherette was back. Assured that the movie club projectionist and his Marine dad escort had arrived early and were already in the projectionist's booth, Maureen next made a quick tour of the lobby. The candy counter looked well-stocked and the popcorn machine popped merrily. Inside the theater, as Frank Hubbard had promised, the stairway to the balcony had been roped off with a yellow DO NOT CROSS banner and a large uniformed cop stood at the foot of the stairs.

She returned to the outdoors, feeling confident that this evening would run smoothly, that the movie would remain intact, that the audience would enjoy the show, and that

Haven House Inn's figures would be in the black, even if only by a little. The crowd seemed to be in a holiday frame of mind, and almost everybody Maureen spoke to said they looked forward to the lighthearted movie. When it was nearly showtime, Maureen, as she had the previous night, took a seat in the back row of the theater, putting the blue cashmere shrug on the seat beside hers, in case Ted might have time to join her there later.

The houselights dimmed, the curtains parted, and soon the audience was laughing along with Daffy Duck, Elmer Fudd, and Road Runner. Maureen stole a peek over toward aisle four, but her vision was blocked by tall Looney Toons fans. The mood turned more solemn with the start of a 1964 newsreel showing the Bob Hope Christmas in Vietnam show. Bob was joined by Anita Bryant, Janis Paige, and Jerry Colona as they presented their annual Christmas show to US forces stationed in Vietnam. The laughter returned with the opening scenes of *Home Alone*.

Maureen found her attention wandering while young Kevin figured out that there are bad guys on the premises. She glanced around her, trying to identify people from the inn or others who'd been at the dinner earlier. Aster and her friend Edith were easy to spot—two gray heads together just a few rows in front of Maureen. She hoped Aster would give some thought to the proposed aquarium. The words Edith had spoken earlier played back in her mind. "Frank surprised me with the tickets this afternoon." And she'd added that Aster was free for a last-minute dinner date. But Hubbard had told her when he bought the tickets that his mother had requested them. Somehow, it didn't add up.

The whispered "Did you save my place?" announced Ted's presence. Maureen snatched up the blue sweater and he eased into the seat beside her. "I'm glad you could make it," she told him.

"Sam and Leo and the girls have everything under control," he assured her. "I thought it would be okay for me to sneak down here and catch half the movie."

"I'm sure you've seen it a couple of times before," she said. "So has probably everybody here, but it's one of those you look forward to every December."

"You're right. I've got a nice pot of that wassail on low heat, waiting for the return group. Nice night for it. Everything going smoothly here?"

"Almost too perfectly." Maureen smiled. "I keep waiting for the other shoe to drop. Or the other film to flop."

"Not a chance," Ted said. "This movie's new enough to be digital. Piece of cake for the projectionist."

"Fingers crossed anyway," she said.

"Ssshhh!" came the hissed command from the row in front of them. Chagrined, the two watched in comparative silence while Kevin was reunited with his family. The audience began to stir from their seats when the "Previews of Coming Attractions" flashed onto the screen. When Maureen and Ted stepped into the theater lobby, there was already a line at the candy counter. Katherine and Harry, holding hands, were at the head of the line.

"Butterscotch Life Savers," Maureen whispered.

"Butterscotch Life Savers? You want some?" Ted reached into his jacket pocket. "I'm buying."

She touched his hand. "No. Not for me. Harry Henshaw doesn't like to be without them. Katherine filled her purse with them last night. They must be stocking up."

"Do you have a favorite? I'm still buying."

"I always wanted to try a Sky Bar," she said. "Just one will be fine." She moved to the side, standing in front of a giant iconic poster of Macaulay Culkin, both hands to his face in horror. Ted joined the candy counter line. He returned holding the promised confection toward her. "You know, we should find out where they get the old-fashioned candies. We could sell them at the inn."

"I already e-mailed the owner about them," she said, slipping the four-sectioned bar into her purse and heading for the waiting golf carts.

Chapter 19

Haven House Inn looked like a virtual Christmas card to returning moviegoers. Single electric candles glowed in every window of the old building, and the porch Christmas tree flashed varicolored bulbs. Potted poinsettias brightened the wide front staircase. Inside, the dining room welcomed guests with Ted's fragrant hot wassail in pressed-glass punch cups—from one of Penelope's many "collections." Aster Patterson's locally famous shortbread cookies, these with frosting holly berries on top, completed the late evening holiday snack.

Maureen carried her hot drink into the lobby and took her position behind the reservation desk in order to invite guests to join the others for wassail and cookies, and at the same time to man the phones in case there might already be some response to the matinee lunch promotion. She was disappointed when the Browns and the Henshaws left without stopping at the inn. She would have liked to talk with them some more—with Harry in particular. At exactly eleven o'clock, Frank Hubbard appeared to pick up his mother and Aster, both of whom were so reluctant to end their night out and leave that he was persuaded to join them in a cup of wassail—"The kind with the brandy in it," Edith specified—and a decorated cookie.

Turning the desk duty over to Shelly, Maureen, at a discreet distance, followed Hubbard and the two women back into the dining room, intending to speak with Aster about the aquarium plan. It had also occurred to her that at the same time she might learn whether Mrs. Hubbard had asked her son for tickets or whether it had been his own idea. Both Edith and Aster had certainly seemed to be surprised by their good fortune.

"Yoo-hoo, Maureen," Aster called. "Come and join us. This drink is wonderful. Have you tried it?"

"I have," Maureen said. "It's delicious. I hope you girls have enjoyed your evening. Did you like the movie?"

"It was a real treat," Edith said. "Especially since neither Aster nor I had plans for tonight. Frankie's surprise was just what we needed." She reached across the table and patted her son's hand. "Such a good boy."

Hubbard flushed, averted his eyes, and pulled his hand away. "No big deal," he muttered. "Thought you'd like it."

There's something more than being a good son involved here. What the heck is he looking for? She couldn't very well come right out and ask him. Maureen accepted a second cup of the lovely orange/cider blend, appreciating again Ted's innovative touches to the inn's growing reputation as a good place to dine.

"Everybody loves the decorated cookies, Aster," she told the woman. "I meant to stop by the store to thank you for the extra Christmas frosting touch, and I need a new dog-story book for Finn. I also need your advice about the possibility of putting a good-sized aquarium behind the bar. What do you think?"

Aster squinted and focused her eyes on the bar. "You'll need a stronger base. A tank full of water weights a lot. That rickety thing George banged together won't hold it. Has Finn read *Old Yeller*?"

"I don't think so," she said. "It might be too scary for him," then she hurriedly added, "do you think we should stock our tank with angelfish, like yours?"

"People seem to like watching them. Very relaxing. We liked the previews of coming attractions they showed tonight." She tilted her head toward her friend. "We'd both like to see *The Bishop's Wife.*"

Edith bobbed her head enthusiastically. "Oh, that Cary Grant. What a movie." She looked toward Frank. "What do you say, Frankie? Want to pop for a couple more tickets for us?"

"Yeah," Aster said. "And this time give us more than a couple of hours' notice."

Maureen watched the policeman's face. Did he realize that she'd figured out that his buying the tickets was a cover for . . . for what? All he did was watch the elevator go up and down.

Hubbard's expression didn't change one bit. "Sure," he said. "What day is the Cary Grant one?"

"Day after tomorrow," Maureen said. "Tomorrow it's *Prancer.* It's a kid movie so there'll be children in the audience. The moms will go because Sam Elliot is in it. The matinee is at two o'clock every day. Lunch is at noon."

"Couple of tickets for Cary Grant." Hubbard reached for his wallet.

"And dinner," Edith prodded.

"And dinner," Hubbard repeated.

"Tickets are in my office," Maureen reminded him. "We'll get them when you leave."

"Fine," he said. "Ready to go, Mom? Aster?"

"We were just talking about having another one of these hot toddies or whatever you call them. The ones with the brandy in them," Edith announced, waving her cup back and forth. "Come on, Frankie. Be a sport."

Aster waved hers too. "*Here we go a-wassailing*," she crooned. "Come on, Frankie."

"Okay. Sure." Hubbard signaled for a waiter, his expression glum. Edith beamed at her son and Aster clapped her hands together in delight. "Some more cookies too."

"Enjoy." Maureen excused herself and began a slow walk around the room, stopping now and then to speak to a guest. The second day of Christmas was going a great deal better than the first day had, and Maureen was grateful. Glancing back toward the round table where Frank Hubbard watched his elderly dates sip and nibble and chat, she enjoyed his obvious discomfort.

He knows that I know he's up to something, she thought, *and he can't be sure that I don't know exactly what that is.*

Maureen returned to her post at the reservation desk, gratified by a sudden rush of business. Several new room and suite reservations came in by phone and she sold several matinee tickets for *Prancer*. She'd brought the tickets from her office to the desk so she was ready to dispense them as soon as Frank and his slightly tipsy companions appeared. "Two movie and dinner tickets for *The Bishop's Wife*, right?" she said.

"Right." Hubbard exhaled a sigh of apparent resignation and handed her his credit card. "Thanks, Doherty. They had a wonderful time."

"I can see that," she said. "You should do it more often. Next time stay for the movie."

"Sure," he said. "I'll do that." And with a giggling woman on each arm, he walked carefully to the exit.

The after-movie crowd had begun to break up. Hilda, the night manager, had arrived, but Maureen remained in the lobby. "Good night. Thanks for coming. See you soon. Glad you enjoyed it." The words and phrases came easily and honestly. She realized, somewhat surprised, that she was getting pretty good at this innkeeper hosting business—and that she was sort of loving it. Not just the business, but the old building itself and the staff that had come with it, and the visitors who stayed overnight or longer, and the little city of Haven and its residents, and even its ghosts.

"What do you think?" Ted's voice from the doorway behind her brought a smile.

"I think it's been a good night," she told him. "A good time was had by all. What do *you* think?" She motioned for Hilda to take over the desk and joined Ted.

"I think you're right. We're on a roll. Let's keep this party going. Looks like the porch has cleared up. Want to grab a couple of rockers and talk?"

"An excellent idea," she agreed. "Let's do it." She didn't object when he took her hand and led her through the green doors. In fact, it seemed quite natural. Although the four rockers in the front row were vacant, they chose two in the far left-hand corner. There was a good view of the Boulevard with its twinkling Christmas lights and lamppost displays of alternating angels, candy canes, and stars. Neither spoke right away, yet she felt no awkwardness in the mutual silence. It was just restful. After a moment she began the conversation. "I spoke to Aster about the aquarium. She thinks it can be done if the back shelf is replaced with something a lot stronger."

"She's an expert," he said. "I'd trust her judgment completely about the size and weight of the tank. "

"How do you feel about angelfish?" she asked. "Aster says people like to watch them. Very relaxing."

"She's right," he said.

"I seem to have a thing for angelfish." She spoke hesitantly, not quite sure if she should tell him about the coin she kept in the drawer along with the Zoltar cards. It was a 1983 Bermuda nickel. Queen Elizabeth was pictured on one side, and an angelfish decorated the other. On the day she'd left

Bartlett's of Boston, that coin had rolled from under her desk and come to a stop at the toe of her shoe. "Keep it for good luck," her boss, William G. Bartlett III, had advised. So she had kept it. Then she'd inherited an inn with a restaurant named after the beloved queen even though hardly anybody called it "Elizabeth's" anymore. Now angelfish had assumed special meaning too. She hadn't talked with anyone about it except Finn. Not even Lorna.

"What kind of thing?" he asked.

She told him everything about the coin—how it seemed to have some special meaning for her. "Is it some crazy kind of coincidence, or is it possible that such things are—oh, I don't know—meant to be?"

"Like you finding a picture of yourself in Penelope's office? A picture taken when you were a kid holding a fish that I might have cooked for you in my mother's restaurant?" His expression was solemn. Totally serious. "A coincidence like that?"

Yes. I meant a coincidence exactly like that.

They rocked together, quietly, wordlessly in the glow from the Christmas lights.

Chapter 20

There was no doubt about it. The Lunch and a Movie promotion would make money for the inn. Maureen felt confident enough about that to start the day right after a pumpkin pancake breakfast by calling carpenters about rebuilding the wall behind the bar. As soon as Will Goudreau walked into her office she had a good feeling about him. He was dressed for work in overalls and sturdy boots. His handshake was firm, eyes clear and friendly, nose a little bit crooked, graying hair thinning. His business card read GOUDREAU AND SON. Was Will the father or the son? She showed him the decorators' sketch of how the finished project should look and walked with him to the bar. He pulled a measuring tape from one of his many pockets and silently went about measuring, tapping on the existing wall, crawling under the counter, and aiming a flashlight into all the corners and crevices of the underpinnings of the whole thing He quoted her a price a little below the highest estimate she'd had but well above the lowest. He seemed knowledgeable about types of wood. He showed her catalog pictures of wood carvings of sea creatures that could be applied to the new structure. He pulled up photos and weights of fish tanks on his phone.

It didn't take long for her to make the decision. She stuck

out her hand. "Okay, Mr. Goudreau, when can you start?" Did she detect a slight hesitation before he grasped her hand? Before he agreed to take the job?

"I'm going to run this by my dad, first, if you don't mind." *So he's the son.*

He pulled out his phone. "I'll tell you the truth. He wasn't crazy about me bidding on this job. He did some work here a while back, when Ms. Gray owned the place. He says the inn is haunted." He smiled and gave an apologetic shrug. "I don't believe in that stuff myself, but, well, he is my dad."

"Of course. I'd like very much for you to do the work. I'll be in my office." Maureen left the man, the phone to his ear, and mentally crossed her fingers as she returned to the lobby. *He understands just what I want. I hope he'll do it even if his dad thinks the inn is haunted. Which it is.* While he called his father, Maureen pulled up the information on the next carpenter on her list—just in case.

Only a few minutes had passed before he knocked on the office door. "Come on in, Mr. Goudreau," she called. "It's open." His expression told her that the dad had okayed the job. "Dad says it's okay for me to do it, Ms. Doherty," he reported, "but he doesn't want to work in here with me unless I absolutely need him. The ghost he met up with really scared him."

I can relate. She shook his hand once again.

"If you want me to, I can put up a temporary screen so the people in the dining room won't have to see what's going on," he offered. "Maybe we can set up a temporary bar somewhere too."

"I'll check with my executive chef about it," she said. "I'm guessing he'll want to do that. Let me know when you can get started on the project as soon as you can after Christmas so we can coordinate everything."

"I sure will. I'm looking forward to doing the job," he

said. "I'm glad you're fixing the old place up. Too often lately they tear down something grand like this place and put up a T-shirt store or a parking garage."

She agreed, stood, and walked with him to the front door. "I'm looking forward to working with you."

"Me too," he said. "I just hope the ghost lady won't bother me when I'm working."

"The ghost lady?"

He looked down at his shoes. "Yeah. My dad said he was minding his own business, installing a picture window, and all of a sudden there she was. Standing right next to him."

"I'm quite sure you won't be bothered by any ghosts," Maureen assured him, hoping she sounded convincing. *A picture window? What picture window?* She was afraid to ask.

"I hope not. He finished the job even though he was scared. He didn't want to frighten Ms. Gray so he never did tell her there was a ghost right in her own living room—even if the ghost was a real pretty woman."

Maureen had no ready reply to that. "I'll look forward to your call," she told him, "and Merry Christmas." She returned to her office, picking up the stack of drawings on her desk. The next one after the rendering of the bar was the sketch of the gift shop at the end of the porch and she looked at it for a long minute, wondering how soon she'd be able to have Goudreau and Son give an estimate on that. Closing her eyes, she thought about how it would look stocked with beachwear and sea shells and hard-to-find candy.

"One thing at a time," she told herself and quickly returned the Someday file to the file cabinet. "Someday is later," she said aloud. "Today is right now." She leaned back in her chair, trying to settle her mind on exactly *what* she should do right now. A brisk knock on her office door presented an answer.

"Ms. Doherty?" Molly's voice was hesitant. "Sorry to

bother you, but you might want to turn on your TV. But . . . um . . . we're kind of on it."

"We are?"

"I mean the inn is." Maureen reached for the remote. Clicked on Channel 9. Molly was right. There was the inn. The Christmas lights looked fine but the flashing lights of the police cars were a jarring note. The camera lingered on the people climbing the stairs to the front porch. An announcer's voice-over described the scene. "Potential witnesses to the recent murder of Decklin Monroe return to the Haven House Inn, where the late Mr. Monroe had been staying. Monroe, a motion picture projectionist, had been hired by the Paramount Movie Theater in downtown Haven to show a series of holiday movies. The Haven House Inn had organized a dinner-and-a-movie promotion and much of the audience present on the night of the killing were guests at the inn. An investigation is ongoing."

Some of the guests were recognizable, even in the dim light. Maureen saw the Browns and Mrs. Henshaw, the couple from the Babe Ruth Suite, and several other guests as well as a number of people from the neighborhood. "Where did this come from?" Maureen wondered aloud. "I didn't see any TV mobile units around that night."

"You don't need mobile units these days," Molly offered. "Just a cell phone with a good camera. Be in the right place at the right time, and you can sell your video to local, maybe even national, news channels."

"Maybe my guests aren't going to like being classified as potential witnesses to a murder. And some of them are easy to recognize. Look, there's that nice couple from Wisconsin."

"Uh-oh," Molly whispered. "I'm not sure they're married. They sure aren't going to want to be photographed holding hands like that if there's some hanky-panky going on. And hey, look, that's you at the foot of the steps. That's a great red dress."

Glad when the film clip came to an end, Maureen turned the set off, hoping that not many had seen it.

Unfortunately, many had. The buzz about the TV report was immediate. Those who hadn't seen it were told about it in enthusiastic detail. Some said they hoped it would be on again in the evening local newscast so they could see how they looked. If any of the people who talked to Maureen about it were upset about the "potential witness to a murder" idea, nobody said so. Once again, she was surprised by human nature. It seemed that being part of the "Christmas Movie Murder" was somehow cool. If the nice couple from Wisconsin were worried about being recognized they didn't show it, and had happily signed up on the waiting list for the matinee showing of *It's a Wonderful Life* on day six, which was already a sellout.

Frank Hubbard showed up late in the day to dismiss the officer guarding Decklin's room. "We're bagging up his personal possessions in case some of his family wants them," he told Maureen. "You can go ahead and rent the place again if you want to. The ME has finished with the body and a nephew from New Jersey has arranged for cremation and is coming to Haven."

"Will there be any services? Or a memorial of some kind?" she asked. "I feel as though we should send flowers or something. He'd made a few friends here."

"You'll have to check with the nephew about that," Hubbard said. "He'll probably be calling about staying here. I gave him your number."

"You did? Thanks."

He shrugged. "Yours is the only hotel we've got besides a couple of dinky little mom-and-pop motels."

"Yeah. Well, thanks anyway. What did the medical examiner find? Anything you hadn't already figured out?"

"Not really. Small-caliber gun used at close range. Probably used a silencer. Looks like it was somebody he knew, to get attacked from the front like that. He didn't even try to deflect the shot." Maureen was surprised to get that much information from the usually close-mouthed Hubbard. He continued, "Don't think you're getting the inside dope. It's already in the Tampa papers."

And our pictures are already plastered all over the Tampa television too. She wasn't sorry to see him leave.

Chapter 21

Maureen wasn't surprised when the Babe Ruth Suite couple stopped at the reception desk to buy tickets for *Prancer* and lunch. "Oh, Ms. Doherty, we're having such a good time. We drove over to St. Petersburg to see Babe Ruth's house. It's for sale, you know. Simply gorgeous. And did you see all of us on the news? We were kind of in the shadows, but I taped the whole thing so I can play it back for the folks back home. If you lighten it a little you can see us just fine." A happy giggle. "I wonder if they'll take pictures of us after the movie tonight. Wouldn't that be fun?"

"I'm so pleased that you're enjoying Haven," she said, quite honestly. "I think you'll enjoy the movie."

The woman rolled her eyes, "Sam Elliot is in it. I know I'll love it and the food here is fantastic. Did you have the Eggnog French Toast yesterday? To die for. Any chance of getting the recipe?"

"I'm sure the cook will be glad to share it. You're not the only one who's asked. I'll print a few copies. They'll be here on the desk later today."

Another idea. Print a cookbook of Haven House recipes and sell it in the gift shop. When we get a gift shop, that is— and I'll talk to Ted about the French toast, she thought. So many ideas had bombarded her senses lately. Some were doable. Some were just so much pie in the sky. The thoughts continued. *I have such plans, such dreams for this old place. A year ago, back in Boston, I never imagined I'd have such deep concern about a century-old, falling apart inn.*

What was that line on the new Zoltar card? "*Questions, rumors, deep concern,*" she said aloud.

"What? Did you say something?" the woman asked.

"Sorry. I guess I must be talking to myself." Maureen blushed. "It's been quite a week."

"Sure has. Well, see you in the movies!" The couple left, chatting happily to one another.

There's not much doubt about the question and rumors, she realized, *and the deep concern fits in perfectly.* She put the BACK IN FIVE MINUTES sign on the desk and opened the louvred door to the dining room. She'd talk to Ted right now, before something else turned up to distract her. She tapped on the kitchen door before pushing it open.

Ted hurried to meet her. "What's up? Anything wrong?"

"Not this time." She smiled and asked about the French toast recipe.

"No problem," Ted said. "My mother used to make it around the holidays. I'm pretty sure she got it from my grandmother. I'll write it out for you right now." He reached into the breast pocket of the immaculately white chef's jacket for a pen. *How does he stay so clean around all this food?* He wrote in a neat, round-lettered cursive on a lined index card.

"Only half a dozen ingredients," she said. "My kind of cooking."

"The trick is in the day-old bread and the right spices." He handed her the card. "I saw a guy measuring the bar," he said. "So we're ready to move ahead on that?"

"I think we can manage it. Thanks for this." She held the card up. "I'll get out of your way."

"You're never in the way," he said. "I understand we made the local TV news."

" 'Fraid so. I haven't heard any complaints about it yet, though. You?"

"Not at all. I think people are used to the idea that no matter where you are, there's a good chance you're on somebody's camera."

"Or in the paper," she said. "I guess you've seen the *Times*. They've figured out what kind of gun killed Decklin—and there was apparently a silencer on it. Hubbard says his nephew is coming here to make the . . . um . . . the final arrangements and to pick up his belongings. Such a sad death. Hubbard says they think it was somebody he knew."

"That makes even worse, doesn't it?" Ted's eyes were downcast. "I mean, if somebody just sneaked up behind him and shot him, he'd never know what hit him. But to look the killer right in the face—it must have been terrible."

"I know," she agreed. "I just hope it wasn't somebody he thought was a friend."

"You liked him," he said.

"Yes, I did."

"I did too. I'd better get back to work."

Her five minutes were nearly up. "Me too." She walked back through the dining room, this time thinking about how the walls might look with beachy bleached wood paneling and the round tables with centerpieces of big shells like conch and whelk and helmet with flower arrangements in each one.

When Maureen arrived in the lobby Shelly was next to the reception desk writing on one of the many pink While You Were Out pads that Penelope Josephine Gray had purchased. "Oh hi, Ms. Doherty. I heard the phone ringing so I answered it. Here's the number for you to call." She handed Maureen the pink slip. "A guy named Monroe made overnight reservations for tonight and tomorrow night. He says he's Decklin Monroe's nephew."

"Thanks, Shelly. I'll call him right away." The name on the paper said Roger Monroe. She dialed the number.

The man picked up after the first ring. "Hello?"

"Mr. Monroe? This is Maureen Doherty at the Haven House Inn in Haven, Florida." She smiled as she spoke, hoping that the facial expression made her voice sound friendly, welcoming. "Thank you for your reservation. Sorry I missed your call. How can I help you?"

"I'm not exactly sure," he said. "I'm in a bit of a pickle here. Seems my uncle Decklin got killed down there and I need to come down, sign some papers, sort out his belongings and . . . well, figure out what to do with his remains. I guess what I need is somebody who knows their way around town, knows who to call for what, that sort of thing."

"I'll be happy to help you, Mr. Monroe. I'm fairly new to the area myself, but there are members of my staff who are natives. They know everything and everybody there is to know in Haven."

"Good to hear. I'm at the airport now. I expect to land in Tampa at five o'clock this afternoon. I'll grab a cab. Do you have a restaurant?" He sounded hopeful. "I know I'm going to be starving by then."

"We certainly do and we'll look forward to seeing you soon." She paused. Should she express condolences about his uncle? "I'm sorry about Decklin's passing," she said. "He'd made friends here."

"Thank you," he said. "I barely remember him. He was my mom's brother. She's gone too. Guess I'm the only one left."

"I'm sorry," she said again. "We'll expect to see you at around six."

At first she'd planned to type the French toast directions onto Haven House stationery—Penelope had left plenty of that too—but Ted's handwriting was so distinctive and easy to read, she decided to copy the recipe just as it was onto card stock. Before long she had a small stack of the duplicates on the reception desk as she'd promised, and had moved on to printing the paper menus for the week's breakfasts, lunches, and dinners. For these she used the inn's letterhead along with some Christmas clip art. *Someday*, she thought, *maybe we'll have these done professionally. And maybe that won't be as much fun.*

Gert poked her head in the door. "Maureen," she whispered, "I overheard some customers complaining that someone was smoking in the elevator last night."

Maureen sighed, halting the copier mid-run. "Did they see anybody smoking?"

"Nope. Just smelled it."

"I'll take care of it," she said. "Can you answer the house phone until I get back? I won't be long."

She didn't wait for an answer but lost no time in heading for the elevator and pressing the penthouse button. She detected no tobacco smell, only the faint lingering scent of Molly's signature fragrance—*Charlie*. If Reggie wasn't there she'd give Lorna a good talking-to and let her give him the message. Once she stepped out onto the third-floor corridor she heard Finn's happy "woof."

"I hope I don't have to ban Reggie from the inn," she mumbled. But how do you ban a ghost from anywhere? Sneaking a smoke here and there didn't really call for going to all the trouble of an performing an exorcism. She'd have to depend on his British good manners. She turned the key in the lock.

Lorna looked great in the red Victoria Beckham, which translated into black and white nicely. It hadn't taken her long to grab that essence, had it? The ghost sat on the couch, book in her lap, dog at her feet, handsome Englishman looking spellbound beside her. She looked up at Maureen. "Oh, hi. We're just getting into *Call of the Wild*. I'd almost forgotten what a great book it is. Do you have time to join us? You haven't missed too much. We're just at the part where Buck gets stolen from his home."

"Some other time, thank you." Maureen tried to keep the impatience out of her voice. "Reggie, it's about your smoking in the hotel. I've asked you politely not to do it. Now the guests are complaining that there was an odor of pipe tobacco in the elevator last night."

Reggie at least had the good grace to look ashamed. Lorna gave him a playful slap on the arm. "Reggie, you naughty boy. If you don't follow the rules she'll have to toss you out."

"I'm sorry, Maureen," he said. "Really I am. I was just in such a hurry to get up here to see Lorna last night that I hopped right into the elevator even though it was occupied. I won't do it again."

"No smoking at all in the building," Maureen emphasized. "None at all. Got it?" She pulled the door open, prepared to leave.

"I understand. I truly do. They have that rule in the courthouse over in Clearwater too. I especially like their lift. It's one of those fast ones. But Maureen, I completely forgot that I was smoking in yours last night because I was interested in the conversation the women were having."

Maureen stopped in the half-opened doorway. "Women? Why? What were they talking about?" She stepped back into the room.

"Just lady's gossip," he said. "I shouldn't have been listening, but . . . well . . . that's part of the fun of being invisible."

By then Lorna, interested, had closed the book. Finn woofed sadly and nudged at her hand. "I'll read some more in a minute, Finn. What did they say, Reggie? Come on. Give."

"It was two women. Names Edith and Esther."

"Aster," Maureen corrected. "But they aren't guests here."

"I know. Apparently the two had sneaked away from the wassail party. They were both a bit tipsy."

"Sneaked away?" Maureen wondered. "Why?"

"Mostly they wanted to ride in the elegant elevator," he said. "Can't fault them for that. It's quite a treat."

"What else?" Maureen grew impatient. "Where were they going?"

"The Edith woman said she knew the room number of the poor fellow who got himself killed in the movie house. She wanted to get a peek at it." He touched his mustache thoughtfully. "She wanted to see if he'd left anything the police might have missed. She said that sometimes a woman can spot things in a room that a man might miss."

"She's right about that," Lorna said.

"There was still an officer guarding that room," Maureen said. "They wouldn't be able to get in."

"They got off on the second floor." Reggie looked pleased with himself.

"That's where Decklin's room was. Everybody knew that," Maureen said.

"I followed them." The pleased look became a smirk. "The constable at the door seemed to know them. At least he knew the Edith woman. She must have said something convincing because he actually opened the door enough for them to peek in—not enough for them to cross the threshold, of course, but it looked like one of them used her phone to take a picture. Then they scooted back to the elevator, giggling like a couple of schoolgirls."

"Edith's son is the top cop around Haven, so she must know the door guard. He could have thought it wouldn't do any harm to let them peek," Maureen reasoned. "I wonder what they saw?"

"I know what they saw," Reggie said. "Want to know what was in there?"

"You went in?" Lorna slapped his arm again. "What did you see?"

"Actually, it looked like a normal hotel room." He counted on his fingers. "Bed, chair, desk, television, luggage stand, bureau. Nothing special."

"What else?" Maureen prodded. "Anything out of place?"

"Hmmm. There were three shirts laid out on the bed. Nice shirts. Dress shirts, I'd say." He paused, then snapped his fingers. "There was one of those shoeshine buffer things you get sometimes in hotel bathrooms along with the shampoo and such."

"Penelope left us a good stock of those," Maureen said. "They're in every room. Anything else, Reggie?"

"No. As I said, there was nothing special there."

"Just the usual furniture, three shirts, and a shoeshine buffer," Lorna repeated. "Do you see what I see, Maureen?"

"I think so." Maureen said. "He tried on at least four shirts and shined his shoes before he left."

Lorna nodded. "Dressed to impress, I'd say. Like you would for a hot date, not to sit in the dark in a projection booth."

"Or maybe like you would for an important interview," Maureen countered. "He wanted to buy the Paramount. He told me that he had some meetings lined up with big-money people—that he'd need to make a good impression."

Chapter 22

Maureen had stayed away longer than she'd meant to and now hurried down the two flights of stairs. The elevator was fun, but not very fast—especially if there were other passengers in it who wanted to stop on a different floor. She paused at the entrance to the lobby, admiring the little tree with its shells and sand dollars and starfish decorations, and the garlands of tinsel and greenery festooned over the doorways. From the dining room the piano plinked out "Rudolph the Red-Nosed Reindeer"—and was she imagining it, or was there was even a faint smell of gingerbread in the air?

Gert looked up from the reception desk and smiled. "Did you figure out who the phantom pipe-smoker is?" *Phantom is close,* Maureen thought.

"Just a friend of a friend, who apparently didn't understand the rules," she explained. "I think it'll be okay now." *It had darned well better be.* "I'll take over here. Thanks, Gert—and by the way, while we're alone, there's something I've been wanting to ask you."

"Sure. What is it?'

"Those stories about Las Vegas—I mean you and Decklin hanging around with Frank Sinatra—is it all true?"

Gert lowered her voice. "To tell you the truth, Ms. Doherty, I don't know for sure. Decklin seemed so sure about it all, and frankly, there was a lot of drinking going on—some other stuff too. Anyway, I sure loved listening to him telling me about all the grand times we had together with Frankie and Dean and Sammy and all them. I know I was there back then, but did Decklin have me mixed up with some other showgirl? I don't know. I hope it was me. I *love* those stories." She stuck out her chin. "And I'm sticking with them."

Maureen smiled. "I don't blame you. So would I. Say, is that gingerbread I smell?"

"Sure is. Molly made it. She says it smells like Christmas. We'll be serving it with whipped cream after dinner tonight. Shall I save you a piece?"

"Yes, please. I'll be in my office making copies, but I'll leave the door open so I can hear the push bell if anyone needs me."

Maureen activated the copier once again. The machine whirred and the colorful menus whished into a neat pile. The easy automation of the job gave her time to think, to process what Reggie had revealed about what Edith and Aster had seen in Decklin Monroe's bedroom. Had they perceived the same thing she and Lorna had? How tipsy were they? Had Edith shared what they'd seen with her son? Would Frank figure out by himself that Decklin had been expecting company in the projection booth? Important company?

"It's not up to me to bring it up," she told herself, "even if it really means something. Anyway, how could I explain that a ghost friend of mine had followed Aster and Hubbard's mother to a secured site they had no business seeing—or photographing—let alone talking a police officer into opening the door for her? Nope. None of my business."

Separating the menus into neat stacks, she put one of each into the slots reserved for guest mail and messages, then carried the remaining ones into the kitchen for the servers to place on the tables. The gingerbread smell was even more tantalizing there. She paused, impressed as always by the way the kitchen crew worked together. Sometimes it reminded her of an orchestra playing in harmony with Ted, in his still-spotless white chef's jacket, with a wooden spoon in his hand instead of a baton, directing the symphony. The illusion brought a grin—and the grin caught Ted's attention.

"Hi there." He lifted his hand—without a spoon—and waved. "That's a happy face. Everything moving along like it should?"

"So far, so good." She held up crossed fingers. "It smells wonderful in here. Like Grandmother's house at Christmas."

"That's Molly's work. We've got a good crew here, Maureen."

There's that "we" again. I like it. "I've got your menus for tomorrow here." She put the stack on a counter. "Let me know as soon as you have the Cary Grant dinner figured out. I'll make an extra special one for that."

"Did he ever stay here?"

"Cary Grant? I wish. No, not as far as I know. If he had, that room would be booked a year ahead, I'll bet."

"Don't worry," he said. "Before you know it there'll be some of today's top movie stars lining up to stay at the Haven House Inn."

She laughed aloud and most of the kitchen crew looked up. "I appreciate the encouragement about the old place, but that's a little bit overboard, isn't it?"

"Well, maybe a few mid-list movie stars will stop in for lunch some day. How's that?"

"We could handle that." Now she was using that "we." *Interesting.*

"I'm almost finished here. I can stop by your office and show you the suggestions for the *Bishop's Wife* movie dinner. Okay?"

She looked at her watch. "I'm expecting Decklin's nephew

to check in around six," she told him. "I'll be in my office at least until then."

He gave her a thumbs-up and returned to stirring with the wooden spoon. She offered a quick wave to the kitchen crew, trying to ignore the knowing winks and smiles aimed in her direction. They surely wondered if something besides business was going on between the executive chef and the inn's new owner. She wondered too. But—back to business. She'd already personally checked the suite she'd reserved for Roger Monroe. She'd assigned him the Milton Berle Suite. Berle had appeared at the St. Petersburg Bayfront and had stayed for two nights at Haven House back in the 1950s. Some newspaper research had revealed that the mid-century comedian's nephew lived in Tampa and he'd shared some great family photos of "Uncle Miltie" to decorate the walls of the suite.

So far, Frank Hubbard hadn't asked if or when Decklin's nephew had made arrangements to come to Haven. Maybe Roger Monroe had already phoned the police station and told them his plans. If he had, she hoped that Hubbard wouldn't barge in the moment the man arrived at the inn to barrage him with questions. If he hadn't, she had no intention of sharing that information with anyone. How could the nephew feel about spending some of the Christmas season away from home, attending to final arrangements for an uncle he barely knew? This was certainly not going to be a fun trip for the man. She'd plan to do everything she could to make his stay at Haven House as pleasant as possible under the circumstances. He'd mentioned needing someone who knew the area—someone who could show him around. She decided to wait until she met him before picking out that special someone.

Roger Monroe had said he'd be starving by the time he arrived. She didn't doubt it. Airplane fare wasn't what it used to be. A bag of peanuts or a cookie was about all a flier could expect these days. Anyway, she knew he'd enjoy dinner in the inn's dining room. That was a pretty sure thing. How old was he? She hadn't been able to tell from his voice. Would he be interested in the area's nightlife or would he like a glass of warm milk from room service at nine o'clock?

Her thoughts about Decklin's nephew were interrupted by the vibrating phone in her pocket. Caller ID announced Aster Patterson. "Hello, Aster," she said. "Did you find that new dog book for Finn?"

"Dog book? Oh yes, sure. I have a good one. Local writer too. It's *For the Love of a Dog* by Elizabeth Rose. He'll love it. But that's not what I'm calling about. I've done something I shouldn't have, Maureen. I don't know who to talk to about it." Aster sniffled. "I shouldn't involve you, but I have to tell somebody." Another sniffle. "And there's something I need to show you."

"Oh, Aster." She spoke soothingly. "It can't be all that bad." *This has to be about the illicit elevator ride to the second floor.* "Do you want to come over here and talk? Or I could stop at your shop tomorrow morning after my run on the beach."

"Are you busy right now?" It sounded like a plea. "I could run over there in just a minute."

"If it's important to you, Aster, of course. Come right on over. I'll be in my office. We can talk there."

"Thank you, Maureen." There was relief in the woman's voice. "I'll bring cookies."

She'd barely returned the phone to her pocket when there was a knock at the partly open office door. "Hi. Can I come in?" Ted didn't wait for an answer. He put a sheet of paper on her desk. "Here you go. Menu for tomorrow night's movie." She recognized the distinctive handwriting.

"Wow," she said. "Prime rib? Can we afford it?"

"I was able to save a little here and there on the vegetables," he said, "and we've got quite a few of Molly's apple pies and plenty of ice cream in the freezer—and hey, it's Cary Grant night."

"You're right." Maureen laughed. "There seems to be some extra excitement about this one. I told my mother about it and she said she's tempted to fly here from California just to see it again."

Ted eased into the chair across from hers. "I'm thinking about making up another batch of wassail for the after-the-movie crowd," he said. "What do you think?"

"I think it's about to become a Christmas staple at the Haven House. Everybody loved it."

Another knock at the door. A timid one. "I guess you have company." He stood, prepared to leave.

"That'll be Aster," she explained. "New dog book for Finn."

Ted opened the door. "Hi, Aster. Come on in. I'm just leaving."

Aster wore one of her unique outfits—colorful print yoga pants under a red-and-black lumberjack shirt, and pink Crocs, with matching pink rollers in her hair. An aluminum foil–covered platter was balanced on top of a book. She was, as usual, oblivious to the stares of the people in the lobby who didn't know her. "Hi, Teddie. Hi, Maureen. I brought cookies. Here's the book for Finn." Placing book and platter carefully on Maureen's desk, she looked up at Ted. "You said you were leaving?"

"Huh? Oh, yeah. See you both later." With a wink in Maureen's direction, he closed the door behind him.

"Pull up a chair, Aster," Maureen directed. "What in the world has you so upset?"

"I swear I never would've done it if I hadn't been drinking." The woman sat, pulling her chair close to the desk. "I don't know what made us think his ghost would be in there."

"His ghost? Whose ghost?"

"Decklin's. He was very interested in the afterlife, you know. He came into the bookstore several times when he was here. He bought ghost books and ghost magazines and we talked about how people come back after they die, you know?"

Maureen remembered that Decklin had denied believing in ghosts to her, but then, she'd denied believing in them too. "I didn't know that about him. Where did you think his ghost might be?" she asked, knowing the answer.

"Why, in his room. In this old inn. We were both a little sozzled on that wassail, and Edith knew the cop who was guarding his door. He let us have a quick peek, but that's all you need to grab a picture of a ghost and that's a fact."

"I'd heard that," Maureen admitted, recalling when not many months ago a professional ghost hunter had claimed to have a photo of Billy Bedoggoned Bailey playing the piano.

"I grabbed a picture of his room," Aster said.

Oh, please. Not another haunted room. "What did you see?" she asked.

"No ghosts." Aster sounded disappointed. "And Edith tells me that Frank has finished with that room. Bagged everything up for his relatives to deal with. That right?"

"Yes. His nephew will be checking in here later this evening."

Aster reached into the shirt pocket, pulled out a photo, slapped it onto the desk. "Here's the way Decklin left his room. Edith and I knew something was up that night for sure as soon as we looked at the picture. We don't think Frank noticed it and we don't dare to tell him because we shouldn't have even been up there. The cop should never have opened the door for us. We don't want to get anybody into trouble." She tapped the photo. "Do you see anything unusual?"

Maureen examined the photo. Took her time before answering, lowering her voice.

"He tried on four shirts before he left for the theater. He was meeting somebody."

"That's what Edith and I think. But we can't tell Frank."

I think so too and I can't tell him either. She paused, looked around and spoke softly. "I think Frank Hubbard will come up with the right answer using all the police methods he has at hand. He'll figure it out without your picture. Let's just get rid of it."

Aster pushed the photo closer to Maureen. "Will you do it?"

"Yes," Maureen agreed and shoved the thing into her pocket. She spoke in her normal tone of voice and opened the door. "Thanks, Aster, for the cookies and the dog-story book. I'll see you tomorrow night for the Cary Grant movie and dinner."

Chapter 23

As soon as Aster had left, Maureen searched her clip art for good color photos of prime rib and apple pie. She worked in some artwork of holly berries, Christmas wreaths, and a black-and-white studio shot of Cary Grant and Loretta Young, then struggled to write appropriate copy describing the many benefits of buying Dinner and a Movie tickets for *The Bishop's Wife*. Words wouldn't come. The darned picture of Decklin's room seemed to be burning the proverbial hole in her pocket.

Making sure the office door was closed, she pulled the thing out and took a close look at it. It was just as Reggie had described it, four dress shirts in a jumbled row on the bed, along with the shoe buffer. Why had she promised Aster that she'd destroy it? Perhaps the fact that it might indicate a meeting with someone important—someone local, someone Decklin had felt that he needed to impress—would help Frank Hubbard narrow his search for a murderer.

She turned the picture over, putting it facedown on her desk. "This isn't exactly 'withholding evidence,'" she told herself. "It isn't exactly evidence at all, and it's just a photo of something Frank Hubbard has already seen." *But maybe he didn't put two and two together the way his mother and Aster and Lorna and I had.* There were lots of people in the

theater that night, but there were probably not many who
Decklin Monroe would dress up for, let alone shine his shoes.

Maureen still had a tiny niggling feeling of guilt because of
the more-than-a-few minutes she'd delayed in calling 911
after she'd found Decklin's body—but she'd quite success-
fully justified that with the panic-in-a-crowded-theater explanation. But this was quite different. There was a real
possibility that Decklin was not the victim of some random
acquaintance that he'd offended or cheated or had an argu-
ment with or owed money to, who'd sneaked up to the projection booth. It was an indication that Decklin himself had
invited the killer—had made his own appointment with
death.

How could she suggest all that to Hubbard without involving a long-dead movie starlet or telling him his own
mother was a snoop or that one of his officers had opened a
door for ghost hunters? She looked up when Gert knocked
and entered in one motion. Good thing the picture was facedown. "The Milton Berle Suite is all ready for the nephew.
Do you want me to do the bottled Evian water and the complimentary Christmas cookies in the room?"

"That would be nice. Sure. Please do that." Gert was
about to leave when one of those invisible light bulbs of inspiration flashed over Maureen's head. "Gert, wait a minute,"
she said. "You're pretty much in charge of housekeeping. I've
been wondering something. Did you happen to go into Decklin Monroe's room before the police came and roped it off?"

"Sure. I was the one who made sure it was locked. I didn't
go inside—after all it was kind of like a crime scene. I just
looked around to be sure everything was the way it should be
then closed the door."

"Tell me what you saw," Maureen encouraged. "What do
you remember about it?"

"Well, first it bothered me that the bed was unmade.
Looks messy, you know?"

"Go on."

"And he'd left clothes on top of the unmade bed." She shook her head. "Men!"

"What kind of clothes?"

"Three perfectly good clean shirts just tossed on the bed. He even left a used shoeshine rag right on the pillow case. Disgusting." She wrinkled her nose. "Men!"

"Thanks, Gert," Maureen said. "It seems like he was trying to look his best, trying on shirts until he found one he liked."

"That's true," Gert agreed. "I do that too—but then I hang up the clothes I decided not to wear. I guess men don't bother." She touched on finger to her chin. "Say, maybe he was dressing up for somebody. Did he have a girlfriend?"

"Not that I know of," Maureen said, "but I think I should tell Hubbard. It might mean something to him."

"I guess it could. Well, if he needs to ask me about it, you know where to find me." She left the office as quickly and efficiently as she'd entered.

Maureen experienced a moment of pure relief. Now she had a way to share with Hubbard what might be a step toward solving a murder—without implicating ghosts or tipsy girlfriends or a careless cop. She put the photo into the shredder and picked up the house phone. She was about to hit Hubbard's number when Gert reappeared at the door.

"A cab just pulled up out front," she said. "Might be the nephew."

"Thanks, Gert." She hung up the phone, patted her hair, smoothed her skirt, and hurried to the reception desk. There were a few guests seated in the white wicker chairs in the lobby and heads, both male and female, turned when the man came through the green door.

Roger Monroe was striking looking, no doubt about it. Tall, with a broad-shouldered athletic build, dark hair tousled just enough, warm brown eyes, and a winning smile. He put his suitcase on the floor and extended his hand. "Ms. Doherty? I'm Roger Monroe. You're expecting me?"

The accent was markedly New England. She shook his hand, pushing the guest registry toward him. "We certainly are," she said. "Welcome to Haven, Mr. Monroe."

"Glad to finally be here." He picked up the pen, then fixed the brown eyes on her. "Do I hear a little bit of Boston in your voice, Ms. Doherty?"

"It's hard to hide, isn't it" she said. "I'm from Saugus. You?"

"Marblehead," he said. "Almost neighbors."

She handed him a room key. "You're on the second floor, end of the hall. You'll have a little bit of ocean view. Still hungry? The dining room's open until ten."

"Starving." He picked up the suitcase. "I'll toss this into the room and be right back down."

She gave him a warm smile and a wave and ducked back into her office, leaving the door ajar, and once again picked up the phone. This time the call went through. "Frank Hubbard," came the gruff salutation.

"Hello, Officer Hubbard. This is Maureen Doherty. One of my housekeeping staff just shared some information about Decklin Monroe's room that might be important."

"About his room after he was dead or before?"

"After. She was the one who secured the door. She didn't go inside but took a good look at the condition of the room." She paused, waiting for his response.

"So? What did she see?" The tone was brusque. "Can you hurry up, Ms. Doherty?"

"He'd left several shirts on the bed as though he was taking particular care about how he looked. And he'd shined his shoes." Another pause.

Impatient sigh. "Yes. We know that. What about it?"

"It occurred to both of us that he may have been dressing to impress somebody," she said. "He may have arranged to meet somebody important at the theater that night."

She could almost see the eye-roll. "Yes, Ms. Doherty. That occurred to me too. Do you and this observant chamber maid have any idea of who that might be?"

So he saw it too. Maybe he's more perceptive than any of us thought. "When Decklin and I were in the theater that day when you spoke to me in the parking lot," she continued, "he told me that he'd made contact with someone who might help him with funds to get the renovation of the Paramount started."

"Interesting." The tone was friendlier. "I didn't know that. Might be useful. Thank you, Ms. Doherty." *Click*. He was gone.

For a moment she stared at the silent phone, than hung it up. She heard the whirr of the elevator descending and returned to the lobby just as Roger Monroe stepped out of the elegant brass and glass sliding door. He'd changed to jeans and a white Aran knit sweater and looked fine in both.

"Sweet ride," he said, "and the suite is great. Thanks for the cookies, but I'm still starving."

She walked to the dining room door and pulled the louvred panel aside. "Here you go," she said. "Enjoy."

From inside the room the *clink* of china, the *plink-plink* of the player piano, and the smell of good food seemed to tumble into the lobby, reminding Maureen that she hadn't eaten since breakfast. She pushed open the green door to the porch, noting that the four staircase-side rockers were occupied. She approached the group. "Can one of you watch the desk while I grab some dinner?" Molly volunteered. "And George," she added, "I have a special job for you. Decklin's nephew is going to need someone to drive him around, to help him meet the people who can help him get his uncle's affairs straightened out. I think you're the man for that job. Okay?" George, his chest puffed out noticeably, agreed immediately.

"I'll be in the dining room if you need me." Maureen opened the louvered door, chose the empty table closest to lobby, and picked up the menu. Waitress Shelly appeared beside her in less than a minute and took her order for a glass of white Zinfandel, a bowl of New England clam chowder, and a Caesar salad.

Goudreau had mentioned building a temporary bar to serve the public while the renovation was happening. Where should that go? She sipped a creamy spoonful of chowder, appreciating the fact that Florida-born Ted could create the familiar New England staple so perfectly. At the same time, she tried to decide which round table would have to be removed to make room for a short-term bar. She should get the barstools reupholstered right away so that they could be used at the temporary bar and be ready for the new one as soon as it was finished.

Removing the table closest to where the bar was now located seemed to make the most sense. Maybe she could send the barstools to the upholsterer one or two at a time. She narrowed her eyes, trying to picture what a temporary bar might look like in the selected spot. She held up both hands, using thumb and forefingers to form an oblong frame the way she'd seen artists and photographers do.

"Yes," she decided. "That would work."

Then she realized that someone was seated at the table designated to be the bar site, just outside her finger-frame. The white Aran sweater was easy to figure out. The puzzled look on Ralph Monroe's face was not.

Chapter 24

She felt her cheeks coloring. Should she give a friendly wave or keep eating her salad, pretending she hadn't just sent him some strange hand signal? Or should she get up and rush back to work, hoping he'd forget all about it? There wasn't time to do either one. While she watched, he signed the check, put some bills on the table for Shelly, and headed across the room toward her.

"Hi," he said. "I recognized the picture-frame sign language, but I'm not sure I was supposed to be in the picture."

"I'm so sorry," she said. "You must think I'm crazy. I'm in the middle of planning some improvements in the place and, well, you were sitting right on the edge of our temporary new bar."

"A temporary new bar?"

"Just for the time it takes to rebuild the old one," she explained. "I'm upgrading the inn one little piece at a time."

"Pay-as-you-go plan? That's usually the best way."

"I hope so." She smiled. "I haven't forgotten your request that I introduce you to someone who can help you find your way around town and answer your questions."

He returned the smile. "I was hoping you'd be able to help me with that."

There was a longer than necessary pause. "I'll do what I

can personally, of course, and our houseman, George, will be glad to drive you wherever you need to go. He was born in Haven and knows every inch of the place. Knows everybody in town too, I'm sure."

Another pause. Did he look disappointed? "Thanks. I'll look forward to meeting him. Well, I'll leave you to your dinner. Mine was delicious. See you tomorrow."

"Yes. Sure, Mr. Monroe. Just call the desk if you need anything. See you tomorrow."

She watched him leave the room. Shelly refilled the water glass, and watched him too. "Nice-looking guy. Good tipper too. Leo says he's Decklin's nephew. Right?"

"Right. He's here to take care of his uncle's . . . uh . . . final arrangements."

"Hope he stays a while. You want dessert?"

"No thanks. I need to get back to work." She finished the chowder, played with the remains of the salad, signed the check, and went back into the lobby where Molly chatted happily with a few guests seated there enjoying cocktails.

"Thanks, Molly. Is everything okay?"

"Smooth as silk, Ms. Doherty. Took a couple of reservations and I signed for a special delivery letter for you." She handed Maureen an envelope. "Here you go."

Maureen accepted it, noting the creamy texture of the ecru paper. It was a fairly large oblong, not a business-size letter. *Probably a Christmas card*, she thought. She turned it over. It was addressed to her at the Haven House Inn. There was no return address. She thanked Molly again, said hello to the assembled lobby guests, and returned to her office, once again leaving the door ajar.

Her hands shook a tiny bit as she slid a letter opener along the top fold of the envelope. She knew what to expect inside. The typed address was familiar. So was the ecru envelope. She knew without looking at it that this was a Christmas card like the ones she'd found in Penelope's bureau drawer.

Of course she was right. The inside of the envelope was of gold foil and the front of the card showed a nativity scene. Like the ones she'd seen earlier, there was no signature, but unlike the cards Penelope had received, there was a typed message below the "Merry Christmas" greeting.

> Maureen Doherty. We had expected that you would sell the property since the previous owner had spent virtually all of the money which had accompanied the original bequest. Since it appears that you have made an attempt to maintain the Haven House Inn as a viable business, we are depositing the amount of fifty thousand dollars into your bank account to assist in your efforts. We will send instructions as to your future disposition of the inn at a later date.

She read the words again. And again. Someone would send instructions as to her future disposition of the inn? Was this the way Penelope had been instructed to select her as heir to Haven House Inn? And maybe even more importantly, could it be true that the mysterious "someone" had deposited fifty thousand dollars into the inn's account? That was easy enough to check. The computer was right in front of her. She brought up the current statement. A deposit in the amount of fifty thousand dollars had been made within the past hour.

Who was the depositor? Maureen clicked with trembling fingers. Not much help there. The depositor was identified as the Greater Haven Improvement Fund.

Whoever my benefactor is knows that the Christmas card

has been delivered. They know that the first thing I'd do is look at the bank statement. What else do they know about me? Am I being watched?

The thought actually made her shiver. The influx of money into the struggling business was certainly welcome, but the idea that she had somehow been previously selected—maybe even as far back as her childhood—was just creepy. The whole thing was totally bizarre.

The typed note mentioned the "original bequest." That could mean Penelope Josephine Gray's inheritance of the inn. Had there been others before her? The attorney had told her that the inn was "around a century old." George had told her that he remembered when Penelope came to the inn. It was in the fifties, he'd said. That meant that someone else must have operated the place for around half a century before then. Had that person had a strange inheritance too? Her attorney, Larry Jackson, should have that information. She reached for the phone.

She pulled her hand back. Prime rib and apple pie. Getting the menus out on time was more important than ancient Haven history. Phone Larry later. Figure out the best way to use the newfound money later. Make sure George had the company car gassed up for Ralph Monroe's needs. Later. For now, do the menu—a nice, calm, boring task, nothing mysterious, exciting, bizarre about it. It was just what she needed.

The color photos slid into place, the descriptive copy came effortlessly. The printer whirred out the requested number of copies. Job done. Reserving a few for the reception desk, she carried the menus to the kitchen. Ted looked up as she entered. "Prime rib menus already? That was fast. You should give yourself a raise."

"Good idea," she said, placing the menus in their usual spot on a shelf away from the cooking surfaces. Ted's remark about getting a raise was funny, considering that she'd just received a large one. From the "Greater Haven Improvement

Fund." She started for the door, then turned back. "Ted, you say you've lived in Haven all your life. Did you ever hear of the Greater Haven Improvement Fund?"

He frowned briefly. "Sounds familiar. I know I've heard of it before—a long time ago—maybe when I was a kid." His brow furrowed. He snapped his fingers. "My mom—no, it was my grandmother. She had something to do with a club or an organization or something that sounded like that."

"I wonder if it's still in business. Have you heard anything about it lately?'

"No. Sorry. It was a long time ago. Is it important?" There was concern in his voice.

"I'm not sure," she said. "The name showed up today in some . . . um . . . paperwork about the inn. I'm curious about it. I'm going to call Larry Jackson. Maybe he can figure it out."

"Sure. Say, if you think it would help I could call and ask them about it."

"Call who?" she asked.

"Mom and Grandma. They're just over in Miami."

"Oh, Ted, I didn't know you had family so nearby. And here I am expecting you to work on Christmas. Shouldn't you spend it with them?" *There is so much I don't know about this man.*

"No. Don't worry." He waved her protest away. "They came here last Christmas. This year they go to my sister's place in South Carolina. We have it all figured out. A regular routine. So, should I call them for you?"

She hadn't even known he had a sister. "If you don't mind," she told him, "that would be really helpful."

"No problem. I'll do it as soon as we finish cleaning up in here." He pointed to the menus. "Thanks for these. I hope we get a good crowd."

"Hope so." She heard the lobby push bell *ding-a-ling*. "Duty calls."

Duty called in the person of Molly, who explained that she'd dinged the bell to tell Maureen that Mr. Monroe was on his way down to talk to Ms. Doherty. "I think it's best if you handle it—whatever it is," Molly said. "I asked if his room was satisfactory and if there was anything I could do for him. He said he'd rather talk to you."

"Okay. I'll handle it. Thanks, Molly. And will you remind George to be sure the company car has plenty of gas?" She sat on the tall stool behind the counter and watched the elevator doors. She checked her watch. The night manager was due any minute and she would be able to relax, go up to her suite, and concentrate on the things she'd been putting off— first of all, how to put the newfound money to good use. And tomorrow morning she'd see what Larry Jackson knew about the Greater Haven Improvement Fund.

Between the lawyer and Ted's family's recollections, maybe I can finally learn exactly why I'm here in Haven at all, she thought.

Hilda, the night manager, arrived on time and Maureen gave her a quick rundown of the day's business along with the list of pending reservations. "We have a full house. Should be a quiet night for you. I'll hang around for a minute. I need to wait for a guest who has some kind of problem and insists on speaking to me."

The woman gave an understanding nod. "Oh yeah. One of those."

The elevator door slid open and Roger Monroe bounded out, happy-faced, apparently rested from his trip. Maureen wished she could match his energy. It had been a long, tiring day. She looked forward to taking Finn for a quick walk, putting on comfy pajamas, and getting her thoughts in order. She attempted a cheerful smile. "Good evening, Mr. Monroe. How can I help you?"

"Here's the thing, Ms. Doherty. I thought I'd be ready for a good night's sleep, after getting up early and changing planes and wandering around in airports, but—hey, I'm wide awake and your hotel is . . . well, kind of quiet. Is there anything to do in Haven? I mean at night?"

"Not a great deal, I'm afraid," she admitted. "There's the L&M Lounge, just down the street. I believe they're open until two. It's kind of a neighborhood sports bar. Lots of TV screens, pool tables, arcade games."

"Sounds good. What does 'just down the street' mean, though? I'm a stranger in town." Big, bright smile. "Why don't you come along with me? So I don't get lost."

"Can't do it, Mr. Monroe," she said. "Busy day tomorrow. Thanks anyway. I'll tell you what, though. I was just about ready to take my dog for his nightly walk. We go right past the L&M. You're welcome to join us."

"Sounds good." He sat in one of the wicker chairs. "I'll wait for you right here. What kind of dog?"

"He's a golden retriever, name of Finn."

"Nice breed," he said, then repeated, "I'll wait for you right here."

"Okay," she said and headed for the elevator.

Chapter 25

Maureen pulled Finn's leash from the hook behind the kitchen door and hurriedly attached it to his collar. "Here we go, boy," she told him. "A quick walk before bedtime, and we've got company tonight."

"Woof?"

"It's okay. I think he likes dogs. Anyway, we're just walking him down to the L&M."

She decided to take the stairs. Lately sometimes Finn seemed nervous in the elevator. That wasn't surprising since it had become apparent that ghosts could ride unseen in it—especially tobacco-smoking ghosts.

In the lobby, Roger Monroe was still in the wicker chair, eyes focused on the elevator. Finn strained at the leash, bounding toward the man, pulling Maureen along behind him.

"Hello, boy. You must be Finn." He scratched behind the golden's ears, looked up at Maureen, then stood. "It looks like he's ready for his walk. We'd better not keep him waiting."

The night manager didn't bother to hide her curious stare as the three passed the reservation desk. Neither did George and Sam from their rockers on the porch.

"I'll get that car gassed up first thing," George announced.

He gave Roger an up-and-down look. "Will you be coming along on the ride tomorrow too, Ms. Doherty?"

She frowned. "Me? No." *What are people thinking? That this is some kind of date?* "Mr. Monroe is interested in learning what he can about Haven during the short time he's here, George. I'm sure you'll be an excellent guide."

"Looking forward to it." Roger offered George a fist bump. "See you in the morning."

"Yes, sir. I'll be ready whenever you are."

With Finn leading the way, they started down the boulevard toward the beach. Some of the shops were open later than usual because of the Christmas shoppers. "If you want to do any Christmas shopping while you're here, we have quite a nice variety of shops," she said.

"I got the shopping done before I left home," he said. "I'll pick up a few souvenirs while I'm here, though. Everyone is jealous that I get to spend time in Florida while they're up to their ears in snow."

Maureen wondered about the "everyone" but didn't ask. *He'd said on the phone that he was the last, so he probably doesn't have any kids.* Finn stopped to visit the hydrant near the closed book shop. "This is one of my favorite places," she said. "The owner has a great assortment of Florida books. They make nice souvenirs."

"I'll be sure to check it out," he promised. "I'm surprised that you don't sell some souvenirs at the inn. Postcards, at least."

"I know," she said. "It's on my list. This is my first Christmas in Florida too. I arrived only a few months ago. I'm sure George will tell you all about it on your journey tomorrow."

Finished with his business, Finn tugged on the leash again and Maureen and Roger moved forward.

"Haven looks just about the way I'd pictured it so far," Roger said. "The shops and houses, the palm trees, even the streetlights." He turned in a half circle, waving an arm toward the thrift store across the street and encompassing the Quic-Shop. "It's a lot different from New England. How do you like living here?"

"So far, so good, I guess," she said. "Running an inn is a lot different from buying sportwear for a department store—but the warm weather is a bonus and I lucked out with inheriting a good staff along with the building."

"It was an inheritance?" he asked.

"Yes." *He doesn't need to hear my whole life's story.* "There's the L&M, just ahead there on the right. "

"Want to come in with me? I'll buy you a beer," he offered.

"Sorry. No dogs allowed," she said. "Finn and I will take a quick run on the beach and go along home. See you tomorrow." She turned toward the beach, confident that Roger Monroe could find his way back to Haven House by himself.

The beach run was, just as she'd said, a quick one. She kept Finn leashed and ran along beside him. They stayed within sight of the Casino as she admired the Christmas lights on homes and businesses along the edge of the beach. She cleaned up after Finn with a plastic bag, deposited it in the bright green receptacle, and, as she'd promised, headed for home.

The front porch was all but deserted. She spoke a soft "Good evening" to a couple rocking in a shady corner and went inside. The lobby was empty except for the night manager concentrating on her phone. There was no sound from the dining room. It was almost eerily silent when she and Finn climbed the stairs to the penthouse. She unlocked the door, listening before pushing it open, half expecting to hear Lorna and Reggie in conversation. Finn woofed faintly and the two entered the darkened suite, where only the window candles glowed.

She pressed the light switch, illuminating the living room, and moved quickly to the kitchen and lit up that room too.

She hung Finn's leash behind the kitchen door, then followed him into the bedroom. "Time for bed for us, Finn," she told him. "I'll take my makeup off, jump into my pjs, and join you."

Twenty minutes later, still wide awake, listening to Finn's soft snores from the foot of the bed, Maureen gave up on dreamland. Careful not to wake the sleeping dog, she slid out of bed, tucked her feet into slippers, and returned to the still-lighted living room. Feeling conflicting thoughts ricocheting around in her brain, she pulled a chair up to Penelope's desk and took a lined yellow legal pad from the top drawer. She drew a line down the middle, dividing the sheet into two columns.

Heading column one she printed MONEY PRIORITIES. The second column was headed GHIF (Greater Haven Improvement Fund)—POSSIBLE CONTACTS.

There were lots of ways to spend the money on Haven House, but the first item she put in column one was "Souvenir Shop," the very suggestion Roger Monroe had made earlier. Not that she hadn't thought about it before. She'd planned to have it built in the far corner of the wraparound porch, in the area where nobody like to sit because that's where the ghost hunter had died. Maybe Will Goudreau's father would agree to help with the project if it was on the porch and not inside where he claimed to have seen a ghost. She'd already thought of a couple of items to sell besides post cards: old-fashioned candies and beach-themed décor. Her experience as a department store buyer would come in handy too. She still had a list of associates in the retail business. She'd call Goudreau and get a cost estimate.

She turned her attention to the "GHIF—Possible Contacts" column. So far Ted's mother and grandmother were the only possible contacts she knew of and she didn't even know *their* full names. "Let's see," she said. "Ted and I are about the same age, so his mother must be in the same age range as mine—somewhere in her mid-sixties. So *her* mother—Ted's grandma—is around eighty-something. Who else do I know who'd remember things about Haven from back then?" Molly and Sam and George were in their late sixties. They might know something. *Who else?*

Lorna! Although Lorna's ghost seemed to be in her twenties, she'd died at the age of sixty-five, back in 1975—more than forty years ago. And if she was as gossipy back then as she was now, there was a good chance she knew plenty about the Greater Haven Improvement Fund. The clock showed past midnight but Maureen tapped the push bell anyway.

Lorna arrived in a glamourous whirl of green velvet. "Hello, Maureen. What the heck are you doing up so late?" She sat on the couch, carefully arranging the circular skirt of her dress.

Maureen was suddenly aware of her own flannel pajamas and bunny slippers. "Wow! Look at you," she said. "Did I call you away from something fabulous?"

"Yes and no," the ghost replied. "I wasn't at a party or anything. Just shopping. All this talk around Haven about Christmas movies made me think of clothes."

Maureen chucked. "Lorna, *everything* makes you think of clothes."

"True. Anyway, I've been at the wardrobe department at Paramount Pictures studio." She stood and twirled around. "Like this? Edith Head made it for Rosemary Clooney in *White Christmas*. We had great clothes in the fifties."

"You remember the fifties?"

"Of course I do. I was in my forties then, but still looking good enough for some nice bit parts." She smoothed the velvet skirt and played with the skinny straps at the neckline. "But why did you ring for me?"

"I need to know about some things that were happening in Haven back when Penelope Josephine Gray inherited this place."

"Shoot. I'll help if I can."

"Do you know anything about something called the Greater Haven Improvement Fund?"

"Didn't we talk about this before?" Lorna looked puzzled.

"I don't think so." It was Maureen's turn to look puzzled. "I just heard about it myself."

Lorna raised a hand, pointed one finger into the air. "I remember. We were talking about washing dirty money. What did you call it? Money laundering. That's what it was."

"That's what *what* was? What are we talking about?"

"That organization. The Greater Haven whatchamacallit. Buddy told me about it." She frowned. "That was how they were washing the money from their crooked deals back then. They had illegal slot machines all over. It was a way to clean up the cash. Remember? There was something about hiring out-of-state contractors to build the inn too. I told you that the cops thought Monroe and Henshaw were involved but they couldn't prove it."

"Yes, I know we talked about it but nothing about an improvement fund ever came up," Maureen recalled.

"It was a long time ago. As soon as you said that name, though, I remembered. That was the name Buddy told me. I'm sure."

Here was a connection Maureen hadn't considered. *Now Buddy and Decklin Monroe are both dead*, she thought, *and it seems there's chance my inheritance of Haven House and even the unexpected new money in my account both came from some kind of criminal business dealings.*

"Was that all you wanted?" Lorna asked. "I was just about to try on Rosemary's black velvet mermaid-style gown. I'll probably wear it to Elvis's Christmas party at Graceland along with a nice diamond necklace and earring set I saw in Tiffany's window."

"Oh, sure. Have a good time. Thanks for answering my ding-a-ling. You were really helpful."

"Glad to help." Lorna began to fade, then popped back into focus. "I hope you get some decent pajamas for Christmas." And she was gone.

Maureen considered her lined yellow list. Dreams of the new souvenir shop began to fade like a visiting ghost. Could she accept money from an unknown source if that source turned out to be an old-time crime ring? And what about the "possible contacts" side of the sheet? Ted's mom and grandma certainly couldn't be part of anything shady. Or could they?

And what about Harry Henshaw? She wondered if Frank Hubbard's newfound interest in the Buddy Putnam cold case had turned up any useful links. She tore the yellow sheet from the pad, crumpled it up and tossed it into the wastebasket, and went back to bed. She lay there in the dark, imagining the conversation she might have with Haven's top cop.

"Say, Frank, I've been wondering about that cold case you're working on. The ghost that haunts my suite mentioned that a century-old organization called the Greater Haven Improvement Fund—which, by the way, I believe may have given me the inn and has offered some more financial support—is somehow involved in Buddy Putnam's and maybe Decklin Monroe's murders . . ."

Chapter 26

In the light of morning, her thoughts seemed a bit less jumbled. If Ted noticed that she was unusually quiet during their run on the beach, he didn't comment on it, and knowing how busy he was preparing for the Cary Grant Dinner and a Movie, Maureen didn't press him about contacting his mother and grandmother. That could wait. She did, however, have some further thoughts about the Greater Haven Improvement Fund. She dressed casually for the busy day ahead in jeans and Tampa Bay Bucs T-shirt, and once back in her office she placed the call from the do-it-later list to Larry Jackson, the handsome attorney who'd informed her of her inheritance in the first place. "Larry? Maureen Doherty. Do you have a minute to answer a question?"

"Is everything all right, Maureen?" There was concern in his voice, and no wonder. Her previous calls to Jackson, Nathan and Peters had usually meant that she was in legal trouble of some kind.

"I'm fine," she quickly assured him. "You know I'm interested in the history of the inn and I wonder if you know who's owned it before me—even before Penelope Josephine Gray."

"I don't have that information here in the office, but we

can research it for you," he said. "Any hurry for it? We're a little short-staffed here because of the holiday."

"No hurry," she told him. Those records went back to the turn of the twentieth century. They'd surely keep for a while longer. "If it's not too much trouble."

"Not at all. As soon as I get a chance I'll check with the registry of deeds, or maybe we'll have to search old building permits," he promised. "Don't worry. We'll find it. A history of the old place will be interesting for your guests. Is that what you're planning?"

She hadn't been planning that at all, but a short history booklet about the Haven House Inn would make a good item for the proposed souvenir shop. "Something like that," she agreed. "As soon as I have time to pull it all together. Thanks, Larry. Looking forward to talking to you soon."

That had gone well, she thought, and decided to call Frank Hubbard after all—naturally omitting any reference to late-night conversations with a ghost or theories about century-old money laundering.

"Hello, Officer Hubbard," she said. "I've been thinking about that cold case involving Buddy Putnam you told me about. I was talking to my lawyer this morning about the old records on Haven House and I wondered if your research has turned up anything about a Greater Haven Improvement Fund. It was an organization that was active around here at just about the same time Buddy died." She knew she'd fudged the truth a little but the basics were sound.

"That's amazing, Doherty," he said. "See? I told you that you have some kind of 'gift' about these things. That name— the Greater Haven Improvement Fund—turned up a couple of days ago in Buddy's records. He made regular donations to it. Strange thing. The guy wasn't what you'd call the char- itable type. He'd be more likely to steal money than give it away. It might have been some kind of money laundering scheme. We're looking into it."

"That would seem out of character for sure," she said. "Have you figured out what the fund did with the donated money? And who else might have donated to it?" *Slow down with the pointed questions,* she told herself. *Don't tip your hand.*

"Oh, the fund itself was legit," he assured her. "Still is. It's a nonprofit. Every once in a while it funds repairing a sea wall or broken windows on city property. Nothing much going on anymore with either donations or projects. There's not much money left in the old fund anyway. I checked with the Historical Society. Back in the early nineteen hundreds they had donation jars—goldfish bowls, actually—all over town for people to throw money in. They've even got one of those jars over there in the little museum. Anyway, the first thing they did was break ground for your hotel. Florida tourism was just heating up and Haven needed a place for tourists to stay. They did the movie theater next, so the tourists would have entertainment like vaudeville acts and silent movies—and then the Coliseum so they'd have dancing and music and a place for wedding receptions and birthday parties. There was a lot of talk around town about hiring out-of-state construction companies that overcharged for darn near everything they did. The newspapers even looked into the possibility of the money laundering, but nothing illegal was ever proven about that."

Maybe they never proved it, but Lorna says it happened. But visiting the Historical Society—she should have thought of doing that right away. *That's why he's a cop and I'm not,* she thought. "Thanks a lot," she said. "I'll run over to the Historical Society as soon as I get a minute. I'm writing a little souvenir book about the history of Haven House."

"Good idea," he said. "Mother and Aster really enjoyed the movie and the food."

And the wassail. "I'm glad they did. I'm sure they'll enjoy the Cary Grant night too. Thanks for the information."

"No problem. Merry Christmas."

"Merry Christmas to you too."

Had her relationship with Frank Hubbard become a lot less toxic lately? This conversation had been not only helpful but almost friendly. *Probably due to the Christmas season. Good will to men and all that,* she decided and moved on to the next do-it-later item on the list. Pop into the kitchen and see if Ted had talked to his mom.

Breakfast was well under way when she turned front desk duty over to one of the holiday hired extra staff women from the neighborhood, and arrived at the dining room where Molly presided over the buffet table. The pumpkin waffles with whipped cream, along with a cup of coffee, were irresistible. Maureen picked up her tray and headed for the closest table.

"Ppsst." Molly signaled. "Ted said if you came in to send you out to see him."

"Thanks, Molly. I'll do that." Hoping Ted didn't have bad news about anything, balancing the tray with one hand, she knocked to be sure no one was coming through from the other side and pushed the kitchen door open—making a mental note to ask the Goudreaus about installing a kitchen door with a window in it to avoid collisions.

Ted sat at his small desk beside the walk-in cooler. Concentrating on a stack of papers in front of him, he didn't look up as she entered. Maureen sat on a low wooden stool beside the desk, her tray on her lap. "Molly sent me," she whispered.

Ted looked up, smiling, pushing the papers to one side and brushing his hair away from his forehead. "Maureen. Glad to see you. Here. Put your tray down. How do you like the waffles? Wait a sec. I'll grab a cup of coffee and join you."

She watched him draw a mug of coffee from the tall, stainless steel brewing machine, unable to tell from his expression what was on his mind. Was she here to talk about business or did he have answers about the GHIF? She took a bite of a waffle, savoring the whipped cream topping, and peeked at the top of the paper pile. A bill from a vendor, no doubt. Produce. Five hundred and thirty dollars and change! Did lettuce and carrots and potatoes cost that much? At this rate, along with a few improvements to the property, even an extra fifty thousand dollars wasn't going to last very long. Maybe she needed to stop worrying about the inn's past history and start concentrating very hard on its future.

"I talked to my mom this morning," Ted told her, "along with my sister, some nieces and nephews, and Grandma too." With another forkful of waffle midway to her mouth, she waited for him to go on. "Mom and Grandma knew exactly what I was talking about. Grandma even served on the GHIF committee for a while. She says she still has a purple satin badge with the letters on it. She thanked me for reminding her about it and she says she's going to send it to the Haven Historical Museum."

"Good idea. They've already got one of the fishbowls they had around town for people to donate money to the fund." Maureen borrowed the information Frank Hubbard had so recently shared. "The badge will make a nice addition to the collection."

He smiled. "I can see that you've already done some investigating. Do the museum people have the information you've been looking for?"

"I haven't actually talked to anyone over there yet," she admitted. "Frank Hubbard told me about the fishbowl. I'd love to know what your grandmother has to say about what she did on the committee. I wonder if she knew Penelope."

"Yes. She did. They were friends. Grandma came to Miss Gray's funeral." He reached across the desk and gently brushed her upper lip. "Whipped cream," he said, smiling.

"Grandma told me that it was her understanding that the GHIF raised the original funds to build the inn, and besides that there was a bank account with enough money in it to keep the place going for a long time. According to Grandma, Miss Gray found out that it had been left to her through a letter from a lawyer. She never knew why it was given to her or who had selected her to have it. She devoted her life to running it, though. Grandma was glad that Penelope died without knowing that Elizabeth had been tearing through the operational funds like a drunken sailor."

"I'm glad she didn't know that too," Maureen said. "But she'd be smiling if she knew I'd inherited you and Sam and George and Molly and Gert, even if the money was mostly gone."

"We're all pretty happy about that too," he said. "And we all know how hard you're trying to keep the old place afloat and everybody's excited about the improvements for the bar. When do you suppose we'll be able to get started on that project?"

"Sooner than I thought," she told him. "We've been blessed with a sudden influx of money. It came from the Greater Haven Improvement Fund."

He leaned back in his chair. "Wow. So someone is still pulling the strings in the old organization? Do you know who?"

She shook her head. "Not a clue. But I think maybe Decklin knew."

"You think that's why someone killed him?"

"I don't know what to think. Frank Hubbard says the GHIF is a legitimate charity, but I found out that Buddy Putnam—the man who was shot in the Paramount—had something to do with it too, and he was far from an upright citizen. Besides that, he was one of Decklin's associates. So was Harry Henshaw."

"Leslie Brown's daddy?"

"Yes. Hubbard thinks that because Decklin and Mr. Henshaw were involved in the Putnam murder investigation, and I happened to be vaguely acquainted with both men, that somehow I know something about the Putnam cold case he's suddenly become obsessed with."

Ted frowned. "Does that make sense?"

"Not to me. At least not yet. but I can't resist digging into it." Maureen shrugged. "Call me crazy. It definitely has something to do with the history of the inn, so now I feel as if I need to know what the connection is. And why I'm personally connected to the whole mess."

"Sounds to me as if that little history booklet you're planning to write might turn out to be a whole book," he suggested. "Is there anything I can do to help?"

"Maybe. I mean, you know a lot of Haven people and I don't. If you hear or see anything that connects the inn to the old charity or to Decklin, Henshaw, and Buddy Putnam— even if it's something that seems unimportant, just let me know about it, okay?"

"Of course I will. I'll keep in touch with Mom and Grandma too. I'll tell them about the book you're writing and see if they have anything else to tell us about Haven and the inn."

"That's a great idea. That little book may turn out to be pretty good," she said. "And I'll check with Aster about any books about Haven that she has in the store."

Ted finished his coffee and stood. "I have to get back to work. Plans for tonight's dinner are moving along without a hitch. Do you think if you said 'pretty please' our favorite cop might share some of whatever he's learned about his cold case?"

"Fat chance," Maureen scoffed. "But I'll ask anyway. Why not? Thanks for talking to your folks for me. I love it that your grandma saved her purple satin badge for all these years. I need to get back to my desk too. Maybe I'll see you at lunch."

* * *

Maureen was at her post behind the reception desk when the elevator whirred to a stop and Roger Monroe stepped out. He wore a brand-new L&M Lounge T-shirt. "Good morning, Ms. Doherty," he said. "Thanks for introducing me to the L&M. I played a little pool, had a few drinks, met some nice people, and heard a few ghost stories."

Maureen pretended surprise. "Ghost stories? About Haven?"

"Well, about the bar anyway. Apparently Babe Ruth stops in occasionally. Isn't that cool?"

"Definitely cool," she agreed. "Ready for your tour of town? Shall I call George?"

"In just a minute. I need to tell you something." His eyes were downcast. "It may be none of my business but while I was waiting for you last night when you went to get Finn, I noticed something."

She recalled that he'd been sitting in a wicker chair, watching the elevator when she and Finn came down the stairs. "What was it?" she asked.

"Did I mention to you that I work for the New England Telephone Company?"

"I don't believe so. No, you didn't." *And why would I care?*

He continued, "I was just looking around the room, you know? Not looking at anything special. But I noticed something unusual about your phone wire." He dropped his voice. "It's none of my business and maybe you already know about it, but I think it's possible that the phone right there"—he pointed to the reception desk—"may be bugged."

"Bugged?" Maureen almost squeaked the word, then lowered her voice and repeated it. "Bugged?"

"May I take a look?" Roger asked. "I'll only take a few seconds."

She nodded agreement, and watched as the man moved to the right side of the desk, knelt on the floor, and reached under the decorative white wicker trim around the edge of the top counter. He lifted a black wire, twisting it. "Thought so." He held up a black oblong shape, less than two inches long. "Here she is. Shall I disconnect it for you? Know anyone who might want to know what calls are coming in and going out of here?"

Maureen remembered wondering why Frank Hubbard had moved from that end of the desk to the other. He'd said he was just watching the elevator. She'd known all along that he was up to something. Now she knew what it was.

"Yes, please disconnect it, Roger. I have a good idea who did it," she said. "I have a *darned* good idea. I'll take care of it. I'll buzz George and he'll meet you in front of the building. Enjoy your day." She accepted the object, thinking that it wasn't much bigger than a good-sized Florida palmetto bug, and, holding it away from her as though it was a *real* bug, retreated into her office, pulling the door almost shut behind her.

As she'd promised, she buzzed George, gave him his instructions, then sat in her office chair and once again dialed Frank Hubbard's number.

Chapter 27

"Hello, Doherty, what's going on? Do you have new information to share with me already?" The man sounded almost jovial.

Maureen struggled to keep her voice level. "Yes and no. It was new information to *me*, but I'm sure you know all about it. There was a big, black, shiny bug hiding under my reception desk counter. Know anything about that, Frank? And maybe more importantly, do you have a warrant for it?"

To his credit, Hubbard didn't try to deny what he'd done. "It's just a 'tap and trace' bug, Doherty, along with legal pen registers," he said. "I don't need a court order for them. I'm not listening to anybody's conversations. One just records the phone numbers calling a specific phone line and the other one records all the phone numbers from the outgoing calls. Perfectly legal. That's all. You didn't disconnect it, did you?"

"Of course I did," she sputtered. "Why wouldn't I? And who or what the hell are you looking for?"

"Here's the deal, Doherty," he said. "The day Monroe got killed, somebody—and we *think* it was Monroe—called a certain number from that phone. And somebody from that certain number called back to that phone. But the strange thing is, after Decklin Monroe was already dead, just a few days ago somebody called that same number from your phone. It might be important. It might be nothing. Maybe it wasn't even Decklin in the first place. I guess anybody passing by that counter can use that phone. Am I right?"

"Sure. Everybody uses it—to call a cab, make reservations, call the babysitter, whatever." Her voice was a little bit calmer. "Even if you don't know who called who, what difference does it make if you can't hear the conversation?"

She heard the long sigh. "I don't know, Doherty. Maybe something. Maybe nothing. I may be running down a rabbit hole here. I'm trying everything I can think of that isn't illegal. All I got out of bugging you is pages and pages of phone numbers with no names."

"Well, I have your bug here. I'll put it in the safe. You can have it back." She almost felt sorry for him.

"Thanks. How did you find it anyway? Just curious."

"One of my guests here works for the telephone company. He spotted it right away." Even with the tiny bit of sympathy she felt, it was satisfying to let him know he hadn't hidden the bug very well. "Can't you check the number the calls from here went to—even if you don't know who placed them?"

"Sure. I've got that." Another sigh. "A known resident. Somebody Monroe knew. Somebody you know. Somebody damn near everybody in Haven knows, along with a few other people from all over this great country."

"Did you bug *their* phone too?"

"Sure. Pages of numbers that don't mean anything. I'm going through them little by little. Nothing interesting has turned up. Dry cleaners. The library. A supermarket." He gave a short, mirthless laugh.

"Why don't you tell me whose number it is? Maybe I can help you figure out who made the calls from here."

"I've thought about that. Maybe I will—but hey, I don't know why I'm talking to you about this, Doherty. This whole bugging idea was just a shot in the dark. I'll come by later to pick up my property. And listen, Doherty, I'm sending extra security to the movie theater tonight. So in case you find any dead bodies lying around, don't clear the place out without telling me first. Got it? Goodbye."

"A shot in the dark." Maureen stared at the phone. *Same as the ones that killed Decklin and Buddy.* She hung up and reached for the business card for Goudreau and Son that she'd pinned to the bulletin board. She'd leave Frank Hubbard to attend to his own business while she attended to hers. And she hadn't needed the snide remark about finding bodies either. There was new money in the inn's bank account and she intended to move ahead with her own version of improving greater Haven. If the Greater Haven Improvement Fund bank balance was as low as Hubbard had indicated, it was likely that she'd be doing her own funding soon enough.

The senior Goudreau answered. She began to tell him about the conversation she'd had with his son. "He told me all about it, Ms. Doherty," he said, "and I'm glad you're working on improving the old place rather than selling it. Are you about ready for us to get started?"

"I'd like to get started right after the holidays. Does that work for you?" she asked.

"I think between the two of us, Sonny and me, we can get 'er done. Some days you'll get one or the other of us, sometimes both. I guess he told you I don't much like working inside that place. Gives me the creeps every time I have to go in there." He paused. "I guess you know by now it's haunted."

She dodged the question. "I'm sure we can work with your schedule. But since the bar is an important part of our dining room, I'd like to have it up and running as soon as possible. Your son said he had some ideas for putting in a temporary bar while the new one is being built."

"Yep. We talked about it. I think it'll be a simple thing to put together—not simple like an ironing board and a couple of kitchen stools, but simple like straight lines, no frills, plywood construction, couple of shelves for the bottles. We can use the bar seats you've got. No worries."

She liked his straightforward attitude and decided not to worry—at least about that. "Thanks, Mr. Goudreau. We'll see you shortly after Christmas, then?"

"You bet. Sonny tells me you're doing a good job over there. I used to worry about old Penelope running the place into the ground. Glad you came along to rescue it. Back when she first inherited the place she had some big ideas too, you know." He made a *tsk-tsk* sound. "We used to talk about it all the time."

"You knew her well?" Maureen asked.

"Oh, sure. Ever since she first came to town. I used to try to help her learn how to manage the money, but she trusted that Elizabeth with everything."

"If you don't mind my asking, did you ever hear about an organization called the Greater Haven Improvement Fund?"

He answered quickly. "Sure. Great people. If it wasn't for them your inn might never have been built."

"I know. I've been trying to figure out exactly how the order of succession of owners works," she told him. "You see, I don't know how in the world I wound up with it. I didn't know Penelope Josephine Gray. Neither did my parents. There must be some sort of system in play that determines who inherits. Do you have any ideas?"

"Ms. Gray tried for years to figure that out too. She was getting cards or letters from somewhere that gave her some hints. She even told me once that she had an idea of who it might be but she wasn't sure."

Maureen leaned forward in her chair, clutching the telephone harder. "Did she tell you who she suspected?"

"No. Never did. We never spoke about it again. I was as surprised as anybody else in town when you showed up."

Not as surprised as I was. "I'd love to talk with you about some of the things you remember about the inn. I'm thinking about writing a little history about it." She realized that every time she said it, the words sounded a little bit truer. "Just a little booklet. Something to sell to the tourists some-day when I can hire you and your son to build me a souvenir shop."

"A souvenir shop? Great idea. Why not put it at the far end of the porch where people can access it from the street as well as from inside?"

"We're on the same page," she said. "Let's think about a design."

"I'll put some preliminary sketches together," he prom-ised. "We'll get together soon."

With the call to Goudreau checked off on the do-it-later list, she moved on. *There's no point in putting off a visit to the Historical Society. That should have been at the top of the list anyway.*

Shelly took over at the reception desk and with the bug carefully placed in the safe, and with her phone in the back pocket of her jeans and a notepad in her purse, she crossed the porch and headed across the street to the building hous-ing the Historical Society and the small Haven Museum. The plaque beside the door read CITY OF HAVEN, FLORIDA, INCOR-PORATED 1910.

Maureen couldn't help smiling. She'd recently left Boston, one of the oldest cities in America—founded in 1630—and she was about to study the history of a city that was barely over a century old. How much history could it have?

She pushed the door open, wondering if she should have made an appointment. A smiling young woman greeted her from behind a desk marked INFORMATION. Information was exactly what she needed. She remembered the woman as one who regularly attended the "Lunchtime Chamber of Com-merce" gatherings at the inn. Fortunately she didn't need to search her memory for a name. A badge on the blue Haven Historical Society smock read Ms. CLAIRE DAVIS. MUSEUM DIRECTOR.

"Good morning, Ms. Davis. Maybe you remember me. I'm Maureen Doherty, from the Haven House Inn," she said.

"Of course. Good to see you, Maureen," the woman said. "I love what you're doing with the place. How can I help you today?"

Once again, Maureen mentioned the very recently conceived idea of the proposed booklet. "I'm particularly interested in the history of the inn. Do you have anything on who built it? How it was financed? I've heard that an organization called the Greater Haven Improvement Fund was involved."

"You've certainly come to the right place. We have plenty of material although it's not all in proper order. Your immediate predecessor, Penelope Josephine Gray, left us a literal trunk full of papers dating back to the turn of the century. We're a volunteer organization, you know, and we haven't had a chance to fully catalog it all yet." Did Maureen detect an eye-roll? "You're welcome to dig into it, if you have some spare time. Ms. Gray was a dear, sweet woman, but not a particularly organized one." Claire Davis put both hands in the air in a helpless gesture. "She was, one might say, a bit of a hoarder."

Maureen grinned. "Don't I know it! I'd love to have a look at the trunk someday. Maybe you can sign me up as a volunteer. I have some experience in sorting out some of Penelope's hoard. I'll be glad to help put it into some sort of order"

"That would be more appreciated than you can even imagine. There's everything in that trunk from rent receipts to greeting cards to stacks of photographs of people—all unidentified, of course. Any time you can give us is more than welcome." The woman's smile was genuine.

"Glad to help," Maureen said. "Hopefully I can get started after the holidays. Meanwhile, I understand that you have one of the fishbowls the founders used to collect money for the inn. May I snap a picture of it to illustrate my little book?"

"Of course. Follow me. Our Haven Museum is in the next room. We have some framed newspaper references to the beginnings of Haven House along with some old photographs and even some souvenir postcards."

Maureen hurried behind the museum director through an arched doorway. The Haven House display was small, attractive, and nicely lighted. *I should have come over here in the first place*, she thought, leaning close to examine a black-and-white photo of the inn. The vintage automobiles parked in front of it indicated that the picture had been taken in the 1920s. *This may be where I'm going to find all of the answers to my questions. On the other hand, maybe it's just another one of those shots in the dark.*

Again, her thoughts returned to Buddy Putnam and Decklin Monroe, both shot in the darkness of the historic Paramount Theater—raising even more questions that demanded answers.

Chapter 28

Maureen dressed early for the Cary Grant dinner event. She wanted to be sure the black dress fit. There'd been no time for shopping so she'd ordered a dress from Dillard's online. This dressing for dinner could get expensive if she didn't watch the pennies. The Antonio Melani round-necked, long-sleeved "little black dress" could be dressed up or down and would be serviceable for quite a while. Besides, it was on sale. Satisfied that it looked good enough, she slipped on low-heeled black pumps, added the silver bangle bracelet and silver hoop earrings, and took the elevator down to the lobby just in time to see Roger Monroe returning from his daylong excursion with George.

"How did it go?" she asked. "Did George show you all the sights?"

"It was a good day. We stopped first at the police station so I could sign some papers, make final arrangements for my uncle, and pick up his stuff. I didn't realize he had a neat old Plymouth. Lucky break for me. I guess his Social Security will pretty much pay for the cremation. Anyhow, once all that was out of the way, we took an all-day tour. Enough to make me sure that I'll be coming back again soon to see some more," he assured her. "You look great. Going somewhere special?"

"It's a special promotion we're doing, a Twelve Days of Christmas dinner-and-a-movie thing. It's Cary Grant night. *The Bishop's Wife* is playing at the Paramount Theater and we're serving prime rib and all the fixings here."

"I've worked up an appetite and I like old movies. Count me in."

"I'd like to, Roger," she said. "We still have a few movie tickets but we're into the overflow seating on the porch for dinner. Will that be all right?"

"Sure. I like your porch. I was planning on putting in some rocking chair time out there anyway."

"Perfect. Let me grab you a ticket and I'll arrange for the seating." She ducked into her office, moved the painting of the poinciana tree to one side, opened the safe, pulled one ticket from the roll, and closed the safe. Replacing the painting, she turned to leave the office and realized that Roger Monroe was watching her from the open doorway.

She handed him the ticket. "Here you go."

"Thanks." He tucked it into his jacket pocket. "Is that a Highwayman painting?"

She looked around. "What? Where?"

"The painting of the red tree. In your office. I couldn't help noticing." He jerked his thumb toward the now-closed office door. "George took me to an art museum in St. Petersburg today. They had a whole roomful of what they call Highwaymen paintings. Yours looks like one of them."

"It was there when I arrived. There's a similar one in my suite. I think they're pretty, but I never actually examined either one of them. Why Highwaymen?"

"From what I understand," he said, "back in the 1950s a group of young African American men—and one woman—from down around Fort Myers way, began to paint Florida scenes—pretty much land and sea subjects like beaches and marshes and poinciana and palm trees. They didn't have any formal training, but they figured out that people liked the simple, brightly colored scenes of Florida. Black folks weren't allowed to show their work in galleries then, so they mostly sold them by the side of the highways, usually from the trunks of cars—for twenty-five dollars each. They learned to paint fast—like sometimes a dozen works a day. Anyhow, the docent at the museum said that they are very collectible. People sometimes pay thousands for one. Maybe you should check yours and see if that's what they are."

Thousands? For my red-tree pictures? "Thanks, Roger," she said. "I had no idea. I'll check them out. I think they both have names signed on them."

Wouldn't that be something? She glanced around at the white wicker and yellow wall décor.

Be prepared for land and sea. Hadn't Roger just said that the Highwaymen painted pictures of land and sea?

Even without checking the signatures on the paintings or researching the Florida Highwaymen artists, she thought there might be a pretty good chance that her red trees were the real deal. After all, she reasoned, Zoltar knows all.

She alerted the kitchen staff that they had another dinner reservation—porch seating. The dinner crowd began to arrive. The door to the dining room was open and ready for the guests. She'd checked and double-checked the flower arrangements, the lighting, the perfect whiteness of the tablecloths and dinner napkins. She stood beside the open door, partly to welcome the diners, but mostly to watch and listen to the reactions when newcomers first caught sight of the twelve tables set with Penelope's wonderful vintage decorations in their red-and-green nests of fragrant branches and flowers.

Edith and Aster arrived together, one on each of Frank Hubbard's arms. Clearly excited, the two had coordinated their outfits for the occasion. They were both dressed in blue, each in her own fashion style, Edith's plain wool suit in navy, Aster's midi dress in a bright turquoise satin. Frank wore blue too—his Haven, Florida, police uniform.

"I'm so happy to see you all," Maureen greeted the trio. "I've reserved the same seats you had last time."

"Looks like you have a full house again," Hubbard said as he turned his mother and Aster over to Shelly, who had taken over the guest seating while Ted, in chef's coat and hat, presided over the carving of the prime rib. Hubbard dropped his voice. "Anything new to tell me about?"

"I think I'm learning more from you than you're apt to hear from me. I went over to the Historical Museum today. Thanks for telling me about the fishbowls. I snapped a few photos for the history book I'm planning to write."

"You're welcome. Speaking of photos, I think you said that some of your guests took pictures the night that Monroe got killed. Did you think to get copies?"

"Most of them e-mailed me copies. A few had videos. I can arrange for you to see them all later when you pick up your bug. Too busy right now. Excuse me." She moved past him, greeting arriving diners.

The Browns appeared, along with both parents. Once again, Katherine Henshaw was stunning. Unbidden, but automatically, Maureen's retail business fashion savvy kicked in. The woman wasn't wearing vintage tonight. She sparkled in an up-to-the-minute blue jacquard Rickie Freeman with a gorgeous Elleme leather tote. Harry Henshaw, his arm protectively around her shoulders, was all smiles.

"I'll talk to you later," Hubbard muttered, turned abruptly, and headed for the open door to the porch.

Once the dining room was full and the guests who'd accepted the porch overflow seating had all arrived, Maureen took a turn around the edges of the dining room, making sure all was going well, then poked her head into the kitchen and got a smiling thumbs-up from Molly.

"Everything's going great," Molly said. "You can relax. Want me to fix you a plate?"

"I'll relax when the whole evening is over," Maureen said, "but I just realized I'm hungry."

"Coming right up," Molly said, and within what seemed like seconds, handed her a perfectly plated meal, complete with medium rare meat, a steaming baked potato topped with sour cream, fresh peas, a side salad, and a dinner roll. "Now sit down somewhere and relax," she ordered. "There are still some seats on the porch."

The porch was a good idea. Maureen could keep an eye on things from there and be within easy reach of the dining room and the reception desk. She accepted the plate, opened the green door, found an empty table, sat in the wicker chair, and almost began to relax.

Waitress Jolene appeared with a glass of wine. "Ms. Doherty?" She pointed. "That gentleman over there sent you a drink."

Maureen lifted the glass, saluting Roger Monroe, knowing without tasting it that he'd learned somehow that she liked rosé with dinner. She began with a bite of the excellent medium rare prime rib, hoping that she wouldn't be interrupted and have to make small talk with somebody while the hot meal cooled in the Florida winter evening temperature.

No such luck. Frank Hubbard had parked his blue uniformed self in a rocking chair next to the front steps. Was he pretending to be armed security for the event, or was he confident that no one would ask a uniformed cop to move? Either way, he was headed to her table. She took another bite, determined to enjoy her meal despite any attempt, official or personal, to involve her in conversation. Or questions. Or anything at all.

He sat, uninvited, in the wicker chair opposite hers. "Sorry to interrupt your dinner, Doherty," he began.

She shook her head and raised her fork. "Then don't," she mumbled, not caring that her mouth was full. "Go away."

"One question," he said.

She shook her head "no" and pointed at him with the fork. "Go away."

He at least had the good grace to look embarrassed, as he pushed his chair away from the table and stood, looking down at her. "Okay," he said. "Have it your way. But I wasn't sitting here to watch *you*. We'll talk when I come later to pick up the girls."

She didn't respond, fixed her eyes on her plate, and sampled the baked potato. She heard his footsteps as he pounded down the front steps, and waited a minute until she heard a car start. *Dear God, don't let him turn on the flashing lights!* He didn't. She sipped her wine and felt tense muscles in her neck and back easing. Once again, she lifted the glass in Roger Monroe's direction—and immediately hoped he wouldn't take the thank-you gesture as an invitation to join her. He didn't. He lifted his own wineglass and returned his attention to his dinner.

She enjoyed every last peaceful uninterrupted bite of her meal. She leaned back in her chair. *Damned wicker is uncomfortable.* Jolene cleared her table and asked, "Coffee and apple pie, Ms. Doherty?"

Maureen looked at her watch. Plenty of time before they'd all leave for the walk to the Paramount. "Yes, thank you, Jolene, I believe I will." She looked across the porch to where Roger Monroe sat, and realized that he was watching her, smiling, his head tilted, one eyebrow raised. *Is that an invitation?* Not at all sure, she smiled and gave the very slightest nod.

He picked up his own coffee cup and strolled slowly, deliberately across the porch and sat facing her from the same uncomfortable wicker chair recently vacated by Haven's top cop. "Was the big guy in blue bothering you? Is everything okay?"

She gave what she hoped was a nonchalant head-toss. "No problem. Officer Hubbard takes his job very seriously and he's been focused on the inn ever since the mur— I mean, since your uncle's passing." *Well, I messed that up.* She tried for a quick change of subject. "Did you enjoy your dinner?"

"Best meal I've had in weeks." He raised his right hand. "Honest. I guess the apple pie will be just as good?"

"It's amazing. Molly's specialty. We serve it warm with a big scoop of vanilla ice cream."

He patted an absolutely flat tummy. "I'll make room for it. Have you had a chance to take a look at the signatures on the paintings?"

"Not yet. Wouldn't that be something if I had a small fortune hanging on my walls? I'm almost afraid to look."

"The docent at the museum said that the Highwaymen sold lots of their work to hotels and motels. It was cheap and pretty. It makes sense that this place would have a couple of them."

Jolene had returned with the desserts. Roger's change of tables brought only the slightest sly smile. "More coffee?" she asked.

"Yes, please," they chorused, then laughed because they'd answered together, followed by a brief moment of awkward silence. This time Roger jumped in to change the subject.

"I hate to admit it, but I don't think I've ever seen a Cary Grant movie before. What am I in for?"

"I've only seen one," she admitted. "*An Affair to Remember*. My mom is a Cary Grant fan. He made a lot of movies. He was very handsome and could do both romance and humor."

"Are you going to the one tonight, or do you have to stay here and 'mind the store'?"

"Oh, I'm going. I get to lead the parade of walkers. We march down the boulevard to the Paramount and back."

"Do I get to join your parade?" he asked.

"Sure, you bought a ticket. You can walk or ride in a golf cart if you want to."

Maureen's hand was in her lap where she could safely sneak a peek at her watch without being impolite. He caught the slight motion anyway. "I know you're busy," he said. "You go on in if you have things to do. I'll just enjoy this great Florida weather from a rocking chair until it's time to leave."

"Thanks for understanding. See you in the parade."

"I'm ready to march whenever you are, Captain." He stood, giving a quick salute. She moved toward the green doors, aware that he was watching and pleased that her little black dress was especially flattering from the back.

The sounds from the dining room indicated that the group was having a good time. She glanced through the door, noting that most of the tables had been cleared of dinner service. Coffee cups and cocktail glasses and a few dessert plates marked the end of the meal. She had a few minutes to spare before it was time to head for the movie theater. Was there time to dash into the office and read the name on the picture of the poinciana? It sounded like poinsettia, the red plants so popular at Christmas. She opened the door, clicked on the overhead light. and moved closer to the painting. "M. Carroll," she read aloud.

There was a polite *tap-tap* on the door. "Ms. Doherty?" It was George's voice. "It's almost time to head 'em up and move 'em out."

"Coming, George," she called, turned out the light, closed and locked the door. She gave the doorknob an extra couple of shakes to be sure it had locked. After all, what if there *was* a valuable painting in there?

The dining room tables had been cleared. Ted had swapped his chef's whites for tan slacks and blue blazer. "Hi, Maureen. Dinner went great, don't you think? I hope the movie is just as good."

"I sure hope so," she said. "If you'll send them out, table

by table, I'll line them up at the curb. Then you'll bring up the rear, all right?"

"It seems as if we ought to have a marching band with a drum major out in front," he said.

"Maybe next year," she promised. "Shall I save you a seat?"

"Yep. See you at the movies."

Chapter 29

The good-natured audience laughed in all the right spots through a Heckle and Jeckle cartoon, then grew quiet as a black-and-white newsreel showed Eleanor Roosevelt making a stirring appeal to the public to donate a much-needed ten million dollars to the Red Cross war relief fund. The audience was totally silent as Mrs. Roosevelt's distinctive voice announced that the horrors of war abroad required help from all Americans. The preview of coming attractions lightened the mood with snippets from *Frosty the Snowman* and *A Christmas Carol*, winding up with *It's a Wonderful Life*.

The opening credits for *The Bishop's Wife* had just started when Maureen became aware of the man standing in the aisle. She reached for the purse she'd put in the seat beside her to save Ted's place. "Is that seat taken?" It was Roger Monroe.

"Oh, Roger. Yes. I'm sorry. It is. I'm saving it for Ted Carr, my . . . um . . . associate."

"No problem." He smiled, held up both hands, and moved toward the rear of the theater.

Within what seemed like seconds, Ted appeared beside her. She moved the purse onto her lap and pulled her feet back to make room for him to take the seat she'd saved. "Did I just almost lose my seat?" he whispered.

"Not a chance," she whispered back. "Everything here seems to be moving along just the way it should, doesn't it?"

"I know. Makes me nervous, like waiting for the other shoe to drop," he said. "You?"

"Same here. I guess we're kind of preconditioned to expect surprises."

"HUSH!" came a not-whispered command from the row in front of them. Maureen put a finger to her lips, leaned back in her seat, and prepared to watch Cary Grant as Dudley, a handsome, charming, debonair yet absolutely proper angel, as he assisted Loretta Young as Julia and David Niven as the bishop, ensuring a happy Christmas for everyone concerned.

There was spontaneous applause from the Paramount Theater audience as the ending credits rolled. Maureen and Ted each hurried for the exit, Maureen gathering her Haven Inn guests. *Like a mother hen rounding up the chicks,* she thought as she waved them into a semblance of a line while Ted directed the golf cart riders to their appointed spots. The hired security guard/traffic cop kept Beach Boulevard vehicle traffic moving while the walking guests proceeded on the sidewalk toward the inn, slowed somewhat by window-shoppers checking out the Christmas displays in the still-lighted storefronts. The two golf carts, driven this night by Sam and George, made trips back and forth from theater to inn until finally most of the guests were situated at their tables, enjoying Ted's hot wassail from Penelope's hoarded collection of crystal punch cups.

Maureen stood beside the dining room door while at the same time keeping an eye on the night manager at the reception desk. "Looks like a good time was had by all."

Frank Hubbard was back.

"Do you think my girls are ready to leave?"

"You can go on in and get them if you want to." She stood aside, motioning him to the door.

"Are they drinking those hot toddies?"

"I'm sure they are."

"How's chances of my getting a look at those pictures your guests took while I wait?"

If she obliged with the pictures would he go away? At least she could give back his stupid phone bug. She decided to take a chance. "Okay. They're on the laptop in my office. I can send them to your office right now. Come on." She led the way, saying good evening to Hilda and unlocking the office door. She went directly to the painting, giving it a long look before she swung it aside, blocking Hubbard's view of the safe. She tapped in the brief combination and removed the bug, holding it in front of her by thumb and forefinger. "Here. Now do you want to tell me whose phone you think Decklin was calling?"

Wordlessly, he slipped the thing into his pocket. After a long pause he said, "I guess it doesn't matter anymore. It's the phone in the Henshaws' cottage."

"I wish you'd told me sooner," Maureen said. "I know who made the call to that number after Decklin died."

"You do? Who was it?"

"Simple. Leslie Brown. She called her mother to tell her she was staying here for breakfast." Enjoying his discomfort she added, "Eggnog French toast."

"And I was going through pages of numbers for nothing." He looked at the floor. "Pictures?" he mumbled.

She sat at her desk, Hubbard standing behind her. "Here we go," she said. "There are about twenty of them. It was dark that night, so some of them aren't real clear." She brought up Hubbard's e-mail and one by one, in rapid succession, she sent the photos. "There you go. All done. I hope they'll be helpful."

"Me too. Thanks," he said. "I'll go get my girls." He paused in the doorway. "That Monroe guy who's staying here. What's up with him?"

"What do you mean?"

"He's signed for the old man's belongings and he arranged right off to get the body cremated. Didn't want the ashes."

"What?" she asked, surprised. "He doesn't want to take his uncle's ashes? That's not right. What will you do with them?"

"I think the undertaker disposes of them somehow. Why? Do you want them?"

Quick decision. "Of course. He had friends here. We'll take care of him now."

"Okay. I'll do the paperwork and you can sign for the ashes. I'll drop him off later. So why is the nephew still here? I'm keeping an eye on him. Something's not right."

The words hung in the air. She remained behind the desk, alone now, staring at the now blank screen. *Something's wrong with one of those pictures*, she told herself. *But what is it?*

She ran through them again, this time more slowly. There were some shots of the well-dressed first-night patrons leaving the inn on the way to see the old Barbara Stanwyck Christmas comedy. There were even more photos of the somewhat chaotic return to the dining room after the early cancellation of the movie. Maureen recognized most of the people pictured, even though she didn't recall all of the names. She ran the slide show back and forth, over and over for a good ten minutes.

"Something. Something," she said. "But what is it?"

"Maureen?" Ted was at the door. "The guests are leaving. Want to come out and say good night?"

"Oh, of course I do." Feeling guilty, as though she'd shirked her hostess duty, she pushed the chair back, switched off the laptop, and turned off the light, taking a backward glance at the painting of the red tree. *This room is full of all kinds of questions today.* She joined Ted in the lobby, putting on a big smile to wish departing moviegoers a good night. She realized that the Browns and the Henshaws, Frank Hubbard and Edith and Aster, as well as Roger Monroe and several of the inn's more elderly guests were among those who'd already left.

"Got time for a wassail nightcap?" Ted asked as they closed the door on the last couple to leave the dining room. "You look as though you could use one."

"Is it that obvious?"

"Probably not to anybody but me," he said softly. "Want to talk? There's nobody on the porch."

"Right now there's nothing I'd like better than to kick off my shoes, sit in a rocker, and have a cup of Wassail with you," she said, realizing as she spoke that she meant every word.

"Pick a couple of rockers," he said, pulling the green door open. "I'll be right out with the hot toddies."

She did as he'd suggested, selecting the same rockers in the far-left corner of the porch that they'd shared before. She kicked off her shoes and wiggled her toes, once again enjoying the glow of Christmas lights and the near silence of nighttime Haven. Ted returned and she held the warm punch cup with both hands, breathing in the citrusy scent.

"What's going on?" he wanted to know. "I see Hubbard's hanging around again."

"He still seems to think I know things that I honestly don't. He asked for the photos some of the guests took on the night Decklin was murdered and I sent them to him. Ted, Hubbard told me that Roger—Mr. Monroe—doesn't want his uncle's ashes. I told him we'd take them—that Decklin had friends here. Was that the right thing to do? Or is it none of my business?"

"You know it's the right thing to do. We'll get with Gert and the others and give old Decklin a good send-off after all this movie business is over."

"Thanks for agreeing with me. I know Gert will want to be involved. But now Hubbard's got some crazy idea that Decklin's nephew needs to be watched because he's still here even after he's taken care of his uncle's final business."

"It looks to me as if he's enjoying a few days of Florida vacation, and after all he barely knew his uncle. George says he's having Decklin's car serviced. He's thinking of driving it home."

"That makes sense." She took a long sip. "Ted, I've got that unexpected rush of money from the improvement fund into the inn's account on my mind. Who's pulling the strings on that?"

"It's found money. Don't question it," he advised.

"I can't help it. I'm not used to money just falling into my lap. And another thing has turned up." She told him about the possibility that the paintings in her office and in her suite might be valuable.

"The inn fell into your lap from nowhere," he reasoned. "Why not enjoy the spell of good luck? Have you looked up the paintings yet?"

"The one in the office is signed by an M. Carroll. I haven't had a minute to go upstairs and look at the other one."

"It must be time for Finn's bedtime walk." He stood, and reached down for her hand. "Let's go get him and see who signed that one. Then we'll look both them up and see if we can afford some more renovations. Aren't you excited about all this?"

There was that "we" again. She liked it. They dropped the cups off at the bar and took the elevator up to the third floor.

Finn began to woof as soon as they stepped into the corridor. "It sounds as though he's anxious for his walk. Poor thing. I've been ignoring him today." She unlocked the door and accepted Finn's happy doggie greetings.

Ted stood in from of the red tree painting. "Al Black," he read aloud.

The golden pranced and performed while Maureen attached the leash. "He really needs to go."

Ted reached for the leash. "How about I take him for his walk while you look up M. Carroll and Al Black and see if they're Highwaymen?"

It seemed like a good trade.

Now alone, Maureen sat at the blond desk and turned on the laptop. She'd just typed in "Highwaymen artists Florida" when her phone buzzed. A text from Frank Hubbard.

What now?

Rpt. on Monroe bullet. 22 cal. Same gun used on Putnam. Ideas?

The same gun that was used on Decklin killed Buddy about forty years ago? Paintings forgotten, she called Frank Hubbard's number.

"The same gun! My God, Frank—that's amazing."

"Thought that would get your attention," he said. "The weapon is a small twenty-two-caliber pistol. Forensics says maybe a Colt Junior Short. Whoever did it must have used a silencer both times or it would have been heard in the theater. Monroe, Putnam, and Henshaw. Looks to me like Henshaw is the last man standing in that group. I'm going to have to have a talk with him. You got any better ideas?"

"You said Decklin and Harry Henshaw both had solid alibis when Buddy got killed. And Henshaw was home sick in bed when Decklin died," she pointed out.

"No witnesses to say he was home in bed. I think he's our killer. Are you having any of your 'feelings' about it?"

I don't have any *feelings about any murder.* She paused before telling him so. She'd had what might be called "feelings" when she'd watched the photos taken on the night Decklin died. "There is one little thing," she said hesitantly. "There's probably nothing to it. It's just a . . . well, a *feeling.*"

"About what?" he urged. "It could be important."

"The pictures I e-mailed to you. There's something wrong with at least one of them. Something is out of order. I've looked at them all again and I just can't place it."

"Keep trying," he said. "Once the press gets hold of this, whoever has that gun—and my gut tells me it's Harry Henshaw—will get rid of it. We don't have a lot of time."

So Frank Hubbard was using the "we" word too, but in his case it wasn't so welcome.

She heard Finn's "woof." "I'll try to figure out what's wrong with the pictures," she promised Hubbard. "And thanks for telling me about the bullet."

"You would have seen it in the paper soon enough," he said. "You're my only connection to all the players in this game, including Roger Monroe. I'll bring those ashes around sometime tomorrow. I'm not sure where the nephew fits in but we need to solve this thing before anybody else gets hurt."

Another "we."

She ended the call as Ted and Finn bounded in. "We had a good run. Did you look up the artists? Are you rich?"

She laughed at the idea that she was rich. "I was just on the phone with Frank Hubbard," she said. "Guess what? He told me that Buddy and Decklin were both shot by the same gun. He thinks Harry Henshaw is the killer. He says he's going to question him about it. Poor Katherine will be devastated."

"The same gun? How is that even possible? It's been what, about forty years?" Ted was clearly just as surprised as she'd been.

"I know. The whole thing is crazy. But as Hubbard says, Harry Henshaw is 'the last man standing' out of that group. Hey, let's stop worrying about guns and look up some paintings."

"With our fingers crossed," Ted said.

"And toes," she added.

Chapter 30

It was true. Roger was right. Both of Maureen's paintings were the real thing. Mary Ann Carroll and Al Black were each Highwaymen painters. Estimates online ranged between $2,000 for the smaller painting and $8,000 for the big one. "Not rich," she told Ted, "but enough to get started on my souvenir shop, I'll bet." They exchanged high fives. Things were adding up nicely. "I'll check with the Goudreaus but I'll bet eight or ten thousand dollars would at least get the thing framed." She grinned. "Or else maybe buy me a couple of Katherine Henshaw's designer handbags."

"You're kidding. Handbags can be that expensive?"

"Sure. An Yves Saint Laurent bag can be two, three thousand dollars." Her eyes widened. "Ted! That's it! Her handbag!"

"Whoa. Slow down. What's *it*?"

"The pictures of the night Decklin got killed. Katherine switched handbags. I'm sure of it." The screen showed Katherine Henshaw smiling between her daughter and son-in-law as they prepared to walk to the theater. "See that bag? It's from last fall's collection. It retailed in Boston for almost two thousand dollars." She tapped the keyboard. "Now watch. See? Here they are back at the inn. Different bag. Still Saint Laurent, but different."

Ted moved closer to the screen. "I see it. But what does it mean?"

"I don't know," she admitted, "but she did and that's a fact."

He frowned. "How did she do it? I mean, she was in the theater with her daughter and son-in-law the whole evening. Wasn't she?"

"I don't know," she said again. "But it must mean something. I think we need to find out exactly what."

"Don't you think this is something you need to share with Hubbard?" Ted asked.

"It could very well be," she said, "but the last time Hubbard questioned Harry he got the whole household upset. He apparently earned his bulldog reputation big time."

"Woof," Finn said.

"Not that kind of bulldog, Finn." She patted the golden's head. "Add this to the gun evidence and he'll probably arrest Harry on the spot. Maybe it will be best if I talk to Leslie about it. There may be a perfectly good reason for the switch. Maybe she spilled popcorn butter on it and ducked home to change bags. She's such a perfectionist about her clothes." She tried for a convincing tone—or at least hopeful.

Ted looked at the clock on the desk. "It's nearly midnight. Much too late to call her now."

"You're right." Maureen fed the two images to her printer. "I truly hope there's a good reason for it. It'll keep until to-morrow. Meanwhile, I'll study the two pictures and see if anything about this makes sense."

"Which two pictures?" He looked from computer to the framed painting over the couch. "High fashion or High-waymen?"

"They're both pretty interesting. I'll toss a coin."

"Okay." Ted stood and moved toward the door. "I'll leave you to your homework, then. See you in the morning?"

"For sure. A good run on the beach might clear some of the cobwebs out of my head."

He reached down and tousled her hair. "You don't have cobwebs in there. Please be careful, Maureen. After all, we're talking about a murder here. Two murders. It might be time to turn it over to the professionals."

"I'm careful," she assured him. "After all we're just talking about expensive accessories here—not accessories to murder!"

Once again, Finn led the way to the bed. Maureen hurried through the mandatory makeup removal and pajama donning—careful to select a fairly new pair of tailored white cotton ones, just in case Lorna turned up during what was left of the night. With Finn snoring gently and a decorated palm tree brushing ever so slightly against the window frame, she drifted into an easy sleep, untroubled by either red trees or black handbags.

In the morning, along with the golden, she joined Ted in front of the Casino.

"Made any decision yet about what we learned last night?" he asked as they jogged along the sand at the water's edge where the shell line met the gulf.

"Yep. I'm thinking I'll sell the biggest painting and use the money toward the souvenir shop, and maybe I should give the small one to the Historical Society. After all, it was given to me and I'm sure they'd love to have it. Then, I'm going over to Petals and Kettles to see what I can find out about Katherine Henshaw's mysterious wardrobe replacement."

"Be careful," he warned again. "George told me about Harry Henshaw's temper." He didn't wait for a response. "Come on. I'll race you to the fishing pier."

The December morning air was cool and bracing and the sand hard-packed at the water's edge made for an easy run.

He had a slight lead but by the time they reached the now fa-miliar fishing charter sign she and Finn had caught up with him. She leaned against the sign with its faded lettering, tak-ing deep breaths. He braced himself against the sign with both arms, one at each side of her head, his face close to hers. It looked—and felt—as if he was about to kiss her.

How should I react? Am I ready for this?

He moved closer. She felt the leash slip from her hand.

With a joyous leap and a happy "woof," leash trailing in the sand, Finn took off after a very tall great heron—its large wings flapping as it headed for the Gulf of Mexico. Thoughts about kissing—or not kissing—evaporated as the two chased the dog, who'd chased the fleeing heron into the water. Both laughed aloud at Finn's expression of disappointment when he ran back onto the beach, shaking away drops of salt water, watching his prey soar out of reach. He seemed to sulk for a minute, then, tail wagging, ran back to where his human companions waited.

Maureen secured the leash once again. "Ready?" Ted faced toward home.

"Ready," she said, and the trio began the run back to the Casino.

They arrived at the same time and walked together along the sidewalk bordering Beach Boulevard. "It's nice here in the early morning," Ted said, indicating with a sweep of one arm the quiet, almost traffic-free street in the pale sunshine, Christmas lights blinking in still-closed store windows

"If someone would meet us here with hot coffee every morning it would be perfect," she laughingly suggested.

"Not likely," he said. "I'm serious about you staying out of any confrontation at the flower shop. Can't you ask what-ever questions you have about Katherine's purses over the phone?"

"I suppose so." Her answer was reluctant and he seemed

to recognize her tone of voice. They reached the inn and Maureen and Finn headed for the side door entrance. Ted stopped at the front steps.

"Anyway," he said, "promise you'll be careful. You can always call me if you need me."

"I know," she said softly and continued through the door, past the guest laundry and the soda machines and up the stairs to her suite. Then, showered, shampooed, and dressed for a Florida December day, she made coffee in the Keurig and popped a frozen waffle into the toaster—avoiding any meeting with Ted in the dining room where she might be talked into changing her plans. She measured the painting, meaning to find something the right size to take its place. Having put it off as long as she could, she took a deep breath and dialed the number for Petals and Kettles and asked to speak with Leslie.

"I could use a few more carnations," she said. "Could I come over and pick some up if you're not too busy?"

"That will be fine, Maureen," the young woman told her. "I'd bring them over to you but we're really slammed already this morning. All four of us are working. Tell you what. I'll have some wrapped and ready for you when you get here."

All four. She definitely didn't want to cause a confrontation of any kind—especially if Harry Henshaw was present. Anyway, Leslie was obviously too busy for conversation. Maybe she'd have to shift to plan B and loop Hubbard in after all.

The chime played "I'm a Little Teapot" as Maureen entered the warm, sweet-smelling shop. Leslie waved from the florist side of the attractive lobby space. "Good to see you. We all loved the Cary Grant movie—especially Mother. Just a sec. I have your carnations in the cooler." Leslie pushed open the sliding glass door and pulled the tissue-wrapped bouquet of red and white carnations from a tall container. "These should last for a while. Just keep them in water. I hope we'll get to join you for another movie before Christmas is over, but Daddy is talking about a cruise to the islands."

So the Henshaws may be leaving town—leaving the country. She knew she was being impulsive but asked the question anyway. "Leslie, I know I'm being nosy really, but something about Katherine—about your mother—has been bothering me ever since the . . . um . . . the Barbara Stanwyck movie."

"Cary Grant was so much better!" Leslie said. "Were you worried because Mother didn't like the movie?"

"No." Maureen was blunt. "I was wondering why she changed handbags before she came back to the inn."

Leslie smiled. "Candy," she said. "Her bag was stuffed with Daddy's favorite candy."

"Butterscotch Life Savers," Maureen said, nodding her head. "She told me about that."

"Exactly. Daddy hates to be without them. Eats them all the time. It's a habit he picked up years ago when he stopped smoking and drinking. She stopped by the cottage on the way back to the inn to deliver them. She wanted to check on him anyway." Leslie shrugged. "I guess she left the whole bag there and switched to a clean one."

Maureen accepted the bouquet. "Of course. That makes perfect sense. I'm such an accessories nut it was driving me crazy." She sniffed the spicy fragrance of the flowers. "Just put them on my bill, please."

"We appreciate your business, Maureen." Leslie walked with her to the exit. "When I get a break one of these lovely mornings, I'll be back for more French toast."

Maureen said goodbye, climbed into the Subaru. After putting the flowers carefully on the seat beside her, she drove away from the shop and pulled into the Quic-Shop parking lot to call Frank Hubbard. He picked up on the first ring. "What's going on, Doherty?"

"I'm not exactly sure," she admitted, "but I have a couple of things I think you need to know about."

"You getting those feelings?"

"No feelings. Just a couple of things I've learned today."

"Shoot."

"First, did you know that Harry and Katherine Henshaw are planning a trip to the islands? A cruise?"

Hubbard raised his voice. "Who told you that?"

"Leslie."

"Okay. I'll check it out. He's not under arrest or anything, but I did ask him not to leave town. What else?"

"This one might be silly," she said, "but I noticed in the pictures I shared with you that on the night Decklin was killed Katherine Henshaw changed handbags sometime between the start of the evening and the time she came back to the inn."

"She did? How did she manage that? And why?"

"Leslie says that her mother had filled it up with Harry's favorite candy and she wanted to give them to him. Butterscotch Life Savers are hard to find these days."

"Life Savers!" The word exploded. "Harry likes butterscotch Life Savers? Why didn't you tell me this before?"

She didn't answer, surprised by his tone. Why would Harry Henshaw's taste in candy mean anything to the police? Or to anyone outside of the Henshaw family?

"Butterscotch," he muttered. "And you didn't think it was important enough to mention?"

She was annoyed and it showed in her voice. "No, I didn't. *Still* don't. Everybody loves those old-time candies they had at the Paramount. They're all hard to get. I'm trying to stock them for the inn."

Maureen heard his long intake of breath, as though he was

trying to calm himself. He spoke then, slowly—like he was talking to someone not quite bright. "It's important, Doherty, because, as I told you, we vacuumed a bunch of snack remains off the projection room floor. And, *as I told you*, candy was included." Again, he lost his composure. "Damn it, Doherty, that vacuum sucked up a full, unopened roll of butterscotch Life Savers."

Chapter 31

A soft "Wow" escaped her lips. "What does that mean? Was Harry Henshaw in the projection room?

"I don't know." There was exasperation in the words. "How long had that junk been on the floor? For instance, was it there when you were spending an hour and seven minutes with Monroe? We printed everything. The only prints on the candy roll were from the lady who was working at the candy counter. Decklin didn't touch it and neither did Harry Henshaw or anybody else unless they were wearing gloves."

"Well, at least you know that they knew each other and they weren't exactly friends," she offered. "Decklin told me that he was planning to ask somebody for money to back his plan to buy the old Paramount."

"That a 'feeling'? Doherty?"

"No, sir. It's an observation. I mean, everybody knows Harry has money—and they were connected in some kind of business in Haven a long time ago."

"Yeah. Along with Buddy Putnam. It was a pretty shady business. Everybody thought so. Nobody talked about it. Nobody proved they were doing anything illegal."

Lorna knew about it.

"Same gun," Maureen said.

"Same gun," he echoed. "According to the records, Decklin and Harry both had bulletproof alibis for Buddy's death."

She resisted snickering at the "bulletproof" description. "Were they together?"

"No. Monroe claimed that he was fishing on a party boat out of Pass-a-Grille. He had the ticket stub and about twenty witnesses and he showed up in at least one snapshot, posing with a red grouper."

She thought of her own long-ago posing-with-a-fish photo. *Some pictures tell more than one story.*

"And Henshaw?" She pressed him for information. "Where was he?"

"He lawyered up. Big-city lawyers, not the locals. There was a deposition. I've read it," he said. "Harry told the investigators that he was over in Tampa during the time in question posting bail for a contractor friend who was in trouble for diverting materials from a city construction job to one of his own projects. He came up with even more witnesses than Monroe had."

"So nobody pursued it after that?" she wondered.

He paused. "The cops dropped the case. Buddy was nobody important." Maureen had heard that before—Lorna DuBois had voiced something similar.

Maureen hesitated, then asked a pointed question. "So Frank, was Decklin a nobody too? Will his murder go unsolved along with Buddy Putnam's? Even his closest relative isn't exactly mourning his death." She almost added *Will there be two ghosts haunting the Paramount Theater?*

She regretted the words almost immediately. Here she'd been congratulating herself on the improved relationship between herself and Hubbard and now she'd challenged him on his integrity as a cop. She braced herself for the explosion to come. *I darn well deserve it.*

There was no explosion. Hubbard's voice was steady.

"Don't you think that's crossed my mind? How much of the taxpayer's money should I spend chasing after a solid citizen like Harry Henshaw? He's a do-gooder. He could probably run for mayor if he wanted to. He has money and influence and good family. So he had a tough reputation when he was young. Hung with a rough crowd. Might have cleaned up some dirty money for some building contractors. No record besides a fistfight fifty years ago and he beat that." He sighed. "Listen, Doherty. Thanks for the tip about the candy. Talk to you later." And he was gone.

She backed the Subaru out of the lot, noticing a few faces lined up at one of the store windows. No doubt the news that she'd used their lot without buying anything would be gossip fodder for a while. She aimed a big smile and a wave in their direction and headed for the inn.

All four of the front-row rockers were occupied and rocking. She waved and smiled at the four occupants with much more sincerity than she'd given the Quic-Shop lookers. She parked in her reserved spot and hurried around to the front of the inn. She pulled the Post-it note with the dimensions of the larger painting from her purse and approached Sam.

"I'm looking for a picture to hang in my office," she told him. "It needs to be this size. Do you think you can find one down at Ms. Gray's warehouse?" Although during the past few months they'd managed to whittle the hoard down to less than half its original size, they still had a way to go before the warehouse would be emptied.

"Sure thing, Ms. Doherty," he said. "You want a picture of anything particular? There's a pile of them. All different sizes. Are you looking for a picture of anything special?"

"Not really. It's just for the office. The size is most important. It has to fit over the safe. Just pick something you think is pretty."

Molly slapped Sam's arm. "No girly pictures, Sam. We all know what you think is pretty."

Maureen laughed with the four, then hurried into the lobby, prepared to check off a few more items from her growing to-do list. *I'll call Larry Jackson*, she decided. *Maybe he's found something by now.* She unlocked the office door, her eyes drawn immediately to the painting. She'd only just started paying attention to it, but knew she'd miss it when it was gone. She dialed the lawyer's number.

"Maureen, how good to hear from you. I've been meaning to call you," he said. "I've done a little research on your project—nothing intensive by any means, but I believe I've uncovered a few interesting tidbits."

"Since I'm starting at zero, all tidbits are welcome."

"So far the Registry of Deeds only has documents back to Ms. Gray's immediate predecessor," he reported. "Somebody ran the inn before that but I have no record yet of who it was."

"But that's a start." Maureen was excited. "Who gave the inn to Penelope?"

"A person named Charlotte Christine Trevaney. Ring any bells?"

"Not a jingle."

"All we have is that name as an owner of record before it got transferred to Ms. Gray. Nothing before that. Strange, actually."

"Strange how?"

"Strange as in, we can find no birth, death, census, or any record at all of a Charlotte Christine Trevaney and we have no idea how she came to own it," Larry Jackson explained. "I think she was a 'straw buyer'—somebody who buys property for someone else who can't have their name on it for some reason. For sure, though, somebody, at some time, has gone to a great deal of trouble to hide the origins of the Haven House Inn."

"At least we have a name. That's a lot more than I've been

able to figure out. Thanks, Larry. Please keep in touch if any more tidbits come your way."

Delighted to have a new name with a connection to the inn, she began a file headed with *Charlotte Christine Trevaney*. It was a new beginning in her search and just typing the name brought satisfaction that there was more for her to learn.

Now there's more for you to learn. Zoltar knows all.

She locked the office and stepped out onto the porch. It was still cool. She might need a sweater today.

Today. Charlotte Christine Trevaney. Buddy Putnam. Harry Henshaw. Decklin Monroe. A murder that happened half a century ago. She'd spent enough time this morning on yesterday. She had more than enough to worry about—to learn about—today and well into her future. She took a deep breath of that soft Florida air and went back inside her inn. It was time to get down to business.

Sam had lost no time in finding the requested picture. She'd just returned to her office desk when he knocked on the door. "I found one right away that's exactly the same measurements as your old tree picture and you said you don't care what it's a picture of—so here . . . What do you think?" He pulled it from behind his back. "Ta-da!"

The frame was much nicer than the one on the Highwayman painting—solid dark wood, carved, and nicely molded. Inside the frame was a map. Maureen stood, moved around her desk, got closer to Sam and the picture. "It looks old, Sam. It says 'Map of Haven Florida, 1928' and it's signed by 'Fred T. Williams, Civil Engineer.' Is this a map of Haven before all the houses and businesses were here?"

Sam peered proudly over the top of his find. "Yep. And look. All of our little lakes are here—and see? They marked out a place for where the cemetery was supposed to go. And there are even some spaces marked 'Indian mounds' and 'homestead sites' and 'land grants.' "

"I absolutely love this, Sam. Thank you so much for finding it." She reached for the new acquisition, then held it up in front of M. Carroll's red tree. She looked upward. "And thank you too, Penelope, for hoarding this treasure."

Later, alone once again in her office, she examined the map with a magnifying glass and camera. Part of it was faded. Perhaps, she thought, it had once hung on a wall in some early Haven settlers home in partial sunlight. She moved the glass around the map slowly, trying to decipher words on the yellowed surface. "I need to visit the cemetery," she told herself. "And the Indian mounds."

The homesites shown on the map were of varying sizes. Some had names attached and some even had house-shaped symbols centered on them. *My little history of Haven project is growing*, she thought as she squinted through the magnifying lens. Some of the names on the homesites were familiar— names of people she'd met or heard about in today's Haven, like Wallace, Haines, and Johnson. She leaned closer to the map, trying to puzzle out a faded name, then sat bolt upright as the letters came into focus.

Trevaney Estate.

Trevaney? Again? This was no coincidence. Charlotte Christine Trevaney, who'd given Haven House to Penelope, must have had deep roots in this old city. Maureen pulled up a current map of Haven and, using the lakes as reference points, tried to line up that Trevaney homestead with the present landscape. She wasn't even the tiniest bit surprised to see that her inn, her parking lot, and part of Beach Boulevard were nicely centered in the Trevaney Estate property on her new, very old, map of Haven.

Chapter 32

A trip back across the street to the history museum was in order. Sure, she had other things to do, but this was simply too tantalizing to dismiss. She snapped a few pictures of the map with her phone, took the poinciana tree painting down, replaced it with the perfectly fitting framed map, and called Shelly to take over the lobby desk. After giving the painting a quick dusting and hurriedly wrapping it in one of the many beach towels left over from Penelope's hoard, Maureen left the building.

Claire Davis greeted her warmly. "I'm happy to see you again. We have a new addition to our little Greater Haven Improvement Fund display." She pointed to the case Maureen had visited before. "A purple satin badge that the volunteers wore. It's not even faded. I thought you might like to take a picture of it."

Maureen put the towel-wrapped painting in a nearby chair, followed her to the display, and snapped a picture. "Thanks. My little self-imposed history assignment continues to grow."

"I understand perfectly. Research tends to do that." The director smiled, pointing to the chair. "Part of your research project?"

"In a way, but mostly it's something I want to give to the

museum if you'd like to have it." Maureen removed the towel wrapping. "It's a Highwayman painting," she began to explain.

Claire interrupted. "It's a Mary Ann Carroll! Are you sure you want to part with this?"

"I'm sure," Maureen said. "It belongs in a museum, not on my office wall. Anyway, I have something new—I mean something old—to take its place." She held up the phone photo of the map. "A 1928 map of Haven. There's a homestead marked where my inn is now. The name is Trevaney. The Trevaney Estate. Do you have any information on a Trevaney family?"

"I'm sure the society will be delighted to accept your gift," she said. "And your map is fascinating. Perhaps you'll send me one of the photos. Yes, the name Trevaney is familiar to me because of a portrait which, I was told, was dropped off at the doorway of this building on the day it was opened back when Haven officially became a city. In 1910. It's a portrait of a woman. The name on the back of the canvas is C. Trevaney."

"The artist? Or the subject?"

"We don't know. We just call her 'the lady in green.' "

"May I see it?"

"Of course. It's in the archives upstairs. We don't display everything we have all at once, you know. The lighting's not great. I'll bring along a flashlight." They started for the staircase. "There isn't room to show all of our holdings, and in this particular case, this is one of those portraits that people talk about because the eyes seem to follow you around the room. Some people find her disturbing."

Claire called one of the volunteers to take over the front desk and together the two women climbed a white painted staircase up one flight to a balcony where several small glass cases displayed household utensils and silverware. Claire opened a white paneled door onto a long, high-ceilinged room quite different in appearance from the quiet elegance of the rooms below. The walls here were of unfinished wood. There were stacks of crates and boxes, some glass cases, and several trunks.

The museum director indicated a large dome-topped trunk. "There's Penelope's trunkful of who-knows-what ready for your inspection when your research leads you there."

Maureen tapped the top of the trunk with one hand. "I'll get to you later," she said.

"The portrait is over this way." Claire pointed the light deeper into the long room. Here rows of metal shelves held more rows of plastic boxes. Maureen followed the light, remembering how Decklin Monroe had lighted her the way up to the projection room at the Paramount. The portrait of the lady in green was a large one. It hung at the end of the room in a place where the roof rose to a peak, so that the woman seemed to be looking down at them from a sort of wooden triangle with a small window at its very top. Claire shone the light onto the woman's face. Her green dress, worn softly off her shoulders, was tiny waisted and full skirted in layers of lace and ruffles. Brown hair was parted in the middle and a pink rose held a loose chignon. She carried a folded fan. Maureen moved closer, noticing the pearl necklace and silver bracelets, then moved to the side for a closer look at a ring with an emerald on a dainty left hand.

She was aware of the feeling that the green eyes followed her every move.

"What do you think of her?" Claire asked.

"She's quite lovely, isn't she?" Maureen said. "Is it all right if I take her picture?"

"Go right ahead. Shall I turn off the flashlight?"

"Yes, thank you. I think the natural light from that high window is good enough." She realized that she'd almost said *Do you think she'll mind if I take her picture?*

She photographed the lady in green from several angles, including a close-up of her face. "I appreciate your letting me come up here," she told the director. "I'm sure not everybody gets to see this part of the museum."

Claire aimed the flashlight toward the floor once again, lighting the way through the maze of artifacts to the doorway. "The fact is," she said, as she pushed open the door to the balcony, "not everybody *wants* to come up here." She gave a nervous giggle. "Some people say the place is haunted."

Maureen had been in Haven long enough so that the statement didn't surprise her. "Really?" she asked, in an unsurprised tone of voice. "Who's supposed to be haunting it? Not the lady, I hope."

"Not sure. I mean I've never personally seen—or heard—anything." The giggle again. "But I don't think I'd come up here alone at night. How do you feel about ghosts?"

Maureen paused before answering. After all, most of the Haven people she'd met so far vehemently denied that there *were* any ghosts—even in the face of pretty strong evidence to the contrary. "Ghosts?" She shrugged. "I guess I can take 'em or leave 'em." She hoped the answer was sufficiently vague.

Claire gave an emphatic nod. "Exactly. Me too. Maureen, I can't thank you enough for the Highwayman painting. It will be our first one, you know. The board of directors will be over the moon."

"I'm glad people will get to enjoy it. And I'm very pleased with my 1928 Haven map that will replace it on my office wall."

"That's a treasure too." She walked with Maureen to the

front door. "Come back anytime, and don't forget you have a trunk here to explore."

Maureen returned to the inn, pleased with her day's accomplishments so far. She'd found a good home for the red-tree painting and she'd also found one more reference to the name Trevaney. Once back inside her office, she took another long look at the 1928 map of Haven, admiring it not only for the historical information it had revealed, but also for the fact that it made an excellent piece of wall art. She took the phone from her purse, about to print the photos she'd taken of the lady in green, when it rang. Caller ID told her that Frank Hubbard wanted to talk to her. Again. She answered it.

"Doherty?" He didn't wait for a reply. "Tell me what you've found out about the Henshaw woman. Katherine Henshaw."

"What I've found out about her? I haven't tried to find out anything special about her. She's a nice woman, seems happily married, has great fashion sense. Why ask me? I met her last week. She's a Haven native. Went to school here. There must be plenty of people around town who know her better than I do."

"I thought you were curious about her. I know you were, or you wouldn't have noticed that handbag switch."

"I was curious about why anybody would ditch one high-end bag for another one in the middle of an evening out," she admitted. "Then I found the answer and told you about it."

"Yeah, you did," he said. "The pocketbook thing was full of candy so she dropped it off for her husband. It's still bothering me. I'm going over to the tea shop to talk to them again about that candy roll. Do you think Henshaw could have dropped it up in the projection room? Or did Monroe bring it up there himself?" His tone softened. "Or did *you* drop it when you were up there for an hour and seven minutes? You told me you were ordering those fancy candies for your own business. Remember?"

"Come on, Frank," she said. "You know better than that. I never knew about the fancy candy until the first day of the Christmas movies. Henshaw was home sick in bed. Decklin might have ordered all that candy himself. I know he special ordered the oil for the popcorn. Maybe he got free Life Saver samples. It makes more sense than old Harry getting out of bed, sneaking into the movies, climbing a couple of flights of stairs, shooting Decklin, then getting out of there and all the way home again without being seen." She hadn't meant to raise her voice, but realized that she was almost shouting at him. "For God's sake, Frank. The man must be almost ninety years old! That stupid roll of candy has you chasing down a rabbit hole. It doesn't mean anything. We have to look for something else!"

She realized she'd said "we."

Frank Hubbard was quiet. Should she apologize for yelling at him? Had anyone in the lobby heard her? She wasn't generally a yeller. The man sure knew how to push her buttons.

"Sorry to bother you about this, Doherty." He spoke slowly, calmly, politely. "I know you're busy. We'll talk some other time. Maybe when I bring over the ashes. Have a nice day."

Have a nice day! She didn't respond, simply ended the call.

Maureen blew out a breath and continued with what she'd started to do. The printer whirred into life and half a dozen color pictures of the lady in green rolled into the tray. "Who are you?" Maureen whispered. She held them up, one at a time, studying the face, the eyes, the flowers in the hair, the delicate details of the green dress. Pulling the folder she'd marked earlier with the name Charlotte Christine Trevaney from the file cabinet, she slipped the prints inside.

I think I'll keep this in my desk upstairs, she thought. *No point in leaving it where people might ask questions I don't have answers for.* Anyway, it was time to walk Finn. She called for Shelly to cover the reservation desk, then carried the folder to the elevator and pushed the call button.

The elevator slowed to a halt and Roger Monroe bounded into the lobby before the door had even fully opened. The man was certainly a ball of energy. "Off to do some more sightseeing?" Maureen asked.

"Regretfully, no," he said. "I'd like to settle my bill. I'm going over to the Plymouth dealership to pick up my car. I'm going to drive home to Marblehead. I've really enjoyed my visit here and I sure plan to come back again. George says he'll take me to a Rays game, and"—big flirty smile—"I'd like to get to know you better too."

"We'll look forward to seeing you soon, then." She knew she was blushing. "Shelly will take care of checking you out. It was nice meeting you," she added, "even under the sad circumstances."

"Oh, yeah. My uncle. Well, that's all taken care of. Next time I'll be on a real vacation." He moved toward the registration desk while Maureen stepped into the elevator. "Say goodbye to Finn for me, in case you're not around when I leave."

"Oh yeah. My uncle"? That seems cold. "I will," she promised, "and in case I don't see you again, thanks for that telephone matter you discovered."

"Did you get that straightened out?"

"I sure did." She gave him a brief wave as the door slid closed.

Finn's happy "woofs" from down the hall greeted her when the elevator door opened on the third floor. "I'm coming," she called. His enthusiastic greeting nearly knocked her over. "Just a darned minute," she told him, tossing the manilla folder onto her desk, and grabbing the leash from behind the kitchen door. They took the stairs this time and exited through the side door. She peeked from behind the hibiscus bush before venturing onto the sidewalk, half expecting to see Hubbard's cruiser nearby. "All clear," she told the dog. "And by the way, Roger said to tell you goodbye. He's leaving this afternoon."

"Woof woof."

"Yeah, he's okay but just not my type."

Finn nodded his golden head. "Woof," he agreed. With the dog setting a brisk pace they headed toward the Casino. After taking care of business, they took a more leisurely stroll along the Boulevard, stopping to look into shop windows. Aster and Erle Stanley were outside on their patio. Finn tugged on his leash, indicating that he'd like to visit. "Okay, we have a little time," she said, accepting the seat Aster offered.

"Just walking, or shopping?" Aster asked.

"A little of both," Maureen said. "I'm interested in books about Haven—especially the ones about the history of the place. I just acquired a nice framed 1928 map of Haven that was part of Penelope's hoard. It has some homesteads and grants marked on it and it even shows where the inn was going to be built. There are some family names on it I'm trying to trace"

"Any name in particular?"

"Trevaney. Ever hear of it?"

"Yes and no. The last time I heard that name spoken was from Penelope herself. Same question. Had I ever heard the name? My answer then was 'no,' and it's my answer now. Never heard of it. Sorry." She stood, shooing Erle Stanley out of her lap. "Come on inside. I'll show you what I've got. I heard you're writing a book yourself."

"Word gets around fast in Haven," Maureen said. "No

surprise about that." She followed woman, cat, and dog into the shop.

"How's that lunchtime matinee going?" Aster pulled several books from a shelf marked Haven History. "George left a flyer about it. The lunches look good."

"People seem to like it. We're thinking of doing more of them."

"I'd like a reservation for the one where you're serving New England clam chowder. I don't care what the movie is. You see, my Peter was allergic to shellfish so I never made it and I just love it." She handed Maureen one of the books. "Here's a good one about the Timucuan Indians who used to live around her. Oh, poor dear Peter. One taste of shrimp or lobster or clams and he'd be sick to his stomach for hours. Both ends running at once, if you get my drift." She selected another slim volume. "Here's one you'll like. *A Culinary History of Florida*. All about Florida food. Local girl wrote it. Joy Harris."

Maureen left with four books and a flamingo-shaped bookmark. Aster followed her outside. "I guess you knew that Penelope herself was planning to write a book too," Aster announced. "She gathered up old papers and letters and maps and stuff for years. I don't guess she ever got around to writing the thing. She used to keep it all in an old steamer trunk somebody left at the hotel." She sighed. "I suppose it's long gone by now."

"Actually, I think I may know exactly where it is." Maureen was delighted. "Thanks, Aster. That could be a big help." That trunk had undoubtedly been sitting in the archives for a long time. Another day wouldn't matter. She and Finn hurried for home. They arrived at the inn just in time to see the vintage Plymouth pulling away from the curb.

She ducked behind the hibiscus and made her way to the side door. Bacall and Bogie had just arrived there too, and the pair darted through the round cat door as soon as they saw Finn. With the cats leading the way, Maureen and the golden passed the guest laundry and the soda machines and took the back stairs up to the penthouse. Finn yelped a happy "woof" as the cats streaked past him through their entrance. She unlocked the door and Finn ran to the desk and sat upright, paw extended as he did whenever he wanted to shake hands.

Chapter 33

"Oh, hi, Maureen." Lorna shimmered into sight, bent, and shook Finn's paw. Bacall made a U-turn on the way to the cat tower so that she could walk through Lorna, who didn't seem to notice. "I was just looking at your pictures." She held up one of the prints of the lady in green. "Where did you run into her?"

"You know her?"

"Not really." Lorna replaced the picture in the folder and picked up another one. "I've seen her around."

"Around here? Around Haven?"

"Yeah. She shows up every once in a while." She held the photo away, then closer to her face. "She dresses way better now. Kind of steampunk—a lot of black leather and chains and fishnet hose and sometimes one of those bird masks. High black boots, long straight hair. Kind of cool. She travels mostly with Goth guys."

The image was difficult to picture. Maureen made a silent pledge to never, ever share that information with Claire Davis. "Do you happen to know her name?"

"I've heard she goes by Absinthe, but I'm pretty sure that's not her real name. Reggie says it's some kind of drink."

"I'll ask Ted about it." Maureen said.

"The cute bartender?"

"Right." Maureen blushed. "Does she ever come in here? Into the inn?" Maureen wanted to know, any thoughts of using the photos for a "Lady in Green Suite" forever banished.

"Not that I know of. She's more the cemetery type. Goths like dark places, always dress in black, hide behind tombstones, stuff like that. Even if you saw one of them in the cemetery you wouldn't be sure of what you saw." Lorna held another photo up to the light. "If she had to dress like this— all ruffles and lace and frou-frou—it's no wonder she went dark. I wouldn't be caught dead in that outfit either." She gave Finn a playful poke on his haunch. "See what I did there, Finn?"

Maureen groaned at Lorna's joke, picked up the photos, and returned them to the folder She placed the newly purchased history books on the desk. "Larry found out the name of the woman who left the inn to Penelope. I was hoping these might be pictures of her."

"No kidding? Is Larry the cute lawyer?"

Maureen rolled her eyes. "Yes. That's him. He says the name of the woman who left Penelope the inn was Trevaney. Charlotte Christine Trevaney. Ever heard of her?"

"I don't think so. I thought Penelope didn't know who left it to her."

"Maybe she didn't. Larry says somebody is—or was—trying to keep it hidden."

After Lorna had shimmered away, Maureen added the Florida books to the bookcase in her room, and made a reservation for Aster to enjoy New England clam chowder and *A Christmas Story*. That sparked a memory, so she picked up the phone and telephoned Leslie Brown.

"Hello, Maureen," the young woman answered. "Do you need some more flowers?"

"No thank you, Leslie. We're all set for now. I've been thinking about how upset you've been about Officer Hubbard's . . . um . . . method of questioning."

"I can't stop thinking about it," she said. "It's as if he doesn't believe Daddy was really sick—and the poor man was so miserable."

"I was speaking with a friend today and she told me that her husband got violently ill if he ate certain things. Did your father eat anything unusual that day?"

"The thing is, Maureen, we all shared exactly the same meals that day. We were all at home, and we knew we were going out to dinner, so we ate lightly. We all ate exactly the same things—breakfast and lunch both—and nobody else got sick."

"Can you remember what you ate?" Maureen asked, searching for answers.

"Sure. For breakfast Dad made scrambled eggs and biscuits out of one of those cans that pops open. Warren had coffee and everybody else had tea. Earl Grey."

"And lunch?"

"Soup. It's sort of a special soup we have once in a while. We call it 'clean out the refrigerator soup.'" Soft giggle. "Like, all the meat and vegetable leftovers from the week in chicken or beef or vegetable broth with pasta of some kind—and whatever spices we feel like throwing in."

"I know what you mean." Maureen smiled at a childhood memory. "My mom used to do the same thing. It was different every time. She even put blueberries in it once."

"Exactly." She could tell that Leslie was smiling too. "We all helped that day, and we were careful about not putting in anything one of us doesn't like. For instance, when Warren joined the family we found out that he doesn't eat canned tomatoes but he likes fresh ones so canned ones were out. I don't like fresh peas, but I don't mind canned ones. Daddy likes grouper or codfish, but can't stand shrimp or lobster.

Mother will eat just about anything, but she's not fond of celery so we hardly ever use it in the soup. We all like pasta. That day it was rigatoni. It was a little more spicy than usual, if I'm remembering correctly. Whoever added the cayenne was a little heavy-handed. It also had little meatballs and cut-up chicken thighs."

Maureen thought of Peter Patterson's allergy. "My friend's husband was allergic to shellfish. You sure there was no lobster or shrimp or clams in it?"

"Impossible." Leslie was firm. "We never have those things in the house. If we want lobster we get it at a restaurant."

Like Aster's clam chowder.

"Thanks for talking to me about it, Leslie. I know none of this is any of my business, but Officer Hubbard seems to think I know things that I don't—so I guess I'm just trying to help unravel this mess."

"I'm happy to have someone to talk to about it, Maureen, and I'm so glad that you're interested in helping." There were sounds of voices and the door-chime tune in the background. "I have to go now. We're swamped right now for both tea and flowers!"

"Talk to you later." She'd just ended the call when another one buzzed. "Hello, Ted," she said. "Is anything wrong?'

"How come when we call each other we automatically wonder if something's wrong?" he joked. "No. I just came up with some figures that may save us some money in the restaurant end of the business. Can you come down and talk about it?"

"I love talking about saving money. Be there in a minute. Your office or mine?"

"Yours is quieter."

"Okay." Maureen made a brief check in the bathroom mirror, yanked a comb through her hair, and touched up pink lip gloss. "See you later, Finn," she said and closed the door behind her. She took the stairs—faster that way—and met Ted in front of her office door. He carried a plump folder and a handheld adding machine. She rubbed her hands together. "Let's go save us some money."

It didn't take long to figure out that Ted's idea was a solid one. "That lunch and matinee we did for the *Prancer* movie was a moneymaker. Look at these figures." He put a sheet in front of her. "See? The matinee tickets are half price. Five bucks. The lunch is simple: soup, sandwich, salad, ice cream and coffee, tea or soda. So food will cost us about another five or six dollars to put together. We'll advertise lunch, dessert, maybe even a Mimosa, and a Christmas movie for 1995. That gives us a little more profit than we made on the dinner package. Want to buy, say, fifty matinee tickets to start? And we haven't announced any more dinner packages, so we'll get our usual dinner customers anyway—at the regular dinner prices. Win-win. What do you say?"

"I say let's do it! It not only makes money for the inn, it saves me time and money personally too. I won't have to keep buying outfits I don't really need or want for every dinner. At lunchtime I can get away with jeans and sweaters and I can carry my old hobo bag instead of trying to coordinate shoes and handbags every night."

"I never thought about it being that much extra trouble for you." He sounded apologetic. "I didn't think about the various wardrobe adjustments involved."

"No reason you should. It's a girl thing. I haven't felt as though, as hostess, I should wear the same dress more than once to these things; besides, changing handbags every time is a pain. I have to take everything out of my regular daytime bag and fit it into a different one— Wait a minute!"

"What?" He frowned. "What's wrong?"

"I'm not thinking about *my* handbag. I'm thinking about Katherine Henshaw going all the way back to her house to change one Saint Laurent bag for another one after the movie. It doesn't make any sense."

"Explain?"

"Okay. She had her purse all set for an evening out. It's a good-sized one—bigger than I'd usually take to a movie. She has all her stuff in it—wallet, compact, comb, lipstick, tissues, pills, hand sanitizer. Then she sees Harry's favorite hard-to-find candy in the lobby. She buys a whole bag of butterscotch Life Savers and dumps them in on top of everything."

"I'm with you so far," he said.

"Good. Then, according to Leslie, her mother stops on the walk home from the theater to the cottage to drop off the candy and to check on Harry," Maureen recited. "She leaves the first bag at home and picks up the other one."

"Yes," he agreed, "I guess she would do that."

"No." Maureen was vehement. "No. It's not that easy. If she just dumped out the Life Savers, she'd still have all the necessary things in purse number one with no need to change to the other one."

"What if she left the whole thing for Harry to sort out?' Ted wondered.

"Then she wouldn't have her comb and mirror and lipstick and all in the second bag. It doesn't make sense. In fact, it's impossible. Either Leslie or Katherine is lying. Don't you see?"

He put his folder down on her desk. "Yes I do," he said, "and I think maybe you should tell Hubbard about it."

"I do too—and Ted, just as soon as you figure out menus for the remaining matinee movies we'll get some local publicity going."

"A poster in the Quic-Shop ought to do it," he joked.

"For sure. Can you schedule servers for both lunches and

the regular dinners for what's left of the Twelve Days of Christmas?"

"I'm on it."

"I'll call Hubbard now and try to explain the strategy behind women's handbag switching." She hit Hubbard's number.

"What have you got, Doherty?" he growled. "I'm busy."

"Maybe something. Maybe nothing," she told him.

"You got a feeling?"

"Yes sir," she answered immediately. "I've got a feeling."

Chapter 34

Frank Hubbard was silent while Maureen explained, step by step, how Katherine Henshaw's story about changing expensive designer purses mid-evening didn't make sense. "I thought," she concluded, "that you might want to question Mrs. Henshaw about her reason for substituting one handbag for another the way she did."

"You some kind of an expert on handbags, Doherty?"

"Actually Frank, I am. I have a degree in fashion merchandising and I spent ten years buying accessories for a major department store in Boston."

"Good point, Doherty," he said. "I think I'll have a conversation with Mrs. Henshaw and maybe the daughter too. Nothing official, you know? No uniform. No difficult questions. Just a friendly conversation to help me tie up some loose ends."

Maureen thought about what Leslie had reported about Hubbard's recent questioning of the family. "To tell the truth, Frank, I doubt that either of them would voluntarily sit down for a 'friendly' conversation with you. Last time you left the women in tears and the men wanting to fight you. Anyway, this is a busy time for the florist shop and the tea room both. They can't close everything down to talk to you."

"Just doing my job," he muttered. "I can be friendly when I want to be. But you're right about the businesses. Maybe I'll do it one person at a time over a nice cup of tea at their place. Do you want to come along? The women might relax, talk a little more if you're there."

"Can you do that? Bring me in on a murder case? I'm nobody."

"Baloney. You're an expert on handbags. You just told me so yourself. I'll write you up as a consultant. I might even be able to get you a few bucks for your time."

She couldn't help smiling. *Maybe I'll add "expert consultant" to my résumé.* "If you think it would help I'll be there," she said, "but I doubt that Harry Henshaw will let you talk to Katherine alone. He's very protective of her and he has no love for you, that's for sure. If you can set it up, let me know when and where. I've got a lot going on here. I'm busy too."

"It'll be soon," he promised. "I've been thinking about what you said about old Harry sneaking into the movie house, climbing up all those stairs, and sneaking out again. It's kind of hard to figure, isn't it?"

"Sure is," she agreed. "Shooting Decklin had to happen some other way."

"Right," he said. "I still think Harry did it. I just don't know how. I don't believe that bellyache story for a minute. If he sits in on my chat with the missus, maybe he'll slip up and tell us something."

"Maybe," she said, doubting that such a thing would happen. "Talk to you later." She'd been serious though, when she'd told Hubbard that there was a lot going on at the Haven House Inn, and some of it was happily on the positive side—like having enough money to have Goudreau and Son get started on some much-needed improvements. "No time like the present," she told herself. She called the carpenters and gave the official go-ahead for updating the bar and constructing the temporary one. Goudreau Jr. agreed to get work started immediately after the holidays. Then she looked up auction houses with an aim to selling the remaining Highwayman painting, chose a local one and sent them a photo. She ordered fifty matinee tickets for *Miracle on 34th Street*. She congratulated herself on making quick work of several jobs, then thought about more items on the to-do list. *Measure the painting in the living room and ask Sam to check Penelope's hoard for something pretty to fill up the empty space on her wall. Ask Ted what he knows about absinthe. Do some planning for Decklin's memorial.*

One more thing. She looked around the compact office, trying to visualize where a vintage roll-top trunk might fit. "It would be great if I could bring Penelope's trunk over here. I'll never be able to afford the time away from the inn it will take to go through it properly if I have to go to the museum to do it. I wonder what it would take to get permission to move it."

There was still something she could do immediately. She needed to prepare a basic layout for the Lunch and a Movie flyers. There were eight Christmas films left in the twelve-day rotation and she found poster art work for each of them on line. Within an hour Ted had produced the lunch menu along with file photos of each item and the flyer layout was ready for the printer.

Now if Hubbard calls and I have to drop everything for my temporary role as an expert consultant, I won't feel quite so guilty.

Maureen didn't have to wait very long for the anticipated call from Frank Hubbard.

"I called the tea shop," he said, "and I talked to old Harry himself. I told him I had some questions about how come Mrs. Henshaw had changed pocketbooks in the middle of a dinner date. I told him I was sure there was a good reason and I'd appreciate it if she'd clarify the situation."

"How'd he react to that?" she asked.

"At first I thought he'd blow up, but he just said, 'She did that?' and I said, 'Yes, sir, she sure did. I have pictures.' "

"So he said you—we—could come over and talk to her? And to Leslie?" It seemed too easy. "I hope he won't be angry with her." Maureen was concerned, remembering his reaction to Katherine having tea with Decklin. "I've seen him treat her rudely."

"Rudely? What the hell does that mean?" He raised his voice. "Does he beat her? Call her names? What? There's all kinds of spousal abuse. Do you think she needs protection from him? The only record I've got on him was when he was in a drunken fist fight with Decklin Monroe."

"Leslie says he stopped drinking years ago and I don't think he'd actually hurt her. I mean, all I saw was kind of an elbow grab and a shove," she explained. "I called Leslie right away and she told me they'd already kissed and made up. Apparently, Harry hadn't liked the fact that his wife had had a brief chat over tea with Decklin Monroe. Leslie says he's very possessive and that they're madly in love with each other. They've been lovey-dovey every other time I've seen them together."

"Okay, if you say so. Harry says we can come over there tomorrow morning at seven a.m. They don't officially open until eight, so we'll have the place to ourselves. Is that good for you?"

"It'll work," she said, pleased with herself about checking off all those topics on the to-do list. "See you at seven."

If she was going to be dressed and ready for a seven a.m. date at Petals and Kettles, that meant that she'd have to cut her morning run short—or else start earlier. She'd better let Ted know about her change in plans.

The night manager had arrived. Maureen went over a few notes with her and headed through the dining room to the kitchen.

"Hi, Maureen." Ted stood behind the big gas range, stirring something in a copper pot. "Trying out a new recipe for hamburger soup." He held up a spoon. "Have a taste. I think it's perfect for cool-weather lunches, nice and filling, and it uses ingredients we always have on hand."

She tasted. It was delicious, as she'd fully expected it would be. "Perfect," she said. "They'll love it. I had a talk with Hubbard and he's set up a meeting at the tea shop for early tomorrow morning."

"Early? How early?"

"Seven. I either have to cut my run short or start earlier."

"How about we start at five? And who's going to be at this meeting?" He motioned for Gert to take over the stirring. "Low flame," he instructed. "About three more minutes." He wiped his hands on a towel and pointed to his desk. "Let's talk."

She pulled a chair up close to his, hoping to keep their words confidential. She spoke softly. "Hubbard talked to Harry and told him about the handbag switch. Harry seemed surprised but he said that both Katherine and Leslie could talk to us."

"Harry knows you're going to be there?"

"I guess so. I mean Hubbard said 'we.

Ted looked doubtful. "I'm not crazy about you getting involved in this, but the tearoom is a pretty public place, so what could go wrong?"

Maureen grimaced. "Um, not exactly public. They don't actually open until eight."

He leaned back in his chair, frowning. "So you're alone in there with Hubbard and a possible murder suspect and his family? I don't like it." He moved forward again, closer to her. "But I guess it's none of my business, is it?"

"Of course it is. You're an important part of my life. I value your opinion on everything," she said. "And we won't be alone. They have waitstaff and flower arrangers and others who probably show up early for work." She

246 Carol J. Perry

waved a hand toward Gert the pot stirrer and the other kitchen workers. "Just like here. I'll be fine. Besides, I'm sure Frank Hubbard is armed."

"True. But so is whoever shot Decklin and Buddy."

"I'll be fine," she assured him again. "You sure you don't mind starting our run at five tomorrow? It'll barely be light."

"Maybe we'll catch a nice sunrise." His smile was back.

"I have a question I've been meaning to ask you," she said. "What do you know about absinthe?"

The smile grew broader. "That's quite a change of subject. Absinthe is green, tastes like licorice, is classified as a spirit, not a liqueur, and it has a really high alcohol content—over ninety proof."

"A high spirit," she joked.

"For sure. Edgar Allan Poe used to drink it. Ernest Hemingway too. People used to think it was addictive. A hallucinogen. They called it *la fée verte*—the green fairy. Back in the early nineteen hundreds it was banned in the United States and most of Europe."

"Do we have it in our bar?"

"Sure. I don't get much call for it. Sometimes I use a little of it in a mixed drink along with elderflower liqueur and pineapple, lemon, and lime juice—I call it a Fairy Godmother."

So is absinthe the lady in green, and is the lady in green Charlotte Christine Trevaney? And is Charlotte Christine Trevaney the fairy godmother who gave Penelope the inn that Penelope gave to me?

Will I ever know the answers?

Maureen was about to leave the kitchen when Gert, pot-stirring duty completed, followed her to the door. "Molly and Leo and George and Sam and Ted and I have been talking about what we want to do for Decklin's celebration of life." She looked a bit self-conscious. "I guess that's what they call it nowadays. It has a nice sound to it, don't you think so?"

"I do," Maureen agreed. "What do you have in mind?"

"We plan to have it on a nice day on the beach and everybody can bring their own chair or beach towel. There won't be many there. He didn't know a lot of people in Haven. The important thing is the music. Decklin loved his music. "Gert pulled a piece of lined paper from her apron pocket. "Here's our play list so far. See what you think. 'My Way' and 'Young at Heart' from Sinatra, then 'Gentle on My Mind' and 'Chicago' from Dean, and wind up with 'Me and My Shadow' and 'The Party's Over,' from Sammy. What do you think?"

Maureen felt a rush of tears burning behind her eyes. "I think he'd love it, Gert. It's perfect. What about food?"

"Ted's going to make up one of those charcuterie boards and some hot dogs and hamburgers and beer and we're all pitching in for a bottle of good champagne. George has a friend with a fishing boat and we'll all go a little way out on the gulf and sprinkle his ashes."

"Count me in for a donation," Maureen said. "And naturally I'll be there for the celebration."

"Decklin liked you, Maureen. He liked the way you're trying so hard to bring this old place back to life." Gert gave her employer an impulsive hug. "Like he wanted to do with the old movie house, you know? I mean, if he could get the money he needed."

"Did he ever tell you where he thought he might get it?"

"No. Just that he'd been in touch with an old friend who had big bucks," she said. "That's what he said. Big bucks. But he didn't mention a name."

"Maybe someday someone else will come up with enough to save the Paramount," Maureen said. "Like the Greater Haven Improvement Fund used to do."

"I hadn't thought about that name in years," Gert said. "I wonder if they're still around."

"They have an exhibit about it at the museum," Maureen said. "It's interesting. Ted's grandmother sent them her purple satin GHIF badge."

"No kidding? I'd like to see that but I don't go into that place anymore." She gave a pretend-shudder. "Not me. There's a ghost in there." Gert looked around and dropped her voice. "Not a friendly one like you-know-who."

Maureen knew that "you-know-who" meant Lorna and acknowledged the fact with a conspiratorial wink—at the same time wondering what sort of ghost Gert had seen in the museum. Could it have been the lady in green or the shadowy Absinthe?

Chapter 35

Finn blinked and shook his head, confused by the ringing of the alarm clock before morning light shone through the windows. Maureen gave him a scratch behind his ears and a kiss on top of his head. "Good morning, sleepy boy," she said. "We're going for our run a little early. It'll be fun."

She dressed in gray sweatpants and matching long-sleeved shirt, anticipating a cool December temperature on the beach. She tucked the flashlight Decklin had given her into her waistband, then she and the golden made their way quietly down the two flights of stairs to the outside door. Beach Boulevard was quiet, the streetlamps all still lighted, seabirds beginning to call to one another. "It's funny what a different an hour makes." She broke into a jog. "I can still see the moon."

"Good morning." Ted's voice came from behind her.

"Good morning, yourself," she said, waiting for him to catch up with her. Silently, the three—man, woman and dog—jogged together, keeping an even rhythm all the way to the Coliseum.

"Want me to take Finn?"

"He'd love it. You run faster than I do." She handed him the leash.

"Use your flashlight," he said, "so I'll know where you're at. I'll meet you at the fishing pier."

There was pale light from the waning moon and some landshine from nearby St. Petersburg, but it didn't take long for Ted and Finn to disappear into the darkness ahead. The bobbing bright beam from the flashlight was as welcome on the broad sandy beach as it had been on the narrow steep staircase to the Paramount's projection room. To keep herself company, Maureen hummed a few bars of "Me and My Shadow" from Gert's playlist and ran a little faster, the lyric reminding her of the witness's account of seeing something or somebody on the movie theater's balcony staircase. "A shape," he'd described it. "Like a shadow."

The flashlight beam picked up a patch of white in the distance. Maureen recognized the fishing pier sign. Too far away to read the lettering, but secure in the fact that she was close to where Ted and Finn waited, she increased her pace again, and heard Finn's welcoming "woof woof woof," and Ted's shouted, "Here we are!"

She spotted Ted's white sweatshirt and watched as the golden streaked toward her, leash dragging in the sand. "Hi, Finn." She knelt and accepted warm doggie kisses, then picked up the leash and walked, heart pounding, toward the sign. Taking deep breaths, she leaned against it.

"You okay?" Ted asked.

"Sure. Just a little out of breath."

He moved toward her, his face close to hers, his hands braced against the sign. "Have you got a good grip on the leash?"

"Got it." She knew he was about to kiss her and this time she was ready.

It was a long, satisfying kiss. More than one, actually. When they finally moved apart there was a sliver of a forthcoming rosy gold sunrise on the horizon. Finn, still securely leashed, lay patiently beside them. He gave a soft "woof."

"He's right," Ted murmured, lips close to her ear. "We'd better get going. We both have a busy day ahead." He took her hand and they began to walk, not run, back toward the Coliseum.

Part of the way back, as if by mutual consent, they dropped hands and jogged, then ran. They reached the stretch of sandy beach behind the building, where the swings and see-saws and monkey bars awaited Haven's local and visiting kids, then walked around to the front of the place, slightly breathless, each pretending nothing special had happened.

Whatever that was, Maureen thought, *or whatever it is, we have to work together so we'd better keep it on the down-low.* Once back at the inn, Maureen and Finn turned toward the side entrance and Ted headed for the kitchen back door on the opposite side.

"See you later," Ted said, and Maureen replied, "Have a good day."

Once back in her third-floor suite, Maureen focused on the day ahead—one thing at a time. Feeding Finn was the first order of business, next shower, shampoo, and figure out what the correct wardrobe might be for helping Frank Hubbard, a not-too-subtle cop, interview Katherine Henshaw, local fashion icon, and Harry Henshaw, jealous husband/possible murder suspect along with their sweet but somewhat confused daughter, Leslie Brown—and she wouldn't be surprised if the Henshaws had an attorney present. She'd told Hubbard so too, and he'd pooh-poohed the idea.

At six forty-five, dressed in a navy linen pantsuit, she climbed into the Subaru and drove around the block to Petals and Kettles, where Hubbard's cruiser was parked across the street from the pretty blue building. Maureen pulled into the driveway beside the shop, approached the front door, and waited for Hubbard to join her. A uniformed deputy accompanied Hubbard. The door was locked. Hubbard gave an impatient knock, then pushed the doorbell. "We're eight minutes early, Frank," she whispered. "I think when Harry said seven he meant seven."

"Eight minutes," he scoffed, knocking again. "Big deal."

Leslie appeared at the door, shielding her eyes, peering through the glass. A few clicks of the locks and the door swung open; the chime played "I'm a Little Teapot," admitting them to the sweet-smelling lobby between the two businesses. The deputy remained outside the door, discouraging early customers.

"Good morning," Leslie said. "We'll be meeting in the tea shop. Mother and Daddy will be along in a few minutes." She led the way to the largest marble-topped table, surrounded by eight chairs. It was the farthest one away from the shop entrance and the service counter. "Can I offer you tea while we wait?"

"Yes, thank you," Maureen said. "That would be nice." Hubbard merely nodded.

Leslie crossed the room and spoke softly to a pink-smocked woman behind a counter and returned with a small teapot and three delicate flower-sprigged cups on a tray along with sugar cubes and tongs, a cream pitcher, and a plate of powdered sugar–dusted biscotti. She filled the three cups, asking the requisite "One lump or two?" and "Cream?" then she sat in one of the ice cream parlor chairs on the opposite side of the table, arms folded, quietly regarding the two. The silence was uncomfortable and Maureen searched for something to say to break it. Eight minutes was beginning to seem like a very long time.

Hubbard spoke first. "So, Mrs. Brown, do I understand correctly that your parents stay in that cottage out back?" He jerked a thumb in the direction of the rear of the shop.

"Yes. During the winter months." Leslie looked at her Gucci watch. "They'll be here soon and you can ask them about it."

Maureen looked at her own Brighton timepiece. At exactly

seven, a door at the rear of the tearoom opened. Katherine and Harry Henshaw came inside, holding hands, nodding and smiling to the pink-smocked staff as though they were walking a red carpet. Over her right arm, Katherine Henshaw carried the two Saint Laurent handbags in question. Walking directly behind them was a woman Maureen recognized at once. It was Nora Nathan, the attorney who'd defended her less than a year earlier, when Frank Hubbard had questioned *her* about a murder.

This meeting, Maureen knew, was simply to determine why Katherine Henshaw had changed handbags after the movie on the night Decklin was murdered and nothing else. That had been agreed to by all the parties concerned. Why had a defense attorney who specialized in criminal law been invited? There was no time to find out.

Katherine and Harry sat directly opposite Maureen and Frank Hubbard. Nora, after giving a nod and a friendly "Hello, Maureen," and "Hello, Frank," sat beside Leslie. Katherine placed the two handbags on a vacant chair between her and her daughter. A pink-smocked lady immediately delivered another pot of tea with cups, sugar, cream, lemon, and more biscotti.

Maureen had assumed that Hubbard would take charge of the meeting, since he'd been the one who'd proposed it, but it was Harry Henshaw who stood up, glanced around the table, and proceeded to act as though he was the host at a book club breakfast. "I believe we all know one another, so let's get started. This shouldn't take long. My wife has assured me that her reason for changing purses is easily explained." He looked down at his perfectly coiffed, manicured, and Versace knit–suited wife. "Darling," he said, "Officer Hubbard would like to know why you chose to change handbags after the showing of *Remember the Night*."

Katherine took a dainty sip from her tea, the enormous diamond on her left hand catching the light from the chandelier above the table. "It was not a memorable movie," she said. "Anyway, I'd seen it before."

"Yes, sweetheart." Harry touched her hair. "Today we're going to talk about your handbags, remember?"

"Oh yes, of course. They had some lovely candy at the movies that night. Better than usual. I bought Harry a whole bagful of butterscotch Life Savers, didn't I, my love?"

"Yes, you did."

Frank Hubbard leaned forward. "Did you put the candy into your handbag?"

"Yes. I dumped the whole bagful in on top of everything else." She returned to sipping her tea. "Except I dropped one roll of your Life Savers somewhere, darling. I'm so sorry." She smiled at her husband.

"Did that mean you couldn't reach the other things you usually carry, like your wallet or your comb or anything?" Frank pressed on with his questioning. Maureen hoped he wouldn't get aggressive—bulldog-like—or Harry Henshaw would be apt to call the whole meeting off. She looked at Nora Nathan, as the lawyer took notes on a tablet. *Nora must be here to be sure the questions don't get off track.*

"Yes, Officer." Katherine smiled at Hubbard. "I was quite sure you'd understand. That's why I had to use another purse. It's a very nice one. Just a tad smaller than the one I began the evening with. I didn't think anyone would notice the difference." She took a dainty bite of biscotti. "You see, I didn't need so much room anymore."

Maureen frowned. "But—" she started, then hastily apologized. "Sorry."

"That's all right, Ms. Doherty," Harry Henshaw said. "Do you have a question?"

"Yes, I do. Katherine—Mrs. Henshaw—since you didn't *know* that your husband's favorite candy would be at the theater, why did you choose to carry the large purse in the first place? Why did you think you'd need all that room?"

Katherine looked up at her husband. "Do I have to tell her?"

"Yes, dear," he answered. "It's a very good question." He looked at the lawyer, who shrugged and nodded her okay.

"If you say so." She reached into the chair beside her, picked up the large handbag, and put it on the table. "You can plainly see that it wouldn't have fit in any of my usual evening bags."

Frank opened his mouth but Harry spoke first. "What wouldn't fit?"

A ladylike eye-roll. "My gun, silly. Look and see for yourself."

Chapter 36

Nora Nathan stood up and reached for the purse, tucking it under her arm. "Private property," she said. "That's all. No more questions. My client has nothing further to say. This meeting is over."

Everyone stood. Frank Hubbard was on his feet so fast his chair tipped over. Harry reached for Katherine's arm. Fearing that the woman might be in danger, Maureen pushed her way between them and Harry grabbed her arm instead. His grip was hard, bony fingers digging into her flesh. "Ouch!" she yelled. "Let go of me!"

"Let go of the lady," Frank said, "and put your hands behind your back. You're under arrest for assault." He produced a set of handcuffs from one of those many places police have on their belts. Harry, eyes downcast, did as he was told and Frank handcuffed him, instructing a grim-faced Leslie to unlock the door and admit the deputy. While Katherine tearfully insisted that Harry had done nothing wrong, that everything was all her fault, he recited the man's rights in a monotone. "You have the right to remain silent . . ." Then with a head toss signaled to Nora. "You his lawyer too, Nathan? You want to ride with him?"

"I am," she said. "What about Mrs. Henshaw?"

"If there really is a gun in that big pocketbook, it looks to me like she might be carrying a concealed firearm without a license. Want to see if she'll hand over the bag and come along voluntarily?"

"I need to speak with both of my clients," Nora said, the Saint Laurent bag still under her arm.

"Go right ahead." Frank took Maureen's arm, much more gently than Henshaw had, and the two stepped back a few feet. The deputy relinquished his grip on Harry and stood with them. It was obvious the pink-smocked tearoom ladies far across the room were paying rapt attention to the scene playing out before them, too far away to hear but close enough to have witnessed the handcuffing incident. Leslie must have texted her husband because Warren burst into the room and, seeing his father-in-law handcuffed and his mother-in-law in tears, demanded an explanation of what the hell was going on.

Maureen wasn't sure what the hell was going on either, and strained to hear the conversation between Nora Nathan and the Henshaws. Harry's voice was indistinct, but Katherine's voice was uncharacteristically loud, between gasped sobs. "It takes up a lot of room, you know, with the silencer on it."

"Ssshh!" Nora shushed her client. "We're not going to talk about it right now. We'll all go down to the police station and get this straightened out."

"Noooo!" Katherine wailed. "Just give the policeman the gun. I don't need to hide it anymore." She lunged at Nora, snatching the bag from under the lawyer's arm. "Here you go, Officer Hubbard." She reached into it and pulled out a gun, not much bigger than a toy—the whole thing including the silencer couldn't have been more than eight inches long—holding it upside down, her thumb and forefinger just above the trigger—almost, Maureen thought, the way she herself had held the phone bug a few days ago, like it was something disgusting.

As though the scene had been choreographed, every person in the large room, including the pink-smocked ladies and the tall deputy—but with the exception of Frank Hubbard and Katherine Henshaw—ducked. Maureen peeked over the edge of the table, just past the flower-sprigged teapot. Hubbard's voice was icy cool, even though the business end of the small, upside-down gun with its black tubular silencer was level with his heart.

"Thank you, Mrs. Henshaw," he said, reaching toward her with a steady palm up. "I'll take care of it for you."

"Thank you," she said, dropping the thing into his hand. "That's that." She dusted French-tipped fingers together. "That's the end of Buddy's little gun."

Harry, arms secured behind him with the handcuffs lunged, toward his wife. "Buddy's gun? What are you saying?" In one swift motion the deputy jerked him back.

"Take him to the station," Hubbard ordered. "I've called for backup. I'll bring her along."

Nora Nathan followed Harry and the deputy to the door. "I'm right behind you, Harry. Don't answer any questions, Kate," she commanded. "I'll be right back."

Within minutes, the sound of sirens signaled one police cruiser leaving as another arrived. A second deputy entered the shop and took a position inside the door. Hubbard acknowledged the man with a curt nod.

Ignoring siren noise and police activity, Katherine returned to her chair, picked up her teacup, and took a sip. She turned toward the service area where one pink-smocked lady had been brave enough, or nosy enough, to keep her head above the edge of the counter. "This tea is cold," she called. "Be a dear and bring a hot pot, will you?"

"I'll get it, Mother." By this time everyone had come out from hiding. Warren moved toward the service area while

Frank Hubbard wrapped the gun in a pink napkin and tucked it into an inside pocket. He pulled a dog-eared card from his breast pocket and sat in the chair opposite Katherine Henshaw while Leslie silently moved to the chair next to her mother.

"I'm going to read something to you, Mrs. Henshaw." Hubbard spoke slowly and distinctly. "You are under arrest for unauthorized possession of a firearm. I am going to read you your rights." For the second time that morning, he recited the words from the Miranda card. "You have the right to remain silent . . ." He'd reached the line informing her that if she couldn't afford an attorney one would be appointed for her when she interrupted.

"Oh, Officer Hubbard, don't be silly. I can afford an attorney. I can afford anything in the world I want. I have jewelry, fine clothes, the best of everything. We travel all over the world, stay at the very best hotels." She waved a hand in the air. "Warren dear, where's my tea?"

Her son-in-law put a fresh cup on the table, and with a shaking hand poured the steaming liquid into it. "Good boy," she said, returning her attention to Hubbard. "Harry will give me anything I want. I just have to make sure I don't do anything to make him angry." She leaned toward Hubbard and whispered, "He's a dear, but he gets jealous sometimes—jealous about other men." She sipped her tea. "Ummm. Good." She took a dainty bite of biscotti. "Imagine that. I'm an old lady and he still gets jealous. He was jealous of poor Decklin, you know. Just because we had a little chat about old times. Pity."

Maureen eased into the chair beside Hubbard that she'd occupied earlier. *Maybe Hubbard was right about Harry killing Decklin,* she thought. *Maybe he was jealous enough, angry enough to do it. But how had the gun wound up in Katherine's handbag?*

"You're free to go along home now, Doherty," Hubbard told her. "Looks like the handbags are all accounted for."

She just stared back at him. As if she'd leave just as it was getting interesting!

"I'm going to read this card for you again, Mrs. Henshaw," Hubbard said. "Please listen carefully." Once again, he read her rights aloud. "Do you understand what I read? Do you want to wait until Nora comes back before you talk to me?"

"No need," she said. "I trust you."

"All right, then. You mentioned 'Buddy's gun,' Mrs. Henshaw." Frank patted his pocket. "Did you mean that the gun you gave to me was once Buddy Putnam's gun?"

"Buddy gave it to me," she said. "He knew that Harry had found out about us going to the movies together. He showed me how to shoot it and take care of it and how to put the silencer on it. He even gave me a little box of bullets."

"So he gave you a gun? Why?"

"Protection." She put the cup down forcefully enough so that some tea sloshed over into the saucer. "He was afraid Harry might beat me again."

"He beat you?" Leslie gasped. "Daddy *beat* you?"

"Just that one time, honey—when he found out about me sneaking into the movies with Buddy. It was pretty bad. I had a black eye and a broken rib. Buddy and I weren't doing anything wrong, but I was afraid Harry might get jealous about somebody else someday and hit me again," Katherine said. "So was Buddy. We arranged to meet one last time at the Paramount. He'd get there first and I'd buy a ticket and meet him at his regular seat in aisle four."

"I don't get it," Warren said. "Did Dad find out and shoot this Buddy guy with his own gun?"

"Oh, Warren dear," Katherine scolded. "Of course not. *I* shot him. I had to. I sat behind him and waited for a part where everybody laughed. The gun made just a tiny pop.

Then I stuck the gun in my popcorn box and walked out. What if Harry had found out I'd gone to the Paramount to meet Buddy again? Buddy had to disappear."

The screech of brakes just outside the shop front window announced the return of the Henshaw's criminal attorney, Nora Nathan. The deputy pulled open the door and stood out of her way as she whirled into the room. "Did he read you your rights, Katherine?" Nora demanded. "Harry will be out on bond within the hour."

"Oh, that's wonderful. Yes, Officer Hubbard read them to me twice, dear." Katherine smiled at the lawyer. "I understand perfectly. I told him about how Buddy gave me the gun and about how I shot him with it."

At this point Hubbard cleared the room of all but Leslie and Warren. He and the deputy took Katherine into custody—no handcuffs—with Nora following close behind.

"I'm coming with you, Mother." Leslie ran after Nora. "Warren, mind the store." Warren, looking dazed, agreed.

Maureen climbed into the Subaru and pulled onto the boulevard, wondering if the report of what had gone down at Petals and Kettles this morning would be under discussion at the Quic-Shop before Frank and Katherine Henshaw got to the police station. It was an easy bet that it would.

It also wouldn't take long for the grapevine to figure out that since everybody already knew that both Buddy Putnam and Decklin Monroe had been shot with the same gun, it only stood to reason that Haven's beloved fashion icon and onetime beauty queen was also quite possibly a killer.

When Maureen arrived at the inn she saw the usual quartet in their rocking chairs on the front porch. They all stood, and started down the stairs as she turned the Subaru onto the driveway leading to the back parking lot, hinting that the four already knew that her early morning meeting had yielded something of uncommon interest.

By the time she'd parked and stepped out of the car, George

and Sam were there to hold the door open, with Molly and Gert not far behind. Sam was first to get a question in. "So, is it true? Harry and Kate Henshaw are both in jail?"

"Not exactly," Maureen hedged. Was anything she'd heard at the tea shop confidential? She hadn't signed anything. She didn't like gossip, but knowing how news traveled in Haven, chances were that her friends already knew everything she knew and more. "Harry will be out on bail," she told them. "Katherine's being . . . um . . . being questioned."

"It's about Kate having a gun that used to belong to Buddy Putnam," Molly announced. "I know because one of my girlfriends works at the tearoom. She said she could overhear some of what you all were talking about. Besides, she's pretty good at reading lips."

"What did she hear?" Gert asked, saving Maureen from having to comment on the chain of custody of Buddy's gun.

"Buddy gave the gun to Kate because Harry used to beat her up." Molly's eyes grew wide. "Protection. That's what Kate said. It was for protection from Harry."

"That's nuts," Sam declared. "Everybody says they have a perfect marriage. They're always holding hands and kissing and all that mushy stuff."

"I don't believe it either," Gert said. "Your girlfriend must be wrong, Molly. Harry treats her like a princess. Always has."

"I'm not so sure." George scratched his head. "Me and Ms. Doherty saw him treating her kind of rough one time, didn't we, Ms. Doherty?"

"We did. That's a fact. And what your girlfriend told you was true, Molly. Kate said that Buddy gave her the gun for protection against her husband."

George's brow furrowed. "So did Harry get the gun away from Kate and kill Buddy with it while he was watching a movie? How'd he get away with that?"

"He didn't kill Buddy," Molly announced. "Kate did. Right, Ms. Doherty?"

"I'm afraid so," Maureen agreed.

"What about Decklin, then?" Gert wanted to know. "Don't tell me Kate shot him with Buddy's gun too."

Maureen didn't want to tell her that, so she didn't. "Let's go inside," she suggested. "Maybe there's something about it on television."

The five joined a small crowd gathered around the TV over the bar. "What's going on?" Sam asked Leo.

"They've arrested Kate Henshaw for shooting some guy a long time ago." He pointed to the screen. "She's at the courthouse in Clearwater right now. They haven't given out much information about it so far.""

The TV camera showed Katherine, wearing the same Versace knit Maureen had seen earlier, getting out of a police car. Still no handcuffs. Nora Nathan was there. A reporter tried to get comments from three people who covered their faces with their hands, easily recognizable to Maureen as Harry, Leslie, and Warren. The newscaster said that Katherine Henshaw was there to be arraigned in connection with the 1970s death of Buddy Putnam.

"Boy oh boy, I'd like to be a fly on the wall in that courtroom," George said.

"Me too," Maureen agreed. "I wonder what Frank Hubbard thinks about all this."

"Looks like you won't have to wait too long," Gert said. "Look who just drove up front."

Frank Hubbard, in full uniform, took the front stairs two at a time, nearly dislodging one of the poinsettias. "Doherty. I need to see you in your office."

"Whew. Bossy," Molly whispered.

"Sure, Frank." Maureen stood, taking her time. "What's up?"

"Your office?" His tone was less demanding, almost pleading. "Please?"

It must be pretty darned important for him to say "please." Maureen gestured toward the front door. "Okay. I have a few minutes." He followed her inside where Jolene was on desk-duty. "Hold any calls for me, will you Jolene?" Maureen unlocked the door, waited for Hubbard to precede her. She sat behind her desk. He took off his cap and sat facing her.

"What's going on, Frank? What are you doing here? I thought you'd be at the courthouse in Clearwater."

"No need. It's just boring routine lawyer stuff. My deputy can take care of it and Katherine and Harry are lawyered up just fine." He leaned forward, his elbows on her desk. "You already know Katherine Henshaw has admitted to killing Buddy Putnam."

"Of course."

"We can be pretty sure she used the same gun on Decklin Monroe, right?"

"It looks that way."

"Yeah, and it hasn't hit the news cycle yet, but we know how she made Harry sick so he had to stay home from the movie." He dropped his voice, looking around the room as though someone might be listening. "The poor guy is allergic to shellfish and the daughter found an empty clam juice bottle in the trash. We figure the old woman dumped it into that soup she made."

"No kidding. That would probably do it alright." *Why is he sharing this information with me? He must want something in return. But what do I have that he wants?* She waited.

"I know you get those 'feelings' of yours when there's a murder." He twisted the blue cap with both hands. "We figure she must have made a date with Monroe about lending him money. But listen, Doherty. There's a piece missing. I need to know how the hell she got up the stairs into the balcony without anybody seeing her."

Maureen knew there was no point in denying that she never had any kind of "feelings" about murder—any murder.

She rubbed her forehead and was silent for a long minute. "Well, there's pretty unanimous agreement that when she shot Buddy in the back of the head, she waited for a noisy, funny part of *Animal House,* right?"

"Sure. There are plenty of those," he agreed. "Some of the old-timers around Haven think it was when the band led the parade into the alley."

"I've heard that," she said, not admitting that she'd heard it from a ghost. "I'm thinking about clothes. About what Katherine wore that night."

"Yeah, yeah. I know you have a fancy fashion degree. We're talking about murder, not high-priced clothes." Hubbard's impatience showed.

Maureen ignored the interruption. "A petite woman wearing a long, fitted black dress with a black handbag and a black scarf. She even wore soft black ballerina shoes," she recited. "What if Decklin had told her exactly what time there would be a dark, nighttime scene. One where the audience would be focused on the screen. What if she pulled the scarf up to cover her face and hair and scooted up the stairs to the balcony at just the right moment."

Hubbard picked up the train of thought. "He would have met her at the top of the stairs and led her up to the projection room while the film was on the first reel."

"Yep," Maureen agreed. "He had a whole forty-seven minutes to work with. He probably would have given her the exact time of another dark scene so she could make her exit. He knew all those reels like the back of his hand. He made that clear when we met."

"So she shoots him," Hubbard's eyes widened. "She waits for the right scene, then scoots back down the stairs and rejoins the family."

"She drops a roll of candy when she pulls the gun out of her purse," Maureen offered. "It all fits, doesn't it? Will that give you enough to charge her with the second murder?"

"It just might," he said. "Thanks, Doherty. You've been a big help—again."

"No problem," she said. Long pause. "Don't you wonder though, if there could have been other men? Other male friends who could have made Harry jealous?"

He stood and put on his cap. "I questioned her about that. About other men."

"What did she say?

"Nothing," he answered. "Nothing at all. She had this strange little smile on her face, looked back at me, fluttered those long eyelashes and just barely lifted one shoulder. I'll tell you, it gave me chills."

It gave Maureen chills too. Later, in her suite, with Finn at her feet, she watched the cats playing with a toy mouse—and wondered how many tiny bullets might be bagged, unnoticed, forgotten, in God only knows how many cold case files around the world.

Epilogue

Katherine Henshaw was found not guilty of killing Buddy Putnam by reason of insanity and was committed to the custody of a Florida mental health treatment facility. She was subsequently charged with the murder of Decklin Monroe but had yet to be tried. Still, most of the news reporters and virtually all of the Quic-Shop pundits declared that she'd probably spend the rest of her life in some kind of hospital. Harry Henshaw and Leslie and Warren Brown were given permission to visit her as much as they wanted to. Harry pleaded guilty to the assault charge, paid his fine, and then, in a burst of generosity, donated the necessary funds to renovate the Paramount Theater as a gift to the newly activated Greater Haven Improvement Fund.

Maureen and Ted and the staff of the Haven House Inn gave Decklin a proper send-off with a surprisingly well-attended beachside celebration-of-life party, complete with hot dogs and hamburgers and a keg of beer, accompanied by a rocking musical loop of Rat Pack favorites topped off with a trip into the Gulf aboard a fishing trawler for the scattering of the ashes and a champagne toast to the departed. A good time was had by all.

Goudreau and Son completed the temporary bar in the

dining room in time for New Year's Eve, and work on the new bar complete with an aquarium stocked with angelfish was finished by Valentine's Day. The sale of the large Highwayman painting brought five thousand dollars—enough to get started on the souvenir shop—and Sam found a lovely watercolor painting of a beach scene to replace it on Maureen's wall. The trunk full of Penelope Josephine's collection of papers and photos and who knows what else, still awaits thorough investigation.

Maureen and Ted tried hard to keep their budding relationship a secret, but they couldn't fool the rest of the staff of the inn for long, let alone the Quic-Shop snoops.

Sometimes, late-night drinkers have reported seeing the form of a shadowy woman dressed all in black, sitting at the end of the beautiful new bar with a green drink in her hand.

Acknowledgments

Linda Bennett is my longtime friend, mentor, encourager, advisor on all things metaphysical, and very real inspiration. We met almost thirty-five years ago. Linda is a psychic and her TV show, *Metaphysically Speaking*, originated at a local Florida station. Linda took on-the-air phone calls from viewers and gave on-the-spot readings. (Readers of my Witch City Mysteries may already see a familiar pattern emerging here—when Lee Barrett becomes "Crystal Moon" and attempts to give psychic advice to callers on WICH-TV.)

At that time I was a moderately successful nonfiction wrier with articles on various subjects in both local and national publications—but I thought sometimes about trying my hand at fiction. Good idea? Bad idea? What kind of fiction? I decided to call Linda. With just my first name and birth date, she "saw" me writing books for young people. Within just a few weeks after that I attended a writers' meeting and met a young woman who wrote middle-grade novels for school book fairs. I bought her book, had an "I can do this" moment, and so began writing. The school book fairs publisher bought my first book for kids, *Sand Castle Summer*.

I shared my success with Linda, was invited to appear on her show, and the friendship solidified as I continued to write for the middle-grade market. When I decided that I was ready to try a "grown-up" mystery, Linda was the total model for Lee Barrett—red hair, cool clothes, animal lover, TV job, and all!

Linda was the first person to read an advance copy of *Be*

My Ghost, the first book in this Haunted Haven series. Her approval was important to me. Her only suggestion was that Finn should have a bigger part. So I've tried to pad his lines—which consist of "woofs"—a little more in this story.

Linda, this one's for you!

RECIPES

Ted's Eggnog French Toast

(Makes 6–8 servings)

1 loaf day-old French bread
  (Ted says if it's too fresh the slices are soggy)
2 large eggs
1 cup store-bought eggnog
2 tablespoons light brown sugar
¼ teaspoon ground cinnamon
¼ teaspoon ground nutmeg
3 tablespoons butter for pan cooking

Slice the French bread into inch-thick slices. Put all of the ingredients except the bread and the butter into a bowl and whisk them briskly. Place a big nonstick skillet over medium heat and put the butter in it. When the butter is melted, dip the bread slices into the eggnog mixture, soaking both sides thoroughly. Put slices into the heated skillet. Cook until they are golden brown—about 2 minutes for each side. Flip and cook the other side. Serve the slices topped with powdered sugar and offer maple syrup or whipped cream for extra toppings.

Haven House Corn and Chicken Chowder

(Makes about 8 servings)

2 leftover cooked chicken breasts, chopped finely
(Ted says it's okay to use rotisserie chicken from the store)
1 large onion, chopped
2 cups chicken stock
2 medium potatoes, chopped
Large can of whole kernel sweet corn, drained
2 tablespoons maize corn flour
2 cups milk
3 tablespoons butter for pan cooking

Melt butter in a large saucepan. Add the chopped onion and cook for 3 to 4 minutes. Add the chicken stock and the potatoes, cover and simmer for 15 minutes. Mix the maize corn flour with a small amount of the milk, then stir in the remaining milk. Add to the soup mixture along with the sweet corn and the chicken. Reheat, stirring constantly until the soup thickens. Season to taste with salt and pepper. Sprinkle in a little chopped fresh parsley if you like. Add a little more milk if it is too thick and serve immediately.

Haven House Traditional Christmas Wassail

Makes 8 servings of about ⅔ of a cup each

1 gallon apple cider
2 cups orange juice
1 cup lemon juice
½ cup sugar
2 teaspoons ground cinnamon
1 teaspoon ground cloves
1 teaspoon ground nutmeg
½ cup brandy (optional)
1 Navel or Florida Honeybell orange, sliced

Blend juices, sugar, and spices together. Add the brandy to make the alcoholic version. Bring mixture to a slow boil in a large saucepan or pot. Boil it for one minute, then reduce the heat and simmer for half an hour. Serve it hot in a punchbowl with orange slices floating in the bowl.

Don't miss the first book in the Haunted Haven series
Be My Ghost.
And be sure to check out the
Witch City Mysteries
available now from Kensington Books,
wherever books are sold!

Visit our website at
KensingtonBooks.com
to sign up for our newsletters, read
more from your favorite authors, see
books by series, view reading group
guides, and more!

Become a Part of Our
Between the Chapters Book Club
Community and Join the Conversation